THE PRISON OF BURIED HOPES

AFTER THE RIFT, BOOK 5

C.J. ARCHER

WWW.CJARCHER.COM

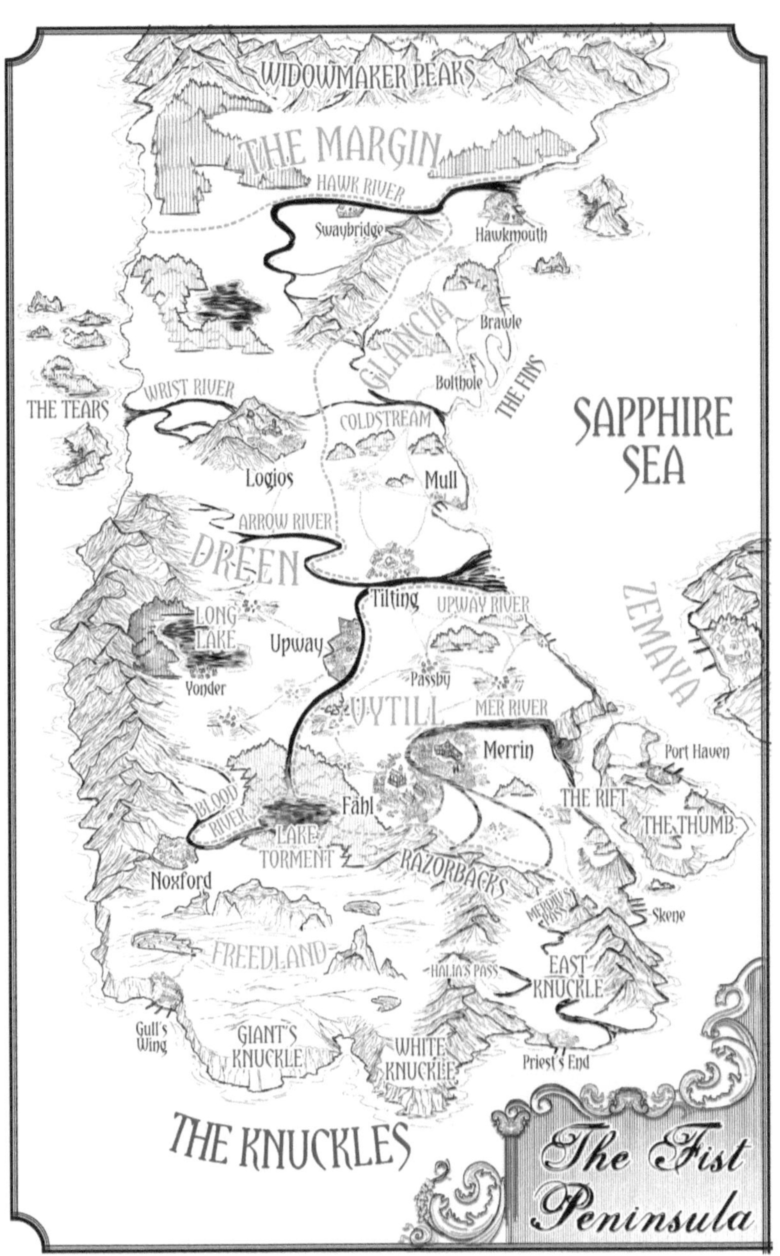

WIDOWMAKER PEAKS
THE MARGIN
HAWK RIVER
Swaybridge
Hawkmouth
GLANCIA
Brawle
Bolthole
THE FINS
THE TEARS
WRIST RIVER
COLDSTREAM
SAPPHIRE SEA
Logios
Mull
ARROW RIVER
DREEN
Tilting
UPWAY RIVER
ZEMAYA
LONG LAKE
Upway
Passby
Yonder
VYTILL
MER RIVER
Merrin
Port Haven
BLOOD RIVER
Fahl
THE RIFT
THE THUMB
LAKE TORMENT
RAZORBACKS
Noxford
MENDUS PASS
Skene
FREEDLAND
HALIA'S PASS
EAST KNUCKLE
Gull's Wing
GIANT'S KNUCKLE
WHITE KNUCKLE
Priest's End
THE KNUCKLES
The Fist Peninsula

CHAPTER 1

"*I*'m uneasy about this," Meg whispered as she eyed the wagon.

"You worry too much," I whispered back. "Kitty will be fine. She knows what she's doing."

"Does she? Anyway, that's not what I meant. I'm uneasy about it because she's still married. She shouldn't be..." She waved her hand at the covered wagon, now rocking in a way that left nothing to the imagination.

"Ignore them, and help me chop these vegetables," I said.

I wasn't prepared to have this discussion with Meg yet again. Ever since faking her death at the river crossing, Kitty's future had taken a dramatic turn. The duchess of Gladstow no longer had to look forward to a life of luxury and pampering. She had to travel with as little luggage as the rest of us, without her servants and with no official status. So if the world thought she was dead, did that mean she could break the vow of fidelity she'd made to her husband?

Kitty clearly thought so, going by the moans coming from the wagon. Meg did not. I was staying neutral on the subject. Kitty could make up her own mind. She was now free to do as she pleased with no husband to give her orders, no noblewomen to censure her, no societal rules to slavishly follow. If she wanted to think of her marriage as nullified by her fake death, then that was her decision to make.

The wagon curtain flipped back and Erik jumped to the ground. He assisted Kitty down the steps, bowed over her hand, and took up his sword from where it had been leaning against the wagon's wheel. With a nod for Meg and me, and another for Balthazar who did not look up from his map, Erik left the clearing to rejoin Quentin, watching the road to the north.

Kitty touched her hair, a satisfied look on her face. "Pass me a carrot, Meg."

"Not until you've washed your hands." Meg pointed to the pail of water, collected from the nearby stream.

Kitty did as directed then crouched alongside us. She accepted the carrot and knife from me and began chopping. Meg and I watched as Kitty held the carrot upright and began slicing towards her body. Her technique wasn't terrible but she had trouble getting the knife through the vegetable and her grip began to slip.

Meg held out her hand. "Give it to me before you slice off your thumb."

"What *can* I do to help?" Kitty asked, looking around.

"Perhaps Balthazar would enjoy your company."

Kitty screwed up her nose and eyed the old man angling the map towards the sky in an attempt to capture the last of the sunlight filtering through the treetops. "He wants to talk about politics and keeps asking me who the duke's friends are. I've answered as best as I can. I'd rather talk about more pleasant things." She cast her gaze in the direction Erik had gone.

Meg sliced through the carrot with the ease of someone who'd been in the kitchen her entire life and the vigor of someone annoyed with her companion. Each slice dropped into the simmering pot of water with a *plunk*.

I handed Kitty an onion. "Cut this up."

Kitty tossed the onion in the air and caught it. "How does one cut something of this shape?"

"Just do your best," I said, plucking a bunch of herbs from the hessian sack.

We'd purchased food and other odds and ends in Tilting

before leaving, then replenished our supplies three days later in the village of Passby. At the end of each day, the men had caught rabbit or fish to add to our vegetable broth, and we'd dined well. Our supplies were running low again, but according to Balthazar, we should arrive in the twin cities of Merrin and Fahl by nightfall the following day. I was looking forward to sleeping in a proper bed, if only for two nights before we continued our journey south to Freedland, where we hoped to find answers.

"I wonder how many attended my burial," Kitty mused. "I do hope the duke put up a gravestone in his family graveyard."

"I thought you hated him, his family and his castle," I said.

"I do, but the graveyard is situated on a hill overlooking the river. The view is quite lovely."

Despite her annoyance with Kitty's broken marriage vows, Meg laughed softly. "Didn't you want to discuss more pleasant things?" she asked. "Or is your death a more pleasing topic to you than politics?"

"Not my death, my burial. They're different things. But you're right, Meg. Let's discuss our men instead."

"We don't have men," Meg said, pointing her knife at me then herself.

"You would if you put in a little effort." Kitty wrinkled her nose as her eyes welled with tears. "Max is very taken with you."

"He might be married," Meg said snippily.

"But—"

"But nothing. I don't want him breaking any marriage vows for me, whether he can remember them or not."

"*You* might think that, but does he?" Kitty sniffed as a tear leaked from her right eye. She dashed it away with the back of her hand. "He doesn't seem particularly concerned. Don't deny it, Meg. I saw him kiss you."

Meg snatched up another carrot. "Kissing is one thing. It's not..." She pointed the carrot at the wagon.

"You ought to do it. It might relieve some tension."

Meg gasped. "I am not tense!"

"If you weren't tense, you wouldn't look upon me with envy after I've been with Erik."

"I do not look upon you with envy. I simply worry about the consequences of your actions."

Kitty lowered the onion she'd been slicing into large chunks. "It is sweet of you to worry, Meg, but you seem to have forgotten. I'm barren. There will be no consequences." She wiped her tears with the back of her hand again. "This is ridiculous. Why am I crying? I'm not sad."

"It's the onion," I told her.

She looked down at the remains of the onion in her hand. "Why is it the onion's fault?"

"Chopping them makes your eyes water."

She sniffed again and tossed the rest of the onion into the pot. "Very amusing, but I'm not falling for it. I may have believed your joke about sausages growing on trees, but I won't believe that onions make one cry. These must be happy tears, that's all."

I shared a smile with Meg. "In that case, chop another." I handed her a second onion while retrieving a turnip from the sack. "I think what Meg's trying to say is that we're worried about you developing feelings for Erik."

"Or Erik developing feelings for you," Meg added. "Nothing can come of your relationship. You're already married."

Kitty waved the knife around, dangerously close to my face. "Don't worry about us. I'm simply having a little fun, and Erik's not the sort to fall in love with just one woman. Our arrangement is temporary, and that suits us both."

I had to agree with her logic. Of all the people to have a casual dalliance with, Erik was probably the best choice. He loved all women, no matter their status, appearance, or even their character. He saw the world as a place filled with two types of women—ones he'd slept with and ones he'd yet to sleep with. Sometimes I wondered if he left the Margin and crossed the Hawk River because he'd been with every woman from his homeland and wanted to explore what the rest of the Fist Peninsula's female population had to offer.

"Look, Bal," said Theodore, approaching along the track. "I caught a rabbit." He held up his prize and beamed. Behind him, Dane carried two more.

"I'm thrilled for you," Balthazar said, rolling up the map. He slotted it back into the whale bone tube and stuffed the tube back into his pack. "Can I help with the cooking?"

"You can chop up this onion," Kitty said, holding it out to him along with the knife.

"No, thank you. They make my eyes water."

She cocked her head to the side. "Honestly, that joke is already rather old."

Balthazar looked to me and I winked back. "We don't need help, but you can come and talk to us while we work," I said.

"Kitty can keep going with the onions," Meg added. "Unless she wants to skin the rabbit?"

Kitty pulled a face and sniffed. "The onions will be fine."

Dane and Theodore gave their catch to Meg, and Theodore sat while Dane headed off again.

"Where are you going?" I asked.

"To check on the others," he said. "We felt as though we were being watched, and I want to make sure no one has approached. Has someone been on guard in both directions the entire time?"

"We haven't seen Max since he left to guard the southern approach," I said. "Nor Quentin. Erik has been with Quentin the entire time except for a brief, er, interlude here."

"Not that brief," Kitty said with a small smile.

Dane nodded his thanks for the report and disappeared along the track that led to the main road. I watched him go, wishing he'd given me a lingering look before heading off. Ever since leaving Glancia behind, he'd been distant towards me. He was civil but didn't instigate conversation or seek out my company in the evenings around the campfire.

To be fair, there weren't many opportunities for us to be alone. He took on the responsibility of leading the group, and that meant having a hand in every task from directing us along the right road to hunting and fixing a broken wheel axle. He even climbed a tree to get a better view of our surroundings.

I preferred to think of him as simply being too busy to spend time with me rather than willfully avoiding me. It made it easier to believe the former when I caught him looking at me from time to time. He always quickly looked away, however, and acted as though there'd been no longing in his gaze.

"I think we should stay longer in Merrin Fahl," Balthazar said as he settled on a log by the fire. "Two days isn't enough time to show our faces in both cities."

Merrin and Fahl were essentially two cities, one on each bank of the Mer River in the middle of Vytill. The city names were usually joined without the "and" between as the population moved freely between them. Merrin, the capital of Vytill, was the economic and political heart of the country where King Phillip and his advisers resided. Fahl was the smaller of the two cities. As home to the supreme priest, it was the spiritual center, not just of Vytill but of all the nations on the Fist Peninsula.

"I suspect you're right," I said. "We need at least two days just in Merrin."

"We should start in Fahl," Theodore said. "The Tilting high priest sent word ahead to his superior so we'll at least be assured of a good meal."

"And a bath," Kitty said on a sigh as she sat on the log beside Theodore. "How I long to be clean again."

"There's a stream through there," Meg said, nodding at the trees. "There's nothing stopping you from bathing in it."

"It's cold."

"Think of it as refreshing."

"There's nothing to wash with. I wish I'd brought a sponge and essence of rose with me. Do you think we can stay at an inn with a bathroom this time? Josie, perhaps you can suggest it to Dane."

"I doubt you'll find bathrooms anywhere outside the king's castle," I pointed out.

"Perhaps not even there," Balthazar said. "The castle is ancient, I believe. I doubt it has the modern luxuries of the palace. Your bath may have to be carried up the old fashioned way and filled by servants."

"I don't care how it's filled as long as the water is warm and smells sweet," Kitty said. "Surely there'll be an inn somewhere in Merrin Fahl that can find me a bath and essence of rose."

"It will cost you," Meg said, not looking up from the rabbit she was skinning with far more expertise than I could manage.

"I have money."

"Very little," I pointed out. "And it needs to last." No one asked how long it needed to last. There was no answer to such a question.

We fell into a discussion about which city we should start our search in. With Merrin being the larger of the two, the chances of there being missing persons was higher, but we might be able to secure the assistance of the supreme priest in Fahl. We all hoped that Balthazar's friend, the high priest of Glancia, had sent ahead his letter as promised and asked that we be helped in whatever manner we needed.

Despite a robust discussion, we could not come to a conclusion.

"Dane will decide for us," Kitty declared.

As if she'd summoned him, Dane appeared out of the dark woods, his strides long and purposeful, his face serious. "Someone has definitely been following us," he said, as if we'd just been talking about it.

"Should we douse the flames?" Theodore asked, rising.

"Leave the fire. Whoever it is already knows where we are."

Kitty clutched my hand. "What if it's my husband?"

"He doesn't know you're alive," I said. "It's more likely to be Brant." The former sergeant of the palace guards thought we had the magic gem. Since he had the remaining two wishes—or claimed to—after killing King Leon, he needed that gem to use them. He didn't believe us when we said it had been stolen before we even left Mull.

"It could be the Deerhorns," Balthazar said.

That put a dampener on our mood. Brant might be angry and violent but we'd so far been able to manage him. The Deerhorns were cruel, calculating, and powerful. Lady Deerhorn and her son, Lord Xavier, hated me with a vehemence bordering on madness.

"Are you sure someone is following us?" Theodore asked hopefully. "Perhaps they're just travelers, like us."

"They haven't revealed themselves," Dane said. "We're not the ones hiding. They are."

Meg tossed one of the rabbits into the pot. "Shouldn't we call back Max, Quentin and Erik? It could be dangerous."

"They'll return at nightfall."

"Wait a moment," Kitty said, frowning. "If the other party is hiding, how do you know there's anyone there at all?"

"Leaves rustle when they shouldn't," Dane said. "And there are footprints in the soil which aren't ours." He headed off to check on the horses, tied up at the edge of the clearing.

Kitty watched him go, blinking owlishly, her eyes still red from her onion tears. "What if we're wrong? What if Gladstow didn't believe our trick and knows I'm still alive. He and the Deerhorns will stop at nothing to actually kill me so he can marry Violette."

I squeezed her shoulder and Meg sat on Kitty's other side. "Would you like to learn a new skill?" she asked gently.

Kitty gave her a valiant smile. "Of course."

Meg handed her the knife and picked up a dead rabbit. "I'll show you how to skin it."

Kitty turned away and made a retching sound. "Some skills are best left unlearned."

As night swallowed up dusk, Max returned, shortly followed by Quentin and Erik who'd been on lookout together. Meg instantly sat up straighter, although she avoided Max's gaze. Erik went to sit beside Kitty on the log.

"You look upset," he said. "Are you unwell?"

"I'm a little worried," she told him. "Dane says someone followed us here."

He put his arm around her waist and kissed her temple. "Do not fear. I will protect you."

She gave him a sweet smile and leaned into him. "Thank you, Erik."

"Protect her from out here," I said. "Not in the wagon."

Quentin chuckled as he peered into the pot. "I'm starved."

"It's almost ready," Meg said.

"You're always hungry," Max grumbled. "You ate leftovers for breakfast *and* lunch."

Quentin patted his stomach. "I'm a growing lad."

Dane rejoined us after standing at the edge of the clearing where I suspected he was trying to listen for rustling bushes or snapping twigs. "I want two of us on watch at all times tonight instead of one. Quentin and I will do the first shift, then Erik and Max will take over."

"I can share watch duties," Theodore said.

"As can we." I indicated Meg and myself.

Dane shook his head. "The four of us will be sufficient." He smiled. It was forced.

Later, when the meal was finished, and the cleaning up done, I went to sit with Dane, not too close but close enough so he knew I wanted to be near him. "You're worried," I ventured.

"Not at all," he said, too jovially.

"You're a terrible actor."

"We can strike that off my list of prior occupations then." He scanned the forest, his body alert, tense. I ought to leave him alone so he could listen for intruders.

But I wasn't ready to do so. "Who do you think it is?"

"It's probably just bandits," he said. "Nothing to worry about."

I laughed softly. "To most people, bandits are worth worrying about."

"They haven't tangled with the Deerhorns."

I swallowed heavily.

His gaze settled on me for the first time since my arrival. "Sorry. It's not something to make light of." We fell into silence as he returned to scanning the forest for signs of someone lurking in the gloom.

"I've hardly seen you of late," he said quietly. "How are you since leaving Glancia behind?"

"I'm fine. Vytill is just the same as Glancia, really. The same sort of trees, the same water, the same soil. Even the company is the same." I didn't admit that leaving my village had been more unsettling than leaving behind the kingdom. I'd lived in Mull my entire life and ventured little further than Half Moon Cove. I felt disoriented and insignificant as I realized how large the Fist Peninsula was. Yet I was hopeful too. Hopeful that Dane would soon learn about his past and that we could be together, somewhere.

"Besides," I added lightly, "whose fault is it that you've hardly seen me of late, hmmm?"

"I don't know what you mean."

"You've been avoiding me."

"Not avoiding, just…" He heaved a deep sigh. "Very well, I've been avoiding you. It's nothing personal."

"It is," I shot back. "Very personal."

"That's the whole problem," he muttered, shoulders slumping.

I sidled closer and placed a hand on his arm. The muscles tensed. He peered sideways at me, his eyes dark and brooding.

"Just so you know, I hate this," he said.

I offered him a grim smile. "I hate it too, but it's the right thing to do. We must wait and see what we learn about your life."

"We're getting closer to answers, Josie. I feel it. I have a strong suspicion Freedland is the key to everything."

So many things pointed to Freedland as being the place to look for answers about the palace servants' pasts. According to the Tilting family of one of the servants, he'd been heading there before he'd disappeared. Balthazar had also bought maps of the republic and been studying accounts of the civil war before he too went missing. It all had to mean something. But what?

"The others want to linger in Merrin Fahl in the hope of finding information about missing people," I said.

"We'll take three days, but no more. The sooner we reach Freedland, the better. And not just for you and me." He nudged my elbow and nodded at Max, where he sat at one end of the log by the fire and Meg sat at the other. They didn't speak yet their stolen glances suggested they were very aware of each other.

Like I was aware of Dane, now and always. When he was near, my entire attention focused on him.

His attention must also have been focused on me. That was why neither of us heard the attackers until too late.

CHAPTER 2

*D*ane shot to his feet and drew his sword. "Go!" he shouted at me as he engaged the first attacker.

Another five descended on him.

Someone behind me shrieked.

Dane parried a strike from one of the swordsmen only to be struck across the shoulder by another before dodging out of the way.

I withdrew my surgeon's knife from my skirt pocket as two of the attackers lunged at Dane. Still reeling from the sudden appearance of the intruders, he was caught off guard and stumbled backwards, almost falling over the log we'd been sitting on. He stood on it and leaped backwards, creating space between himself and the enemy.

Both swordsmen followed and engaged him in battle while the remaining three became distracted as I raised my blade and plunged into the fray.

I didn't advance more than a single step, however. Erik shoved me out of the way as he stormed past, Max and Quentin on his heels. The attackers weren't distracted by me, but rather the armed swordsmen running towards them at full tilt.

"Josie, get back!" Meg grabbed my arm and dragged me out of the way.

Four of us and five of them. It was no contest. Max dispatched his opponent and helped Quentin, while Dane killed the man who'd struck him. His other attacker retreated and the rest followed. Erik, Max, Quentin and Dane raced after them, thrashing through the bushes.

Meg and I clung to one another, staring into the dark forest, listening for sounds of metal clashing. There were none.

"What if there are more in the forest?" Kitty asked, her voice trembling. "What if their plan was to draw our men away from the camp, leaving me exposed?"

She crossed her arms and hugged herself, her gaze darting around the edges of the campsite clearing.

Meg put her arm around Kitty's waist. I tightened my grip around the knife handle and scanned the darkness, straining to hear.

Somewhere in the forest depths, a flock of birds was disturbed out of their nests. They protested loudly before resettling.

Theodore drew up alongside me, a sword in hand. Balthazar passed a knife to Meg. We stood as one, staring into the forest, alert and scared.

Thudding footsteps announced the arrival of a small group before Dane emerged from the darkness at a run. He stopped upon seeing us, looking relieved. Erik and Max followed and Quentin brought up the rear. He leaned over, hands on knees, gasping in air.

"Well?" Balthazar asked.

"They got away," Max bit off. "Their horses were tethered not far from here."

Erik strode up to Kitty and drew her into a hug. She clung to him. Max did the same to Meg.

I gazed at Dane, wishing he would comfort me too. He approached but did not throw his arms around me in unbridled passion.

"All right?" he asked simply.

"Yes, but you're hurt. Take off your shirt. I need to dress your wound."

He gave orders to his men to watch the perimeter then finally sheathed his sword. He removed his shirt and sat on the log. I cleaned the cut on his shoulder, thankful it wasn't deep.

"It'll leave a faint scar," I said as I dressed it.

He inspected it then inspected another, older scar on his right shoulder that extended down his back. It must have been put there by the lashes from whippings he couldn't remember receiving. "They almost match."

"This is hardly a joke, Dane."

He reached for his shirt. "Just trying to lighten the mood."

With my work done, I allowed myself to admire the breadth of his shoulders, the muscles in his chest and arms and across his back. His body might be scarred but it was still more appealing than the marble statues of the male form that graced the palace gardens. Much more.

Balthazar and Theodore approached and Dane rose. He helped Balthazar down to the log then finished tying the laces of his shirt, covering up the chest I'd been admiring.

"Were they bandits?" Theodore asked.

"Hard to say," Dane said. "They were able swordsmen but not highly skilled."

Balthazar placed both hands over the head of his walking stick. "They had mounts just outside the clearing and there were five of them."

"Meaning?"

"Meaning they were organized. They came with more armed men than we have and had an escape planned."

"There's no evidence they worked for someone," Dane said.

"There's no evidence they were merely thieves, either."

"The Deerhorns would send more than five."

I wasn't sure if that was a comfort or not.

Dane made sure the spare weapons were stored in the wagon with Kitty, Meg and me overnight. I hardly slept as I listened for movement outside. Every rustle of leaves had me sitting upright, listening for an attack.

It did not come and we arose in the morning to fresh autumn air and the sounds of the forest surrounding us. Dane looked tired but assured me he was fine when I inquired.

"And the wound?" I asked.

"Also fine."

"Let me know if it becomes more painful."

We packed away our camp things and set off, returning to the main road that led to Merrin Fahl. After spending the morning traveling in the back of the wagon with Kitty and Meg, I decided to walk beside Quentin in the afternoon.

He greeted me from the saddle then yawned. "Say something to keep me awake, Josie. I'm dog tired."

"Tell me about your girl back at the palace."

His cheeks flushed. "She's real nice. Real shy too."

"How did you get to know her then? You're hardly the most outgoing person yourself."

"I fell in her lap. She was sitting on a stool in the kitchen, peeling potatoes, and I tripped over my own feet." He made a tumbling motion with his hand. "I was so embarrassed, I couldn't even talk proper. My words didn't make sense. She thought that was funny and started laughing, so I laughed too."

"Then you got to talking and you charmed her?"

"Nope. The cook yelled at me to stop pestering his staff. I told him I was looking for leftovers, but he chased me out of the kitchen without so much as a lettuce leaf to satisfy my hunger. Ruby came looking for me later in the garrison. She brought me a pie."

"How sweet."

"She is."

He chatted about Ruby for some time, and I found my mind wandering to the head of our procession where Dane and Erik rode together. Erik seemed as relaxed as always on horseback, but Dane's shoulders were rigid. His head turned at every scuttling creature in the leaves at the side of the road, every squawk of a bird in the sky.

"He looks tired this morning," I said to Quentin during a lull in the conversation.

"Who?" he asked around yet another yawn.

"Dane."

"That's because he didn't sleep last night. He was supposed to swap with me but he stayed up so there was three of us on watch during the second shift."

"Typical," I muttered. "He does too much."

"He feels responsible for our safety. Once we reach Merrin Fahl, he'll get some rest. Bandits only attack on the road."

The city wouldn't be any safer if the Deerhorns had indeed sent those bandits to attack us.

* * *

WE ENTERED the smaller of the twin cities, Fahl, before nightfall. It was on the same side of the river as our approach and it was also the location of the inn where we wanted to stay. Rhys, the master of the warrior priests from Merdu's Guards in Tilting, had given us the name of the inn where he and his men usually stayed when on pilgrimage to the religious capital of the Fist Peninsula. Located in the shadow of the supreme priest's temple, it was central, clean and run by an honest innkeeper. Mention of Rhys's name earned us the best rooms and a hot meal upon our arrival.

The following morning, Balthazar was summoned to the supreme priest's temple by a messenger dressed in the simple brown robes of a priest.

"Tell him I'll come later," Balthazar said over breakfast in the inn's dining room.

The messenger's brows rose ever so slightly. "It's not a request, Brother."

Balthazar sighed. "Can I at least finish my breakfast?"

The messenger looked uncertain how to answer. Balthazar sighed again and rose. "At least it's not far."

"His Supreme Holiness has sent a sedan chair for you. It's waiting outside."

"Want me to come with you?" Theodore asked.

"Only Brother Balthazar," the messenger said.

"Friendly," Balthazar muttered as he passed me.

The rest of us finished breakfast and were about to leave to begin inquiries into missing persons when another messenger arrived. He wore a tunic of purple and gold livery, the chest emblazoned with the emblem of a hawk carrying an eye in its beak. The king of Vytill had summoned us.

Dane, Theodore and I traveled in royal carriages across the bridge connecting the two cities. The amount of traffic should have made it a long journey, but carts, carriages, riders and pedestrians all gave way to us.

We carved a path through the crowd towards the magnificent fortress on the hill. It was larger than the Tilting castle of the former king of Glancia but the palace near Mull would have dwarfed it. No matter how grand these old castles were, none could ever amaze me after witnessing the palace.

Like the Tilting castle, this one was built to withstand assault, although the history books hadn't recorded an attack on the kingdom in centuries. Built from the same stone as the outcrops on the rocky hill, it looked as though it had been thrown up, fully formed, by whatever natural forces had created the landscape. With steep slopes leading up to high walls on two sides, and a sheer wall plunging into the river on the third, the only access was via the steep winding road.

All traffic to and from the castle took the same route. Empty carts passed us going in the opposite direction, along with errand boys on horseback, and a gleaming black carriage with the curtains closed. We had to wait at the outer gate for a farmer to move his gaggle of geese to the side, but we traveled freely through the second gate, and the third, without being stopped by the guards on duty. We were expected.

The person who waited for us in the large room was someone quite unexpected. Two someones.

Lord Barborough and a young woman.

The former was dressed as usual in black garb, his right arm limp at his side. The latter wore a sky-blue gown with leaves embroidered in silver thread on her skirt and sleeves, the wide opening at the neck showing off her slender throat and collar bones.

I instinctively curtseyed. As I rose, she bestowed a gentle smile on me.

"You must be Joselyn Cully," she said in a soft voice. "Glancian women really are as beautiful as they say."

I rose, aware that I was blushing fiercely. "Thank you..."

Lord Barborough stepped forward and hurriedly made introductions. "This is Her Royal Highness, the Princess Illiriya."

"Thank you, Your Highness," I said. "That's very gracious of you."

Lord Barborough introduced Dane and Theodore and asked after Balthazar.

"Your messenger missed him," Theodore said. "He was summoned to the supreme priest's temple early this morning."

"What a shame," Princess Illiryia said. "But of course we must allow him time to reconnect with his faith in the god's city."

"You know he was—is—a brother from the order of Merdu's Guards?" Dane asked, his gaze sliding to Lord Barborough, Vytill representative to Glancia and spy.

"We have been informed," she said. "Come. Sit, and tell me about yourselves."

She took a seat at one end of the room where a cluster of cushioned chairs had been arranged before the fireplace. A low fire crackled, throwing out enough heat to reach the chairs but not warm the rest of the large room. Banners of purple velvet edged with gold hung from the high ceiling, and tapestries covered the stone walls, but it would be a cold place in winter. This room wouldn't be the public audience chamber where the king sat on a throne and met his people, but it wouldn't be the more intimate chamber for meeting favorites either.

Princess Illiriya looked regal as she sat on a chair raised above the others on a low dais, her honey-colored hair woven in a complex arrangement of braids high on her head. Her cool blue eyes matched her dress and the single sapphire ring on her finger. She wore other jewels at her throat, ears, wrists, and in her hair, leaving no one in any doubt of her father's wealth. Wealth that diminished every day since the cataclysmic event known as The Rift cut off the Thumb from the Fist and rendered its once-bustling port useless to Vytill. All of those taxes were now pouring into Glancia's coffers via Mull. It must gall this woman's father, but the nineteen year-old princess looked as though she didn't have a care in the world.

Princesses usually didn't. Born to make strategic alliances, and bred to be ornamental, they were nothing more than another jewel in their kingdom's crown. I'd never given princesses a second thought, and certainly not a sympathetic or pitying one, until I'd met Lady Miranda Claypool and Kitty. Now I knew the privileges afforded noblewomen came with a price—freedom. It wasn't a price I would be willing to pay.

"You must be wondering why I've asked you to come here," Princess Illiriya said.

"Asked?" Dane echoed with a hint of steel edging his tone.

I winced. Out of the corner of my eye I saw Theodore shoot him a glare.

"Don't be insolent," Lord Barborough snapped.

"My apologies," Dane said to the princess. "It's been a long journey from Tilting and we have much to accomplish in Merrin Fahl before we move on."

"Of course," she said. "I won't keep you long."

"And the presence of the man who threatened Josie on numerous occasions tends to put me on my guard."

The princess went quite still. "Is that so," she said, her voice chilly.

Lord Barborough cleared his throat. "King Phillip wanted information. I never intended to follow through on my threats." He tapped his limp arm. "I'm quite harmless."

He might be less able than most men but he was far from harmless. He had more power and influence than me, and more cunning. I didn't trust him then and I was yet to make up my mind whether to trust him now.

"Lord Barborough tells me it's an arduous journey to Glancia, although I haven't traveled there myself," the princess went on as though the frosty exchange hadn't happened. "I would have done so this autumn, but…events occurred to render the journey unnecessary."

Most of King Leon's advisors had wanted him to marry this woman. King Phillip of Vytill also wanted the union to take place. Leon had hesitated, allowing Lady Violette Morgrave and her Deerhorn mother to swoop in and carve out a place in his heart.

He would have liked the elegant princess sitting before me,

however. She wasn't as beautiful as Lady Morgrave, and couldn't hold a candle to Miranda, but she had a quality about her that demanded attention. Leon could have used a jewel like Princess Illiriya by his side if he'd continued to rule.

"Lord Barborough returned from Mull with many interesting tales," she went on. "Tales about Mull's unrest and the governor's plans, about the nobles and ministers, about the magnificent golden palace and its strange servants. And about Leon."

Not *King* Leon.

"So you believe in magic," Dane said simply.

"Lord Barborough made a convincing case."

Lord Barborough's lips curved with his smirk.

"Is that why we're here?" Theodore asked. "To confirm his story?"

"Or are you after the unused wishes?" Dane added.

"Lord Barborough says the guard who killed Leon inherited the wishes," the princess said matter-of-factly. "Is that true?"

"Brant claims he has them," Dane said. "But he's not the most trustworthy person."

"And the gem?" Lord Barborough asked. "Do you have that?"

"No."

Lord Barborough scoffed. "Of course you'd say that."

Princess Illiriya put up her hand to silence him. "Miss Cully, you clearly believe in magic too or you wouldn't be here, helping these men find their pasts. You're a long way from home. You're a medical woman, are you not?"

"A midwife," I said.

"With ambitions to become a doctor." She smiled. "If it were allowed."

"Which it is not."

"It's a travesty, in my opinion. Women would make marvelous doctors. Scholars too, and advisors, even queens in their own right. Perhaps one day the laws will change in our favor."

"Perhaps."

"What does your medical knowledge say about memory loss?" she asked, quite seriously.

I hesitated. Beside me, Dane gave his head a slight shake in warning.

"I couldn't possibly say," I said. "I'm not a doctor."

Her eyes twinkled. "A diplomatic answer. You're wise to be careful among strangers. Very well, what would your father say about the servants' memory loss? He was a doctor, I believe."

"He said it's unheard of for so many to be affected at once."

"Does that make it impossible? Or simply improbable?"

I had no answer to that. She was right. It wasn't impossible. Precedents had to start somewhere.

She sat back, smiling. "I'm sorry if I seem reluctant to believe. I'm logical by nature and prefer evidence and reason over speculation and suggestion. Magic is neither logical nor reasonable, and yet..." She spread her hands to encompass Dane and Theodore. "I find myself wanting to believe."

"I, too, was hesitant at first, Your Highness," I said.

"Lord Barborough informed us of Leon's dying confession, how he admitted to finding the magic gem and was granted three wishes. He used only the one, is that correct?"

"Yes, Your Highness," Theodore said.

"Your father, the king, is aware of magic," Dane said. "Did he not want to meet us too?"

She gave a small, elegant shrug. "As you can understand better than most, the demand on a king's time is ceaseless. He wanted to meet you today, but alas it won't be possible. How long are you staying in Merrin Fahl?"

"A few days," Dane said.

"You're going to ask if anyone has been reported missing?"

"We'll make some inquiries."

"You won't find any," Lord Barborough said with a hint of smugness. "I've sent servants into various quarters in both cities. They heard of no missing persons."

"Perhaps we'll get a different result," Dane said evenly.

Lord Barborough's lips tightened.

Princess Illiriya's lips softened with her warm smile. "I wish you well in your search. Where do you think you'll go after you leave here?"

So she didn't know we were heading to Freedland. We hadn't

made a secret of it, but we hadn't told many people either. Not even the servants we'd left behind in Tilting knew.

"We're not sure," Dane said. "Vytill is a big kingdom with many villages that could yet provide answers."

"It's probably wise to remain in Vytill for the time being," she agreed. "There are tensions in Glancia. It might not be safe to return until the next ruler has been chosen."

"You mean until your father has manipulated his way onto the throne."

I sucked in air between my teeth and tried to glare at him but he wasn't looking my way. He watched the princess.

His accusation was a dangerous one to make. While we suspected King Phillip had sent messages to the lords of Glancia, confusing them with lies about which nobleman supported which duke, we had no proof. It was also madness to suggest it within these walls.

"Hold your tongue, Hammer," Lord Barborough snapped.

"It's all right," Princess Illiriya said evenly. "I don't know if what you say is true, but I hope not. I don't want my father to secure the Glancian throne for himself. I'll be forced to travel all the way to Zemaya and beyond to seek a husband. At least if one of the dukes wins the throne, I'll not be too far from here—if I can marry into the successful family, of course. I believe Buxton has a son near my age."

"And Gladstow is now looking for a wife," Lord Barborough said, a thread of glee in his voice that had his princess turning a disapproving frown onto him.

"Have a care, my lord. The poor duchess has not been gone long."

Lord Barborough bowed his head. "My humble apologies, Your Highness. But I warn you, if you desire to marry the duke of Gladstow, we must work quickly. Lady Morgrave is circling."

"How can I desire him when your reports made him seem so unappealing?"

He spluttered an apology. "Gladstow has some fine qualities."

"Chief among them being that he might win the succession race?"

Lord Barborough's head dropped further.

"You would have encountered the duke of Gladstow regularly at the palace," she said to Theodore and Dane. "What do you think of him?"

"I couldn't possibly say," Theodore said. "I was merely valet to the king."

Dane was much less diplomatic. "If Your Highness is looking for a lying, cold-hearted, manipulative and boorish husband, then by all means, challenge Lady Morgrave for the duke. Otherwise, my advice is to stay away."

She stilled and my heart sank. Dane had overstepped this time.

"Thank you, Captain," she said. "Your honesty is refreshing and your consideration for my welfare is kind, even more so because we are strangers to one another." She did not look at Lord Barborough, but her words were as much a stab at him as they were praise for Dane.

Lord Barborough adjusted his limp arm across his lap and looked away.

"I have nothing to gain by withholding my opinion of Gladstow," Dane said.

Princess Illiriya stood and put out her hand to him. He stood too and bowed over it.

"Good day, Captain. Theodore, Miss Cully, it was a pleasure to meet you all. I wish you well in your adventures." She suddenly grasped my hand and held my gaze with an earnest, compelling one of her own. "Do not give up on your dream of becoming a doctor. It may happen in our lifetime."

I curtseyed. "I hope so, Your Highness."

Footmen escorted us from the room and out of the castle into the courtyard where we stepped into the royal carriage. As we drove off, I peered up at the arrow slit windows, the turreted tower, the thick outer wall and the stony-faced guards at the gates. It was a cold, forbidding place, yet the princess had been warm and welcoming.

She was nothing like I expected. I'd been wrong about her. She wasn't bred to be an ornament. She was raised to be a capable leader in her own right. Considering she had a brother to take over the Vytill throne, that meant she was expected to become queen in another kingdom. But with Freedland now a republic, Dreen's king comfortably married and his sons not yet of age, that left only Glancia. And Glancia no longer had a king. If King Phillip succeeded in manipulating his way onto the Glancian throne, then the princess's marital options decreased further. Such a vibrant, clever and regal woman might not want to settle for anything less than a prince. A mere countess wouldn't do.

"Does Zemaya have a royal family?" Theodore asked, peering out the other window at the castle. Clearly his mind was working in the same direction as mine.

"Yes, but their kings are chosen, not born," I said. "When one king dies, the ruling lords come together and fight in a series of physical contests. The new king is the one who wins the most bouts. Besides, Zemayans marry young. A new king will usually already have a wife and children when he takes the crown."

He sat back. "I wonder what she'll do."

"Hope that the duke of Buxton wins," I said.

"Will hope be enough for her?" Dane asked.

Theodore tilted his head and regarded Dane. "You think she'll play a more active role to see Buxton on the Glancian throne?"

"It's possible. I don't know. She might be precisely as she seems—a friendly young princess with few cares. Or she might be as manipulative as her father. All I do know is, I don't trust Barborough, and he was by her side."

We traveled in silence until we reached the base of the hill. Dane opened the carriage door and instructed the driver to leave us there. He assisted me out and indicated the extension of the castle road where it plunged into the city.

"We might as well start here," he said.

I wasn't yet ready to end our conversation, however. "Could Barborough have sent those men to attack us in the forest?"

"Strange way to welcome visitors," Theodore said as the carriage rolled away.

"Perhaps he instructed them to dispatch us and retrieve the gem. He suspects we have it."

Dane scanned the vicinity, his hand on the hilt of his sword.

"We must be very careful. Barborough has influence here. He has the ear of both the king and princess. If he can convince them that we have the gem, they'll send more than a handful of swordsmen to search for it."

Theodore and I exchanged glances. Then we moved closer to Dane.

CHAPTER 3

e spent the rest of the day in Merrin, asking in the market and surrounding streets if anyone had gone missing in the past two years. Only one had, but Dane and Theodore didn't recognize his name and he didn't fit the description of any of the palace servants.

It was a long and strange day. Everywhere we went, people stared. My height and blonde hair marked me as Glancian, and Theodore was clearly from Dreen with his flat features, while Dane was taller and darker than the Vytillians. In Tilting, we'd seen people from all nations, including Zemaya, going about their business. I expected Merrin to be the same, at least certainly with Glancians and Freedlanders since Vytill was situated between the two countries. But everyone looked like the typical Vytillian with brown hair and of medium height, a blend of the people over its northern border with those in the south.

We returned to the inn in Fahl to meet Kitty, Meg, Erik, Max and Quentin who'd been making the same inquiries in the god's city. From the looks on their faces, they'd had no luck either.

"No one," Max said. "Not a single missing person matched anyone we know."

"The same," Theodore told them.

Kitty groaned as she eased herself onto a stool in the

taproom. "My feet ache, my legs hurt, my back is stiff. How do ordinary people walk all day?"

"Practice," Quentin said.

"We have no other option," Meg added.

Erik placed four large tankards of ale on the table. "This is why I ride everywhere. My feet ache too. Later, you can massage them, Kitty."

She pulled a face. "That's disgusting."

"I will massage yours too." He returned to the counter to retrieve the other three tankards, just as Balthazar entered the taproom.

Dane dragged over another stool for him. "You've been with the supreme priest all day?"

Balthazar sat with a shake of his head. "Our meeting was brief. After I explained our predicament and our reason for remaining in the city for a few days, he loaned me a carriage. I drove around Merrin and asked about missing persons."

"What did you find?" Max asked.

"None of the reported missing matched anyone we know," Balthazar said heavily. "It was a disheartening day."

Theodore cradled his tankard between both hands and stared into the liquid. "Does anyone else think it strange we've come up with nothing?"

"It's early days," I assured him. "Merrin and Fahl are large cities. We'll continue tomorrow."

"What did the supreme priest want with you?" Dane asked Balthazar.

"He simply wanted to meet me. The high priest's letter mentioned everything about my disappearance and reappearance at the palace, and the supreme priest was curious."

"The letter mentioned everything?"

Balthazar nodded. "He asked me why I thought magic was involved, and how. He listened without comment. When I finished, he merely changed the subject. He wanted to know what Leon was like, my thoughts on the Glancian political situation, and my plans for the future."

"So you don't know if he believed you about magic?" Theodore asked.

"He's a religious man," Max said wryly. "He's not going to believe in anything that questions the existence of the god and goddess."

"What was he like?" I asked.

Balthazar shrugged. "Intelligent, quiet, considerate. Rather bland, really, when comparing him to the Glancian high priest. I found him difficult to read."

"What about you three?" Max asked Dane, Theodore and me. "Who did you meet at the castle?"

"The castle?" Balthazar asked, his bushy brows arching.

"We received a summons after you left," Dane said.

Theodore smiled into his tankard. "You're not the only important person in this group, Bal."

Quentin chuckled. "He is the most self-important though."

Balthazar stabbed Quentin's leg with the end of his walking stick. "I may no longer be your superior, but you don't get to tease me until you've got hairs on your chest."

"I've got hairs on my chest."

"Those bits of fluff are not hairs," Erik said.

Dane told them about our meeting with the princess and Lord Barborough, as well as our theories about the princess's future.

"Is that why you think she wanted to meet with us?" Balthazar asked. "She wanted an opinion other than Barborough's about the political situation in Glancia?"

"Perhaps," Dane said. "But the king must have more spies than just Barborough. She doesn't need us."

"Perhaps her father doesn't keep her informed and she wanted to make up her own mind."

"Can she do that?" Quentin asked.

I bristled. "We women are quite capable of forming opinions."

Quentin reddened. "I meant can she go behind her father's back and talk to his spies."

"We don't know if the king knew about our visit or not," Dane said. "She implied he did but was too busy to meet us."

"So if you don't think she was simply gathering information, why did she want to meet you?" Meg asked.

"I'm not certain." Dane looked to me. "Josie?"

"I think she wanted to decide for herself if you've truly lost your memories," I said. "She might not have believed Barborough."

"And by extension," Theodore said, "she wanted to decide for herself if magic is behind this." He tapped his temple.

"I wonder what she thinks now," Max said.

We finished our ales and we women returned to the room we shared on the second floor. Kitty flopped on the bed, her feet dangling off the end. She undid her bootlaces and kicked them off before lying back with a groan.

"I'm tired and hungry," she mumbled.

"Then come and freshen up before we rejoin the men for supper." Meg tossed her a cloth and indicated the basin of water. "You can use it first."

Kitty sighed and got to her feet with some effort. "I don't think the boots you bought for me in Tilting are very good. My feet shouldn't hurt this much."

I inspected one of the boots. It was made from the finest leather, but like all new boots, they needed to be worn in to soften. I told Kitty as much.

"How long will that take?" she asked, lifting her hair off her neck and turning her back to Meg so Meg could help her undress. She hadn't shed all of her duchess's ways yet. Perhaps she never would.

"Another day walking around Merrin should do it," I said cheerfully.

"I want to help them find out more about themselves," she said. "I truly do. But surely there's a better way. Can I not ride with Erik? We can cover more ground on horseback."

"The horses need a rest," I said.

"*I* need a rest."

Meg helped draw Kitty's shirt over her head. "It has only been one day. Would you prefer we leave you at the inn while we go out?"

Kitty wrinkled her nose. "No, thank you." She squared her shoulders and tossed her head. "I'm a humble woman now. If I must traipse the streets with my friends, then I will do so and suffer aching feet like the rest of you."

"Please do it quietly," Meg muttered.

Kitty washed and dried herself with the towel the maid had left for us to share. "What was the princess like?" she asked as I performed my ablutions at the basin.

"She seemed nice," I said. "Her bearing was very noble, her manner friendly if a little aloof. She reminded me of Miranda."

"Miranda!" Kitty pouted. "Why not me? I have a noble bearing. I'm friendly and a little aloof too." She sniffed. "I'm also a duchess which is only one rung down from a princess."

"Um…"

Meg cleared her throat. "She looked more like Miranda. That's what you told me earlier, Josie."

"Yes, that's it," I said. "Her hair was more like Miranda's than yours."

My excuse satisfied Kitty enough that she let the matter drop and didn't ask any more questions about the princess.

* * *

HAVING LEFT Balthazar at the inn, the rest of us split into two groups the following morning. Dane, Erik, Kitty and I began our inquiries at the riverside dock and moved through one of Merrin's slums before choosing random streets to wander down in the afternoon. Erik received stares wherever he went, but took them in his stride, even smiling at the children. Most ran off in fear, but a few brave souls asked him what he was doing so far from home.

"Searching for my missing friends," he always said. "You might know them." And that provided us with an opening to broach the subject of missing people. But by the end of the day, we'd not had any success.

"Wait here a few moments," Dane said as we approached a large inn beneath the sign of a rearing white horse.

"Good," Erik said. "I am thirsty. Come, let's drink."

Dane agreed but was the last to head through the archway leading to the inn's courtyard and stables. He checked up and down the street then followed me.

"What is it?" I asked.

"We're being watched."

"Did you see someone?"

He didn't get a chance to answer me. The ostler caught Erik's arm and Erik retaliated by grabbing hold of the man's jerkin.

The ostler swallowed heavily but didn't let go. "I know you."

Erik's fist sprang open and the ostler moved away, out of his reach.

He wagged a finger at Erik. "Thief!" he shouted.

The grooms stopped what they were doing, but did not approach.

"Call the constables!" the ostler told them. "This man is a thief!"

Erik took a step towards him. "I am no thief."

Dane stepped between them, arms outstretched to keep the men apart. While Erik looked like he would engage the ostler in a fight, the ostler looked relieved to have someone intervene.

"I can assure you, this man is not a thief," Dane said. "We only arrived in Merrin Fahl two days ago. This is the first time he has set foot in this part of the city."

"Doesn't matter when he got here." The ostler spat into the straw-covered cobblestones. "The theft happened two winters ago. I never forget a face. Especially one that looks like that."

Dane lowered his arms. "You recognize him?"

"That's what I said, isn't it?"

I went to join the men but Kitty held me back. "Stay here with me," she whispered. "I don't like this."

"Are you sure it was me?" Erik asked the ostler.

"Course it was you. How many other Marginers pass through here?"

"I do not know. How many?"

The ostler looked at Erik as if he were stupid. "None. Just you with your rat-tail hair and these dots on your head." He tapped his own forehead.

Erik rubbed his tattoos.

"Tell us what you remember about the theft," Dane said.

"He turned up here on foot, boots just about worn through, wearing no jerkin or doublet, even though it was winter. He snuck in, all quiet like, thinking we were asleep."

"It was night?"

"Aye."

"If it was dark, how can you be sure it was this man?"

The ostler spat again. "I already told you, he's a Marginer. Ain't been no other Marginers before or since and I've lived in Merrin my whole life. It must be the same one."

"What did he steal?" Dane asked.

"A horse." The ostler jerked his thumb at the stable block behind him where two lads mucking out the stalls had emerged to listen to the exchange. Their wide-eyed stares focused on Erik.

Erik puffed out his chest. If I didn't know any better, I would say he was enjoying the attention. But his gaze was filled with worry. The chest puffing was an attempt to make himself look bigger, more formidable, as if facing down an opponent just before a fight.

I eyed the archway through which we'd come. Two burly men stood there, arms crossed, blocking our exit.

Kitty's grip on my arm tightened and her swallow sounded loud in my ear.

"He came here, speaking in a strange tongue," the ostler said.

"Probably his own language," Dane said wryly. "Did you try to communicate with him?"

"He couldn't understand me, and I couldn't understand him. He gave up and looked like he was going to leave, then a rider came. He dismounted and handed the reins to this fellow without paying him any attention."

"The rider thought he was a groom?"

"Aye. By the time I pointed out his mistake, the Marginer had mounted and ridden out of the yard. We shouted until the constables came, but by then he was long gone."

"If the rider gives me the reins, it is not theft," Erik said triumphantly.

"It bloody well is!"

"Do you know where he went?" Dane asked.

The ostler kept his gaze on Erik but answered Dane. "The sheriff said there were sightings on the south road. He sent word ahead to all the village sheriffs from here to the border to be on the alert. We never did hear if he was caught."

Dane plucked a coin from his pocket and held it out to the ostler. "I can assure you, my friend is not that man. He has never been to Vytill. Please accept this for the information about the thief. It happens that we're looking for him too."

"That so?" The ostler scratched his whiskers and eyed the coin. "Seems an unlikely coincidence to me."

"Yet still a coincidence."

The ostler's lips twisted from side to side. "I don't know."

A commotion at the archway saw the two men keeping guard part to allow in a third on horseback. He was dressed in a constable's uniform of blue tunic and breeches.

He pointed his sword at Erik. "You're under arrest! Get down on your knees, hands behind your head!"

Erik's hands curled into fists at his sides.

"There's been a misunderstanding," Dane said quickly. "This isn't the same man from two winters ago. He has—"

"*Is* it the same man?" the constable asked the ostler.

The ostler scratched his whiskers. "I reckon so."

Dane hissed out a frustrated breath between his teeth.

The constable pressed the point of his sword into Erik's chest. "Get down on your knees and put your hands in the air, Thief!"

"Stop this at once!" Kitty cried in a voice that would have sent palace maids scurrying to do her bidding. She let me go and drew herself up to her full height. "This man is innocent. Move aside and let us pass."

The constable chuckled. "Who're you to give me orders? The princess herself?" He laughed and looked around to see if anyone laughed with him.

Dane moved up alongside Erik and spoke quietly to him.

"Oi!" The constable thrust out his sword, the point drawing dangerously close to Dane's chin. "You're all under arrest until we get this sorted. Understand, Marginer?"

"I understand." It was unclear if Erik was speaking to the constable or Dane.

I took Kitty's hand. It shook, either with fear or anger or perhaps both. "Get ready to run," I whispered.

Her fingers squeezed mine then let go. She gathered up her skirts and marched past the constable, nose in the air. "This is ridiculous. I am not under arrest and nor are my friends. We've done nothing wrong. Come along, Josie. Erik, Dane, it's time we left, not just this inn but this city. Merrin has turned out to be quite the disappointment so far. Mull is more civilized than this pigsty."

"Stop!" the constable commanded. He wheeled his horse around to go after her.

Distracted by Kitty, the move also left him exposed on his left. Dane reached up, grabbed the constable by the doublet and pulled him off the horse. The constable tried to strike Dane as he fell, but Dane caught his wrist and wrenched the sword off him.

"Josie, go!" he shouted.

I looked up to see Erik barreling towards the two self-appointed guards in the archway. They stood their ground, but were no match for a big Marginer running at full speed. One fell over and the other careened into the archway.

With a foot to the chest of the man on the ground, Erik beckoned for Kitty and I to pass.

We ran.

I glanced back to see Erik removing his foot and setting off after us, Dane on his heels. The man on the ground reached up as he passed and grabbed Dane's ankle. Dane stumbled, one hand to the ground to stop himself falling completely, his other hand still clutching the constable's sword. He kicked out and the man released him, but the delay cost Dane precious moments.

The second man charged up behind him, teeth bared, veins bulging in his neck.

"Dane!" I screamed as the man launched himself forward.

Dane turned and struck upwards. The sword hilt connected with the underside of the man's chin, stopping him in his tracks. He fell backwards into the dust with a thud.

"Split up," Dane said to Erik. "Take Kitty."

Erik grabbed Kitty's hand and they went left, only to stop. Erik swore.

Dane and I glanced back and stopped too. Up ahead, Lord Xavier Deerhorn sat on horseback, his jaw slack as he realized he'd stumbled upon us.

And we were running from the law.

"Catch them!" the constable shouted.

Dane and I ran. All around us, shops and houses lined the street without so much as a narrow alley between them offering an escape route.

Behind me, hooves thundered and I could swear I heard Lord Xavier's chuckle on the breeze.

I glanced over my shoulder to see that he'd not bothered with Erik. Hopefully he hadn't even looked at Kitty, his eyes on a different prize—me.

The constable rode out of the stable yard, saw that we were being pursued, and took off after Erik and Kitty.

Dear Hailia, protect them. Protect us all.

I stumbled, only to be pulled upright by Dane. We didn't speak as we sprinted. We didn't have to. We both knew we couldn't outrun Lord Xavier on horseback. We had to find another way.

Just as Lord Xavier rode up, hand outstretched to grab me, Dane jerked me out of his reach. We dashed around a corner into a short alley. It was empty. The upper floors of the houses on either side almost met above our heads. A slender streak of cloudy sky gave us just enough light to avoid hurtling into the cart wheel leaning against a barrel, but not enough to illuminate the dark recesses.

It was into one of these recesses that Dane pushed me. I flattened myself against the door at my back. I expected Dane to join me, but he did not. Merdu, what was he doing! Lord Xavier would surely follow. His horse's momentum would have taken him beyond the alley entrance but not far. He'd soon circle back.

"There'll be another for you after you tell the rider we went that way," I heard Dane say.

Then he was pressing against me, my face in his chest, the spare sword between us. His heartbeat thundered in my ear, matching my own.

The hooves of Lord Xavier's horse passed us and I let out a breath. We were safe.

But Dane did not move and a moment later, the sound of the hooves returned at a more sedate pace. Something crashed and wood splintered. The barrel and wheel, most likely suffering from a blow inflicted by Lord Xavier's sword.

Silence thickened in the small alley. A horse snuffled. A hoof clomped on the stones. "Come out," Lord Xavier growled. "I see you there."

My heart lurched into my throat and my body suddenly felt weak, light, as if I might float away. I was only held up by Dane and the door.

"I said come out, Josie! Or Merdu help me, I'll ram this sword down your lover's throat before your eyes."

"Don't hurt me, sir," came a small, trembling voice.

Lord Xavier swore. "The man and woman who came down here. Did you see where they went?"

"That way."

"Impossible. I would have seen them when I got to the end. There's nowhere for them to hide, nowhere for them to escape."

"There are ways to escape, sir. There's tunnels under the buildings. The entrance is in the house with the sign of the black snake."

Lord Xavier rode away, but Dane didn't move until the sound of the hooves on the cobblestones faded altogether.

"You can come out now," the child said.

Dane stepped back, releasing me. I drew in a deep breath and peered at the boy—or perhaps it was a girl—of about nine years of age, palm outstretched to receive a coin from Dane.

"Thank you for your service," Dane said as he deposited the coin in the child's palm. "But I advise you to leave the area immediately. He'll be back when he discovers you lied about the tunnel entrance. Ingenious, by the way."

"It ain't a lie," the child said defensively. "There are tunnels with an entrance near here. Only it's not at the house of the black snake. That's a bawdy house of a particular kind. The rough kind, if you know what I mean. Pardon me, miss."

"It's all right," I said, trying not to laugh in giddy relief.

Dane and I held hands and raced out of the alley, back the way we'd entered, and headed towards the river. From there, we walked swiftly until we reached the inn where we found Kitty and Erik kissing on the bed in the room I shared with her and Meg.

Kitty sprang up and threw her arms around me. "Thank Hailia, you're safe. We were so worried."

"I can see that." I nodded at the bed.

"I needed distracting. How did you get away?"

"Through trickery and a lot of help from a street urchin. You?"

"I stole a horse," Erik said.

"*Borrowed*," Kitty said. "It was tethered outside a tavern. Once on horseback, we were able to evade the constable. Erik is an excellent horseman, and I'm quite good myself."

Erik puffed out his chest. "We rode around Merrin until we lost the constable and then I ask a boy to take the horse back to the tavern. Then we came here."

"You weren't followed?" Dane asked.

Erik shook his head and smiled. "Today was a good day! We know I was in Merrin two winters ago and took the road to Freedland. We will find answers there. I am sure of it now." He clapped Dane on the shoulder.

"It would be good news if you weren't a wanted man and Lord Xavier didn't know we were here," Dane said.

I sat on the bed, the day's exertions beginning to take their toll on my legs. They felt heavy and my feet hurt. My spirit was affected too. Erik was right, and we had reason to celebrate after he was recognized, but the appearance of Lord Xavier worried me.

"What's he doing here anyway?" I asked.

"Following us," Dane suggested. "His family are not convinced we were telling the truth in Tilting when we said we didn't have the gem. I can think of no other reason why he'd leave Glancia when he should be helping his parents shore up support for Gladstow."

His mere presence proved just how important finding the gem was to the Deerhorns. When we'd last seen her in Tilting, Lady Deerhorn had convinced me she no longer believed we possessed the gem. According to her, we would have used it to our advantage already if we had it.

But sending her son here proved otherwise.

I lifted my hair off my neck to cool myself a little. It had fallen from its arrangement in the pursuit and become tangled. I pulled out the pins and tried to fix my hair back in place but my hands trembled and I made a bigger mess.

Dane sat beside me and drew my hands away. He quietly went about pinning my hair back in place under Kitty's critical eye.

"We'll leave tomorrow at first light," he said as he worked. "It's too dangerous to stay here now."

* * *

"ARE YOU ALL RIGHT?" Meg asked me as we ate a supper of bread, cheese and pigeon pie in the inn's dining room that evening.

I crumbled the pie crust between my fingers and watched it form a little pile on the plate. "I've been better."

"I can't believe Lord Xavier's all the way down here."

"I can't believe we ran into him in a city the size of Merrin." The inn where we'd been spotted was one of the better ones, located on the main thoroughfare that led to the grand homes of Merrin's wealthy. It was where a wealthy traveler would find accommodation, but the encounter was unlucky nevertheless. Neither Merdu nor Hailia had smiled on us today.

"Do you think he'll find us here?" she asked, looking around.

As soon as everyone returned for the day, we'd moved to a different inn. Erik had kept his head low, a hood pulled up to hide his distinctive hair and tattoos.

"I'm sure it will be fine," I said.

I pushed my plate away and caught Dane watching me. He arched a brow, glanced pointedly at my plate, and mouthed, "Eat."

I drew the plate towards me. He was right; I needed to eat. Tomorrow was going to be a long day, and we couldn't take many provisions with us. We'd decided to abandon the wagon and travel on horseback out of Merrin Fahl. I only hoped my poor riding skills didn't slow us down.

"Where are they?" came a growling voice from the taproom beyond.

Dane and the other guards stood and drew their swords. Max and Erik exchanged worried glances while Quentin swallowed loudly. All four settled into fighting stances.

The constable from earlier in the day barged into the dining room, sword drawn. Six more constables followed and then came a man with a sheriff's insignia on his sleeve.

The constable pointed his sword at Erik and Dane. "That's them."

"Arrest them!" the sheriff barked.

"Wait!" I cried, stepping forward.

Balthazar caught my arm and pulled me back. "Let me handle this."

His priest robes caught the constables by surprise. They hesitated. One turned to his sheriff for advice.

"Move out of the way, Brother," the sheriff said. "This doesn't concern you."

"These men are my friends. Why are you arresting them?"

"The Marginer has been identified as a thief."

"*A* Marginer has been identified as a thief," Balthazar corrected. "Unless your witness is confident it was this one, you can't arrest him."

"That will be for the magistrate to decide."

"When will they go up before the magistrate?"

"Tomorrow, or the following day at the latest." The sheriff nodded at his constables. "Arrest them."

"Why both?" Theodore asked, stepping up alongside Balthazar. This time the constables didn't stop. They swatted both men aside and advanced.

Quentin and Max raised their swords, prepared to strike.

"Lower your weapons," the sheriff ordered. "Or you will all be arrested too."

Quentin lowered his sword but Max did not.

"It's all right, Max," Dane said. "We can't fight them. Not in here." He meant not with us standing by. He and the others might be able to defeat six swordsmen, but with three women and two unarmed men to protect as well, they might as well have one hand tied behind their backs. Our vulnerability made them vulnerable.

They put down their weapons.

"You haven't answered my friend's question," Balthazar said to the sheriff. "Why arrest both? You cannot accuse both of the theft."

"I'm not arresting the second man for theft. I'm arresting him for murder."

CHAPTER 4

"No!" I rushed forward only to be caught by one of the constables. I struggled against him, kicking and punching, but it was useless and it was only making him angry.

"I haven't murdered anyone," Dane snarled as a constable edged closer, sword raised to strike.

"He has been here all evening." Theodore indicated the innkeeper and serving girl standing in the taproom, watching proceedings. "Ask them."

The sheriff ordered his men to take Dane and Erik away. "This fellow struck a citizen of Merrin this afternoon outside the inn beneath the sign of the white horse."

"The man got up," I said. "He didn't die."

"He died later from his injuries."

Dane frowned. "That's impossible. I struck him with the hilt of the sword beneath the chin. He remained conscious and didn't strike his head as he fell, and no blood was drawn. He can't be dead."

"I saw the body myself," the sheriff said.

His men hustled Dane and Erik through the door. Erik shook them off, earning a punch in the back. He arched and spat out words in his own language.

"This isn't fair," Kitty said on a sob. "They're good men. Sheriff, you can't do this!"

Theodore blocked the sheriff's exit. "Please, sir, they're innocent."

"If they were innocent, why change inns?"

Theodore swallowed.

"We're fortunate that a concerned citizen of Glancia came forward and identified him," the sheriff said.

Lord Xavier. The cur.

I closed my eyes and groaned. A nobleman would be believed over us, even if he were a foreigner.

"He was able to tell us the most likely inns to find you." The sheriff eyed Balthazar up and down and shook his head. "It's disappointing that a priest from Merdu's Guards associates with such dangerous types."

"They're not dangerous," Balthazar said through gritted teeth.

The sheriff walked off and we all followed him to the stable yard, lit by a series of torches around the perimeter. The inn's grooms held the reins of several horses, two of which were hitched to a cart.

Theodore fell into step with the sheriff. "Captain Hammer is the captain of the Glancian palace guards."

"So?"

"So doesn't that prove he's a good man? King Leon wouldn't employ him in such an important role if he were dangerous."

"King Leon was murdered by a guard, was he not?"

"Not the captain!"

"Then why is he fleeing Glancia? Why change inns after he was seen by a fellow countryman?"

Theodore threw his hands in the air. It was hopeless. The sheriff couldn't be reasoned with.

The constables bundled Dane and Erik onto the back of the cart where they tied their hands together with rope. Neither man resisted.

"This is outrageous," Kitty said through her tears. "If this were Glancia—"

"It's not," the sheriff snapped, showing the first sign of frustration. "We're more civilized in Vytill. We don't have Marginers walking about the streets, frightening the women and children, and we don't let former palace guards get away with murder. I suggest, madam, that you stand back and keep your mouth shut or I will arrest you too!"

Kitty shrank into Meg's arms with a whimper.

From the back of the cart, Erik gave her an encouraging smile. "At least my woman cries for me, Hammer."

No one laughed and his smile became strained as they were driven away.

I watched them go, Theodore's arm around my waist, holding me up; holding me together. I bit down on my wobbling lip to stop myself screaming at the top of my voice.

* * *

BALTHAZAR IMMEDIATELY LEFT to appeal to the supreme priest for help. He returned shortly afterwards with little to report. "He says he's powerless to step in. It's a criminal matter, not ecclesiastical."

"Surely he has some sway," Theodore said. "He must be acquainted with the king."

Balthazar rubbed his hand over his face. When it came away, he looked exhausted. "I tried to explain, but..." He leaned heavily on his walking stick as he sat on a stool in the taproom. "We have to find another way."

"We were just discussing appealing to the princess," Meg said. "Josie thinks it's worth trying."

Balthazar nodded. "Good idea. What else?"

Max put his tankard down with a thud. "Find Lord Xavier and rip his head off."

In Balthazar's absence, we'd discussed the likelihood that Lord Xavier was behind Dane's arrest. It had to be he who told the sheriff where to look for us, as well as giving our names and occupations. Perhaps he'd even suggested Dane was responsible for Leon's death.

"I'll visit the magistrate in the morning," Balthazar said. "If we can't free them with swords or powerful friends, we have to try legal arguments."

"What legal arguments?" I asked.

"The ostler can't possibly be certain, beyond doubt, that Erik was the Marginer who stole the horse two years ago. I'm confident he's basing the identification on forehead tattoos and long blond hair. According to texts I read in the palace, those traits are typical of all Marginers. Legally, that's not specific enough."

Kitty clutched his hand in both of hers. "Oh, thank you, Balthazar. Yes, I think that will work."

"As long as the magistrate is reasonable and follows the rule of the law," Meg muttered.

"What about the captain?" Quentin asked in a small voice.

Balthazar lowered his head.

Quentin's chin shuddered. "This isn't fair. He's done nothing wrong. He hardly touched that man. Right, Josie?"

"Not enough to kill him," I said.

Quentin's face brightened. "So someone else killed him."

"I suppose."

"Then we just have to find out who and force them to face up to the magistrate instead."

"How can we do that?" Kitty asked. "We don't even know where to begin."

Balthazar lifted his head. "We begin at the inn. They'll know the victim's name and where he lived. Then we find out how he died, where, when, and if there are any witnesses. Someone must have seen something."

Max rose. "Let's start now. Tonight."

"Not tonight," Balthazar said. "It's late. We need to conduct this investigation with cool heads. Understood, Sergeant?"

Max sat and swiped up his tankard. "First thing in the morning, then."

I shook my head, earning frowns from the others.

"You don't agree with the plan?" Meg asked.

"I don't need an investigation to know who killed that man."

Kitty gasped. "Who?"

"Lord Xavier. But we're going to have a hard time proving it. He knows how to cover up crimes."

"He does," Balthazar agreed. "But not in a strange city and without his mother's help."

Theodore put his arm around me and hugged. "It's worth investigating, Josie."

"Yes," I said heavily. "Perhaps some luck will go our way."

* * *

BALTHAZAR AND THEODORE headed to the magistrate's office first thing in the morning while I wrote a letter to Princess Illiriya and delivered it to the palace's outer gate. We were not allowed any further without an official invitation.

We had decided that I shouldn't be left alone. Lord Xavier was somewhere in the city, and there was no telling what he'd do if he saw me again. Quentin, Max, Kitty, Meg and I headed to the White Horse Inn, but Kitty and I did not show our faces. Meg and Max asked after the deceased man, claiming they'd seen him fall the day before and were concerned for his welfare.

"The ostler told us all about the incident," Meg said as we hurried away before we were seen. "Jute Weller died at home from the injuries sustained in yesterday's scuffle. Jute happened to be walking past the inn when he heard the commotion and stepped in to stop Erik getting away."

"I said I'd seen the incident and hadn't thought the blow very hard," Max added. "The ostler just shrugged and said he didn't either, but Jute's dead so it must have been. He lived three streets east of here, above his workshop. He was a boot maker."

We headed there, but the workshop was closed, the door locked. No one answered our knock.

"He's dead," said a man dressed in a leather apron from the doorway of the chandler shop next door. "If you want your boots repaired, try two streets down on the left, under the sign of the two black birds."

"We came to speak to Jute's widow," I said. "Or someone who knew him."

"I knew him."

"Did you see him yesterday?" I asked. "After the fight at the inn?"

He glanced at each of us in turn then retreated back inside, slamming the door.

Max pushed the door open. "You didn't answer my friend's question."

Meg put a hand to his arm. "You're frightening him," she whispered.

She approached the counter and watched as the chandler packed away candles in a box carved with his mark then added the box to the top of a stack. "We're making inquiries into the death of Jute Weller," she said. "You see, our friend was accused of his murder and we don't believe he's responsible."

The chandler paused. "Your friend was the one with the Marginer?"

"That's right. Did you see Jute when he returned from the inn?"

He picked up a knife and pointed it at the door. "I was standing there when he ran up, clutching his head."

"His head or his chin?" I asked.

He thought about it before saying, "Head."

"Show me where?" I asked.

He indicated the side of his face, his head, his jaw. Everywhere.

I sighed. This was hopeless. "Did he say anything to you?"

The chandler trimmed the wick of a candle with a flick of his knife. "He told me what happened at the White Horse then went inside his shop. Not long after I heard his wife wailing. I went in to see what was what and saw her standing over Jute, crying. He was dead."

"Did you see anyone else enter Jute's workshop?" I asked.

"No."

"Are you sure?"

"Aye."

Kitty indicated the window. "You were looking at the street the entire time?"

The chandler nodded. "Standing in the doorway, like I sometimes do when it's quiet."

The door opened and a boy entered. "About time," the chandler snapped at him. He indicated the boxes. "All of these have to go to the castle."

The boy collected the boxes, his curious gaze on us and not his task. The top box slid as he turned to go and Max caught it before it fell off. He smiled at the boy as he put the box back.

"I've got work to do," the chandler said. "Have you got any more questions?"

We left and knocked on the boot maker's door again but there was still no answer.

"Now what?" Quentin asked.

"We return to the inn," Meg said. "Balthazar and Theodore might have news."

We returned to the inn in Fahl, but it was some time before Balthazar and Theodore arrived. Waiting for them was excruciating, but worth it—they brought Erik.

Kitty leapt up from the bed and threw her arms around him. He lifted her off her feet and spun her around before planting a kiss on her mouth.

Quentin tapped Kitty on the shoulder. "My turn."

"You would like a kiss too?" Erik asked.

"A hug will do." They embraced, slapping one another on the back.

"It's good to see you," Max said, clutching Erik's arm. "The magistrate agreed with Bal's legal argument?"

"He did," Theodore said. "The ostler couldn't be certain that Erik was the same Marginer who stole the horse two winters ago."

"And the captain?" Max looked to Balthazar, but from his worried face, he already knew the answer. We all did.

Balthazar eased himself down onto the bed. "His trial is set for two days hence."

"Did you tell the magistrate that Dane didn't hit the man hard?" I asked.

"We did."

"Meg and Max spoke to the ostler and he agreed the blow wasn't severe. He'll testify at the trial."

"After we had his accusation against Erik thrown out?" Balthazar shook his head. "Besides, it doesn't matter how hard the blow looked. The fact is, the man died later and no one has come forward to say they saw him in another fight that could have given him further injuries."

"No one has come forward *yet*," I said.

"His neighbor the chandler didn't see anyone come or go," Quentin said heavily.

"We didn't speak to other neighbors. Nor did we see the widow. Hopefully she'll respond to my message. And there must have been other people wandering past."

Quentin picked up his sword where it was leaning against the wall. "Let's go back now."

It was growing late in the afternoon, but there was still enough daylight left. I had something else to do, however.

"You all go," I said. "I have to visit Dane."

"We already did," Theodore said. "But I think he'd like to see you."

I bought some food from the inn's cook and bundled it with a spare shirt in a blanket the innkeeper sold to me for a steeper price than I would have paid at the market. But the market was likely closed already and I didn't want to go out of my way.

I was about to leave when a liveried footman from the castle arrived to speak to me. "You have been summoned to an audience with His Royal Majesty, King Phillip, at the stroke of ten bells, two days hence."

My elation was quickly deflated. "Two days? Is there any way it can be tomorrow?"

The footman looked as though he didn't understand a word I'd said. Then he spun on his heel and marched out.

"I know Leon usually accommodated your visits, Josie," Balthazar said from behind me. "But most monarchs don't adjust their schedules for village midwives."

"But Dane's trial is that day. If the king is going to intervene, it might come too late."

"The *trial* is that morning, not the...the punishment."

My stomach dropped. He'd been going to say execution. That was the punishment for murder.

"Besides, the trial may never go ahead," he went on gently. "If the others find a witness to a second assault, the magistrate will have to set him free." He patted my cheek. "Now go and see him. His spirits need lifting."

The prison in Merrin was located near the river, not far from the castle, in the district that housed the courthouse and other administrative buildings. The warden checked the food and belongings I'd brought, even going so far as to tear the bread into small pieces. I removed my knife from my pocket and placed it on his desk then my person was patted down to check for other weapons. Satisfied I was unarmed, he summoned a guard to take me to Dane's cell.

We descended a series of winding stairs to a corridor lit by torches positioned beside each cell door. The cells themselves were carved into rock and separated from the corridor with thick iron bars. A small, horizontal window high up on the back wall of each cell let in a little light and fresh air from the street above, but not enough to blow away the stench of body odors, human waste, and misery.

A large key hung from a ring beside each door, tantalizingly close yet just out of the inmates' reach. It was cruel, but not as cruel as providing no beds for the inmates to lie on, not even a mattress or chair. At least they weren't chained, but the cells were so small, there was no way they could get any exercise.

The guard stopped at a cell. "Visitor," he announced then stepped to the side.

I rushed to the bars. "Dane?"

He sat at the back of the cell with three other prisoners, his knees drawn up, head resting on folded arms. He looked up at the sound of his name and smiled.

I burst into tears.

"No crying." He reached through the bars and cupped my jaw. "It's not so bad in here, and I'll be out soon."

How could he be so confident? I felt as though I were filled with a well of despair and hopelessness. But I did not tell him that. I smiled and wiped away my tears. I would put on a show of confidence too, for his sake.

"I brought you some provisions." I passed the bundle through the bars and some of the breadcrumbs fell onto the floor.

The other inmates approached, trying to see what I'd brought. Thankfully there was enough for everyone. Dane might not need any friends in prison, but he certainly didn't need enemies. He handed out pieces of the bread but kept the pie for himself.

"You have a bruise," I said, caressing a thumb over his cheek, above the swelling. "Did the sheriff's men do it?"

"One of the other prisoners didn't like my face."

I gasped and eyed them, gnawing at the bread like rats. They were dressed in rags, their beards untrimmed, their faces and hands filthy.

"None of them," Dane said. "He's gone now."

"They released him?"

"Took him to the infirmary."

"He's sick?"

"Injured."

"Oh. I see I don't have to worry about you in here."

He smiled gently. "It's going to be all right."

"Yes," I said with conviction. I told him about our meeting with the king and our attempts to find out who really killed Jute Weller. "If the trial goes ahead, hopefully we'll have enough evidence of your innocence that the magistrate will have to set you free. Or perhaps the king will intervene."

"The princess must have convinced him to see you."

"I'll be sure to thank her."

"How is Erik?" he asked.

"Fine. He's laying low at the inn. Balthazar is keeping him company while the others investigate the murder."

"You should join them."

"I'd rather be here."

"As much as I like your company, this is no place for a woman like you." He glanced over his shoulder at the other prisoners, once more settling on the floor, knees drawn up, heads bowed. "I'd prefer you not see this."

"Is that your only objection?"

"It's not enough?"

"No." I sat on the floor near the bars. "Now sit down and talk to me. Unless you've got something better to do?"

He laughed and sat too. "What shall we talk about?"

"Anything but politics."

"Agreed. Something more comforting and lighter. Something about Mull. Do you know, I miss it. I even miss the palace and especially miss the garrison and the servants we left behind."

I reached through the bars and took his hand. He gently squeezed. "Shall I tell you about the time I tried to hide the fact I'd broken my arm from my parents?"

He drew my hand to his lips and kissed it. "I'm all ears."

* * *

"THE WORKSHOP WAS OPEN AGAIN, but just for boots to be collected," Max said when he and the others returned to the inn. We sat in the taproom, nursing tankards of ale, our mood despondent. I'd known the moment they walked in that they'd discovered nothing of use.

"You spoke to the widow?" I asked.

"In a way."

"We were about to ask her some questions when the chandler saw us," Meg said. "He told the widow we were friends of the man accused of murdering Jute and she chased us off with a broom."

"We tried telling her Dane was innocent, but she wouldn't listen," Theodore said. "She was mad with grief."

"Poor thing," Kitty muttered.

"You've got to get through to her," Balthazar said. "Go and see her again."

Max pushed to his feet and snatched up his empty tankard. "Easy for you to say. You didn't have to listen to her crying and shouting."

"All the more reason to find who really murdered Jute and bring them to justice."

"You think we can bring the Deerhorn lordling to justice?" Max snorted. "I worked among nobles long enough to know who wins and who loses." He went to walk off, but stopped when Balthazar stamped the end of his walking stick into the floor.

"You're giving up?" Balthazar looked at the faces sitting around the table. "Without a fight?"

"No, of course not," Theodore said. "But we're not going to get help from the widow. Not before the trial."

"Then we have to hope the king intervenes," Meg said.

"And in the meantime?" Balthazar asked. "Are you going to sit by and do nothing tomorrow?"

"I'm going to visit the widow," I said. "She saw the body and will be able to describe the wounds to me. If there were injuries other than a bruise on his chin, we can prove Dane didn't kill Jute."

"And if she won't talk to you?" Quentin asked.

"I'll find where the body is kept and inspect it myself."

* * *

THE BOOTMAKER'S door was unlocked but no one was inside.

"Is anyone here?" Theodore called out. "Mistress Weller?"

We had returned to the workshop with Quentin and Max accompanying us. Max insisted, saying I needed an armed escort if I was going into the city, especially with Lord Xavier about. "It's what the captain would want," he'd said.

He was probably right. He stood by the door, looking every bit like a guard with one hand on his sword hilt.

Quentin walked slowly around the workshop, gazing at the floor as if searching for lost coins.

"What are you doing?" Max asked him.

"Looking for signs of where Jute died. His widow found his body here somewhere."

"What's that going to prove?"

Quentin shrugged and continued to scour the floor.

The workshop looked as though it had been tidied. Tools had been put away, and strips of leather organized into batches of similar color and size on the workbench. There were no completed sets of boots, but a small collection behind the counter looked as though they were in the middle of being repaired. A pail full of water sat on the floor beside the stool at the workbench, a scrubbing brush beside it surrounded by a damp patch. The floorboards were discolored in that spot, and not just from the water.

I bent down for a closer look. "He died here."

Quentin and Theodore joined me. "Blood," Quentin announced after a brief inspection.

"There was no blood on Jute Weller after Dane hit him."

The door leading to a room out the back opened and a woman stopped there upon seeing us. She was about to greet me when she noticed the others.

"You!" she snarled. Her face twisted with rage and she flew at Theodore. "Get out!"

"Get out!" The woman pounded Theodore's chest with her fists and kicked him in the shin.

Theodore grunted, but managed to catch her wrists and dodge out of the way before she kicked him again. "Please, Mistress Weller, calm down. We just wish to talk to you."

"I want nothing to do with you! Murderers! Killers!"

"We're not," Quentin tried in a soothing voice. "Nor is our friend. He's a good man and we want to prove he didn't kill your husband."

"Get out!"

I stepped between Quentin and Mistress Weller, still struggling to free her wrists from Theodore's grip. "Dane didn't kill Jute," I told her. "That patch of blood on the floor proves it."

She stopped struggling and stared at the spot I pointed to. Her face crumpled and she began to cry. "I hate him! I hate all of you for coming here and taking my Jute away from me. It's not fair! It's not fair!"

I touched her shoulder. "We're so very sorry for your loss. Dane didn't kill Jute, but perhaps we can find who did."

She sniffed and shrugged my hand off. Then she spat in Theodore's face. "Foreigners."

Theodore instinctively let her go to wipe off the spit.

Mistress Weller picked up a hammer from the workbench and raised it above her head. "Get out!"

Max grabbed my shoulders from behind and dragged me out of the way. I shook him off, hardly noticing him.

"There's blood on the floor!" I pointed to the patch she'd been scrubbing. "Dane's blow didn't draw blood. The ostler will testify as much."

She slowly lowered the hammer. My words must have finally punched through the fog of her grief.

Theodore edged towards her and, when she didn't try to kill him, gently pried the hammer out of her grip. He blew out a measured breath in relief.

Mistress Weller began to cry, great heaving sobs that wracked her body. I put my arm around her and she sobbed into my shoulder. Quentin brought her a stool and I guided her onto it. Theodore passed her a lace-edged handkerchief that drew querying looks from both Quentin and Max, which he pretended to ignore.

"My name is Josie," I said. "My friends and I are passing through Merrin on our way to Freedland."

"With that Marginer," she said, dabbing at her eyes.

"His name is Erik. He's very sweet, despite his looks. He was released from prison since he didn't steal that horse two winters ago."

She handed the handkerchief back to Theodore. "I didn't know he'd been released."

"Our other friend Dane knew Erik was innocent, but he also knew Erik might not get a fair trial. Sometimes people see Erik and assume the worst. Dane is not a killer. He just wanted to help Erik get to safety. Yes, he had to use force, but he also had two swords in his possession and did not use either of them."

"Not the pointy end," Quentin clarified.

Max nudged him with his elbow and scowled.

"Dane didn't kill your husband," I said again.

"Somebody did," she whispered through fresh tears. "Who? Why?"

I looked to the others. How much to tell her?

Theodore squatted down in front of Mistress Weller. "We

suspect it was a man who hates Dane and saw this as an opportunity to get him into serious trouble."

She reeled back. "Are you saying my husband was murdered for no other reason than he was a convenient victim?"

Theodore nodded.

"That's madness!"

"This man is mad," I said, more enthusiastic now that she seemed to believe us. "Mad and vengeful. He followed us here from Glancia, that's how much he hates us."

"Can you prove it was him?"

I hesitated. I didn't want to give her false hope. "I don't know. He's a nobleman and if there were no witnesses..."

She eyed the blood on the floor again. Shudders wracked her body. "It won't come off."

"My father was a doctor," I said gently. "I used one part ash to five parts water with a dash of coleander oil to clean his workbench."

She blinked back at me. "Thank you."

"Your husband deserves justice, Mistress Weller, but not at the expense of our friend. I know this is hard for you, but can you recall what injuries Jute had?"

She indicated her left temple. "There was blood on the side of his head."

My pulse quickened. "That proved someone else came here and hit him. Not only did Dane's blow not draw blood, but he struck Jute on the chin. Did you see Jute when he arrived back from the White Horse?"

"No, but I heard him. I was out the back, preparing supper. He called to me that he was home and I heard him working." She indicated the hammer. "A while later, I came in here to tell him supper was almost ready and I saw..." She gazed at the patch of blood on the floor and her face crumpled.

"Is there any other way in here?" Max asked. "Any way an intruder could have come in unnoticed by someone on the street or by your neighbor?"

"There's a rear entrance that leads to the courtyard, but I was in the kitchen the entire time, from when Jute returned until I came out to announce supper. They would have had to go past me if they used that door."

Max looked towards the door leading to the street. I knew exactly what he was thinking. We needed to have another talk with the chandler.

I thanked Mistress Weller for her help and followed the men to the chandler's shop.

The chandler looked up from where he was serving a customer. His gaze narrowed. "What do you want now?"

The customer paid and picked up the box of candles. She eyed us carefully as she passed. Max closed the door behind her then stood by it, once again taking up guard duty.

"This is getting ridiculous," the chandler grumbled. "You keep coming here and asking the same questions."

"But this time we're providing the answers," I said.

He frowned. "Pardon?"

"We've just come from Jute Weller's workshop. We spoke to his widow. The poor woman has been scrubbing her husband's blood off the floor."

"It's a tragedy. I know she's suffering. I can hear her crying."

"Then let's help her find the real killer."

"The killer is in prison awaiting trial."

"You weren't listening to what I said. Mistress Weller was scrubbing blood off the floor. Dane's blow did not draw blood."

He picked up a crate of candles from the floor and placed it on the counter. "It must have or she wouldn't be scrubbing off blood, would she?"

"You didn't mention seeing blood on Jute's head as he passed by after the altercation at the White Horse."

"Just because I didn't mention it doesn't mean it wasn't there."

"Blood seems like something a person would mention seeing," Theodore said. "It's an important detail."

The chandler merely shrugged.

I blew out a measured breath to calm my rising temper. We needed this man on our side. We needed to know why he'd lied. "You told us you spoke to Jute when he came back from the White Horse."

"That's right."

"And you claimed no one else came by after that and before Jute's wife found his body."

"So?"

"Are you sure?"

"Course I'm sure. I was either standing in the doorway or watching through the window the entire time." His gaze met mine. "No one went inside Jute's shop except for Jute."

"Mistress Weller says she was in the kitchen and no one entered through the back door. That means the killer had to have gone through the front."

"Not if your friend is the killer and he inflicted the killing blow some time before." He lifted a box lid, but I clamped my hand over it, slamming it back down.

He glared at me. I glared back. "I'm giving you an opportunity to change your story," I said. "Now, I'll ask again. Are you sure you saw no one else go in through the front door of Jute's workshop?"

He hesitated. Swallowed.

Quentin placed his hand on his sword hilt, ready to draw.

"Are you threatening me?" the chandler asked.

"No," Quentin said.

The chandler pushed my hand off the box lid. "I was here the whole time, looking out. No one else came or went, just Jute."

Damnation! Hailia and Merdu! I wanted to draw Quentin's blade myself and stab the man through his hand until he agreed to tell the truth.

Max rushed towards him and slammed his palms down on the counter. "Who paid you to lie?"

The chandler reeled back, shaking his head. "N—no one! I, I saw no one. Nothing. Go away, please, or I'll shout until the constable comes."

Theodore grabbed Max by the shoulder. "Let's go. Lord Xavier paid him too well."

The chandler chewed his lower lip.

"Then we'll pay more!" Quentin cried. "Whatever he paid, we'll double it."

The chandler crossed his arms and gave Quentin a smug smirk. "Nobody paid me a single ell."

I grasped Quentin's arm as he reached for his sword. "Probably because he threatened to destroy your stock if you didn't do as he demanded," I said.

The chandler pointed at the door with a shaking hand. "Get out. I have nothing more to say."

I thought Max and Quentin might use their swords to force him to tell us everything, so I bundled them outside with Meg and Theodore's help. We couldn't afford to make the situation worse for Dane by threatening the chandler. Being foreigners already put us at a disadvantage. We had to tread carefully.

"He's lying scum," Max spat. "Deerhorn got to him."

Theodore set off along the street. "Then let's do something about it."

I trotted after him. "Are we going to see the sheriff?"

"We are."

The sheriff was in no mood to see us, however. He spotted us as he was leaving his office with two constables in tow and changed direction to avoid us.

I walked fast to catch up. "We have new information for you that will prove Dane didn't kill that man."

"The trial is tomorrow," he said.

"He should be released today. He's not guilty and we can prove it. There's blood on the floor of Jute Weller's workshop where he died. Dane's blow inflicted a bruise, not blood."

"That's not proof." He quickened his pace.

"Of course it is."

He stopped and rounded on me. "Are there witnesses?"

"The ostler will tell you no blood was spilled at The White Horse."

"I've questioned the ostler. He can't recall."

"He's lying."

"Why would he do that?"

"Because he's annoyed that we got Erik free."

He set off again, shaking his head. "If you have a witness, get them to tell what they saw to the magistrate at the trial tomorrow."

"How, when all the witnesses are lying?"

"I've done my job, Miss," he said over his shoulder. "Let the magistrate do his."

Max pushed past me and grabbed the sheriff's shoulder. The two constables rounded on him, swords pointed at Max's chest. He let go, hands up in surrender. "You're willing to see a good man sent to his death?"

"He might not be executed," the sheriff said. "If the magistrate is feeling generous, your friend will be sentenced to hard labor in a prison mine for accidentally causing a death."

"For how long?" I asked.

"Twenty years."

I reached for Meg, suddenly feeling very weak.

She wrapped her arm around my waist. "Let's go back to the inn. Josie, you need to rest."

"I can't rest while Dane is in prison." I removed her hand and strode off. "We need to talk to the ostler and convince him of Dane's innocence. He must testify that the blow didn't draw blood. If not him, then we'll find someone else who was there. I will produce a witness at that trial, even if I have to employ underhanded methods like Lord Xavier."

Max stepped in front of me and caught me by the arms. His cold gaze met mine. "Quentin and I will find a witness. You go back to the inn. Meg's right, you need to rest and what we're going to do is not a woman's business."

"It bloody well is my business. This is Dane's life!"

"I know, Josie. But I can't involve you in what must be done. Dane'll never forgive me."

"He won't have to know."

"He'll know. Go back to the inn." He let me go and strode off. "Quentin, with me."

Quentin gave me a flat smile then trotted after Max.

Theodore moved up alongside me. "He's right. The time for talk is done. Let them do what they have to do and keep your hands clean."

Meg hooked my arm with hers and we headed back to the inn.

* * *

MAX AND QUENTIN were gone all night. I knew because I couldn't sleep and sat in the room they shared, waiting. When they finally returned at breakfast, I sprang up from the bed.

Quentin jumped in fright. "Merdu, Josie! You scared me half to death."

"Well? Did you convince the ostler to testify today?"

"He wasn't there," Max said. "He didn't come to the inn or return home."

"Where was he?"

They both shrugged.

"What about another witness? Did you find someone else who'd seen what happened?"

Max eased onto the bed and dragged his hand through his hair.

"Quentin?" I asked, voice small.

He shook his head. "A serving girl took pity on us and eventually told us that none of the men who'd witnessed the incident were around. She said we wouldn't find any of them. They're in hiding."

"Hiding!"

Max looked up. His eyes were cast in deep shadow, his face gray beneath the stubble. "They've been paid to disappear until after the trial is over."

I sat heavily on the bed beside him. "Lord Xavier."

"He's a step ahead." He swore under his breath. "I should have known he'd interfere and get to the witnesses first. Dane would have predicted this."

"It's not your fault." I didn't sound particularly convincing, so I took his hand and squeezed. "All is not yet lost. We have the meeting with the king this morning."

If we could explain the situation to him, he would surely see that Lord Xavier had interfered. He'd have no choice but to order Dane's trial be canceled. I had to hope so anyway. A royal pardon was Dane's last chance.

* * *

KING PHILLIP MET us in a long, narrow chamber with a dais at one end and royal purple and gold banners hanging from the beams. A matching carpet covered the floor, deadening our foot-falls as guards led us to the dais. The room would have been a cavern of gray stone without the banners, made darker by the lack of light filtering through the small windows. Dozens of candles on tall iron candelabras had been lit in the corners to keep the grimness at bay, but they only served to remind me that this ancient fortress was outdated when compared to the bright palace at Mull.

The king looked equally grim and somewhat non-descript. He was of average height for a Vytillian, with silver hair and flat gray eyes. His clothing, however, was anything but average. He wore a black doublet covered in a diamond pattern in gold thread, matching shoes with a heel, and a high lace collar of pristine white that brushed his trimmed beard. The white lace cuffs of his shirt protruded from his doublet sleeves and cascaded over his hands but didn't hide long, fine fingers that he flicked to command the guards to retreat. It was the sort of ostentatious outfit King Leon wore.

Princess Illiriya, standing on the dais beside her father's throne, introduced Theodore and me. "And I assume this is Brother Balthazar," she finished.

Balthazar sketched another shallow bow. "Your Majesty," he intoned. "We are honored that you agreed to see us."

"My daughter gave me no choice."

The princess's cheek twitched.

"We are truly grateful for this opportunity to have our voices heard on behalf of our friend," Balthazar said.

"My daughter says you petitioned her to intervene." The king put out his hand to Illiriya. She took it and smiled. "I am not in the habit of interfering in legal matters that have no bearing on Vytill."

"Then we are doubly grateful, Your Majesty," I said. "Clearly you're a man who believes in justice."

He looked down his nose at me.

"My father is an honorable man," Princess Illiriya chimed in. "He does what he can for the innocent."

"The *truly* innocent," the king said.

Everything inside me tensed.

The door behind us opened and the king glanced up. "Ah, Barborough. Finally. You kept us waiting."

Lord Barborough bowed. "My humblest apologies, Your Majesty." He sounded a little out of breath.

"You're just in time," Princess Illiriya said. "Miss Cully was about to tell us why my father should pardon her friend the captain." She gave me an encouraging nod.

"Dane didn't kill that man." I stepped towards the dais, but stopped when the guards moved out of the shadows, hands on sword hilts.

"Yes, yes," the king muttered. "They all say that. Why should I believe you? He struck the man, did he not?"

So he knew something about Dane's case. That was a start. "He did, but the blow did not draw blood."

"A blow doesn't have to draw blood to kill someone later. It's my understanding that a blow need not be too severe, but if inflicted in just the right place on the head, can cause death long after the initial incident."

"It must be severe, Your Majesty, and it must also be inflicted here." I indicated my temple, crown and back of my head. "Dane hit the man on the chin."

The king's nostrils flared and I instantly regretted contradicting him.

"Josie is the daughter of a doctor," Princess Illiriya said quickly. "She has medical knowledge."

"Did she attend medical college?" he asked with a thorough dose of mockery in his tone.

The princess winced. "No, Father."

Lord Barborough tapped the back of his head. "The man fell back, I believe. He most likely hit his head then and that's what caused him to die later. He would not have fallen if Hammer hadn't hit him."

"We had it on good authority that the ostler saw no blood spilled," I said.

"There you are," the king said. "You have a good witness.

There's no need for my interference. This meeting was for naught."

"The ostler cannot be found. Nor can any of the other witnesses."

"That is unfortunate."

"We think someone is paying them, or threatening them, to keep quiet."

The king's face gave nothing away, but Princess Illiriya's lips parted with her silent gasp.

"Why would anyone do that?" Lord Barborough asked with a scoff.

"To cover up their crime," I went on. "Someone killed Jute Weller to make it look like Dane did it."

Another scoff, this time from the king. "What a fantastic tale this is. My dear, you have found some intriguing friends. A pity they're deluded."

My fists clenched even as my heart dove to my stomach.

"We are not deluded," Balthazar said with more patience than I could have mustered. "Lord Xavier Deerhorn wishes revenge on Josie and Dane. We know he's in Merrin. We know he's behind this."

"Then prove it," the king said.

I threw my hands in the air. "How can we when he is hiding witnesses and threatening others into lying for him?"

"Who is lying?" Princess Illiriya asked.

I told them about Jute's neighbor, the chandler, but it did no good. The king pointed out that the chandler could very well be telling the truth.

"If the captain's blow caused him to hit his head, which caused him to die later, of course there was no intruder. I am sorry, Miss Cully, but I cannot interfere in the judicial process."

"But Dane's a good man!"

"Doesn't he go by the nickname Hammer? One doesn't get that name unless one is brutal by nature."

"He's not brutal!"

"He did hit the deceased. That is not in question. I don't know about Glancia, but here in Vytill, we do not condone violence."

"He was protecting his friend," Theodore said, speaking for the first time. He tried to keep his voice reasonable, level, but I heard the strain through it. "Erik was innocent of the crime he was accused of, but Dane knew he would not get a fair trial, being a Marginer."

"And yet he was released," Lord Barborough pointed out.

"Because your magistrate had to follow the letter of the law. A law that Balthazar brought to his attention."

The king put up his hand for silence. "No matter the reason for the captain's thuggery, the fact remains, the man is dead. The magistrate will decide if the captain is responsible or not. I cannot get involved in a matter where there is no evidence to prove the foreigner's innocence. It would not be popular."

Theodore and Balthazar's protests tumbled over one another, but I remained silent. I felt sick. This could not be happening. It was a nightmare; one from which I could not wake.

The king indicated the guards should escort us from the chamber. I appealed to Princess Illiriya, but she merely stood there, her hands clutched loosely in front of her, a stricken look on her face. She mouthed an apology, but I turned away. She had no power here. Her father wouldn't listen to her and she knew it.

Power.

Magic.

I turned back to the king, wanting to wipe that bland expression from his face. He didn't care that he'd condemned an innocent man to death. "We'll give you the gem if you free Dane," I said before I could think it through and stop myself.

Lord Barborough's eyes lit up. "You *do* have it."

"Yes."

"Josie," Balthazar warned.

I tilted my chin. "I also have the two remaining wishes. I'll give you one if you release Dane."

Lord Barborough frowned. "I thought Brant had them."

"You believed his lie?"

Lord Barborough regarded me levelly, as if trying to decide if I were the one lying. "How did you get them? Brant killed Leon, so it makes sense he was the one who now possesses them."

"He struck the killing blow, but the king did not die immediately. We stayed with him until he took his last breath. The wishes transferred at that moment."

"To you? Or someone else who was there?"

I did not let my gaze waver from his as I said, "Not me, but I know who has them, and that person will use one of those wishes on His Majesty's behalf if Dane is set free."

Lord Barborough nibbled on his lower lip as he considered this. Then he looked to the throne. "Your Majesty, if she's telling the truth—"

"I am."

Lord Barborough's face lifted and I knew my conviction convinced him. "Your Majesty, imagine what you can do with a single wish."

The king took his daughter's hand and patted it. "You won't give up, will you?" Was he speaking to her or to Barborough?

"Sire, do not dismiss magic as fakery. I beg you, it's real. I know it." Lord Barborough appealed to the princess, standing very still beside her father. "Your Highness, please. You believe. Tell the king—"

"Enough!" The king shot to his feet. "The princess does not believe in your fantasies. She is a sensible girl. You, Barborough, are already on thin ice. I advise you not to tread heavily."

He strode past us and I went to follow, but it was the princess who stopped me. She held me by the elbow until her father had left the room and was out of earshot.

"It's best not to disagree with him when he's like this," she said. "He won't listen to reason, not even from me."

"But he must be convinced!" I cried. "I *will* sell him a wish if he frees Dane."

"Josie," Balthazar said again. This time it held no warning, merely exasperation.

"We do have the wishes and gem." I wanted to convince the princess, but also let Balthazar know that I planned on following the path I'd set for myself. His warnings would not sway me.

Princess Illiriya clasped her hands together, but her thumbs tapped; a small sign that her serenity was disturbed. "Your offer intrigues me. As Lord Barborough said, I believe in magic. At least, I think I do. I certainly think it's worthwhile buying one of the remaining wishes in exchange for the captain's life."

"What does it matter?" I said, heavily. "Your father will not agree and you have no authority to set Dane free."

"I do have some influence."

"With the magistrate?"

She merely smiled, and I couldn't fathom what it meant.

"What would you wish for, Your Highness?" Balthazar asked.

The princess's smile faded. "That is a secret."

He bowed. "Of course."

"I must warn you," she said. "I cannot free Dane before the trial. There simply isn't enough time. Be assured, if he is found guilty today, he won't be executed immediately. They allow time for the prisoner to get his affairs in order, say his goodbyes, that sort of thing."

I clutched my rolling stomach and managed a weak nod.

She touched my jaw. Her eyes softened, full of concern. "You poor thing. You're being so brave and you're working so hard. He is very lucky to have you. I promise I will do my part and work every bit as hard too."

* * *

"Are you mad?" Theodore asked as we left the castle behind. "What if they learn we don't have the gem or the wishes? They'll probably execute us all for lying."

"That's why we'll get Dane's pardon first," I said. "As soon as he is released, we'll leave the city before meeting with the princess again."

"They'll hunt us down."

"I don't think the princess is that cruel."

Theodore barked a brittle laugh. "You're basing that on two meetings. Josie, I love you and I love Dane, but we cannot dupe Vytillian royalty. It's dangerous. Tell her, Bal."

Balthazar had been silent ever since leaving the audience chamber with Princess Illiriya and Lord Barborough's stares boring into our backs. We kept our progress to his slow pace, but it was too slow for me. Dane's trial would go ahead soon. I eyed the temple bells in the tower, willing them not to chime the passing of time.

"I'm thinking," was all Balthazar said.

Theodore clicked his tongue and brooded until we reached the end of the street where he finally broke his silence. "What if the princess fails to convince her father, or whoever she plans on talking to, and Dane is not released after all?"

"Then we enact Plan B," I said.

Balthazar looked up. "What's Plan B?"

"We free him ourselves."

We rounded the corner and headed to the courthouse squatting on one side of the paved square where several streets fed into it. The area was busy with gentlemen riding past on horseback and ladies in carriages, all jostling for place with pedestrians, carts and street hawkers. Because of the throng, it took some time to realize the three people hurrying towards us were our friends.

"It's Meg, Max and Quentin," Theodore said, squinting at the trio. "What are they doing out here? The trial's about to start."

They quickened their pace and we quickened ours until we were close enough for me to see Quentin's stricken face. I stopped dead.

"No," I whispered as a chill overwhelmed me. I started to shake.

"It's over," Max said, his voice heavy. "They brought the trial forward." He squeezed his eyes shut and pinched the bridge of his nose.

"The verdict?" Balthazar asked.

Quentin let out a sob. It was all the answer we needed. Dane had been found guilty.

My heart plunged to my toes. "The sentence?"

Meg pressed her lips together but failed to stop them trembling. "His execution is set for two days hence."

CHAPTER 6

"We never even had a chance to present our suspicions at the trial," Max bit off. "It was over before we got here."

"They brought it forward deliberately," Meg said bitterly. "I suspect Lord Xavier convinced them to make it earlier so we couldn't present new evidence or find the witnesses in time."

Balthazar shook his head. "He has no friends here. It's doubtful the magistrate would be told what to do by a Glancian."

"Unless he paid the magistrate."

Quentin threw his arms around me and buried his face in my shoulder. "He's going to die!"

I hugged him back, but it was little comfort. I couldn't stop the trembles wracking my body.

"They're going to execute him, Josie," he sobbed.

"That's enough," Theodore snapped. His exasperation was most out of character, stunning Quentin into silence.

Max glared at the courthouse as if he was planning to storm it. "It probably wasn't Deerhorn. My money's on Barborough. Why else would he have been there?"

"He wasn't," Theodore said. "He was at the castle with us."

"He *was* at the courthouse during the trial." At Theodore's blank look, Max added, "It finished some time ago."

Theodore and Balthazar exchanged glances. "That explains why he was out of breath," Balthazar said. "He rushed to the castle after the trial."

"He didn't say a word," Theodore muttered.

Max swore and strode off. Meg followed him and somehow made him stop and return.

I could hardly see them through my tears or hear them as they talked amongst themselves. It wasn't until Meg put her arms around me and urged me to walk with her that I realized she was steering me away.

"I have to see him," I said.

"I know. We're taking you to the prison."

I wiped my cheeks and touched my hair, but it wouldn't do any good. I was a mess.

Theodore appeared by my side. "You look beautiful."

Quentin agreed. "Especially compared to the people he's been looking at behind bars."

* * *

I INTENDED to be strong for Dane, to keep his spirits up, but it was he who lifted my spirits. I entered the prison in tears and left with a plan.

"There is hope, Josie," he had told me upon my arrival at his cell.

I clutched the bars and nodded, not trusting my voice. It felt as though one small word would shatter me completely.

"Witnesses may yet be found." He reached through the bars and tucked my hair behind my ear. "I would offer you a handkerchief but I seem to have misplaced it."

I tried to smile.

"That's better. Now tell me how your audience with the king went. Since you didn't dance in here, I assume it didn't go as planned."

"It did not." Recounting the meeting gave me something to focus on, something to get angry about. By the time I finished, I no longer felt overwhelmed with hopelessness. The way out had become clearer.

Dane, however, went very still. A look of incredulity passed over his face. "You promised him a wish?"

"Yes, but he doesn't believe in magic. The princess seems to and she will work to free you."

He pressed his forehead to the bars and closed his eyes. "Josie…"

"I know what you're thinking, and I've thought it all through. If she succeeds in setting you free, we'll flee the city before she comes to collect the wish and gem. We just have to make it to Freedland safely. They won't follow us across the border. And if she doesn't set you free, I'm going to get you out another way."

He arched his brows. "Should I be worried?"

"You won't have to do a thing. Well, just run when told to. Leave it to me."

"Do I get a hint of this diabolical plan of yours?"

"It involves the same tonic used on both Leon and Kitty's maid."

He smirked. "At least no guards will have to die."

"Not unless the emetic doesn't work on them, and that will only happen if they have the constitution of a horse." I eyed the giant of a guard standing out of earshot further along the corridor. Perhaps I would increase the dose for him.

"Did you think up the escape plan just now or before you promised the princess the wish?" he asked ruefully.

"It doesn't matter. It's too late to rescind the offer. All we have to do is wait. And go to the market to buy herbs."

He tugged on the belt at my waist, drawing me as close to him as the bars would allow. He pressed his head against the bars and I did the same from the other side. "Be careful," he murmured. "You're playing a dangerous game."

"It's not a game."

"I wish you hadn't dangled a magic carrot in front of the princess."

"I had no other choice."

"You did, but she was the safest option. Deerhorn would have been more of a threat."

I drew back. Lord Xavier? I hadn't thought of him, but didn't tell Dane that. He would worry that he'd planted the seed in my head.

That seed took root as I left the prison and headed back to the inn in Fahr with the others. We gave Kitty and Erik the terrible news and told them what we planned to do about setting Dane free. Erik liked it; Kitty thought it was madness.

"You come up with a better idea," I snapped. "If not, then we enact my plan, because letting him hang is not an option."

I headed downstairs to the taproom where I sat in a corner and nursed a tankard of ale, wishing the day would come to an end. It had been the sort of day that shreds one's soul and scatters the pieces to the wind. The more I sat there, the worse my sense of hopelessness became. Our plan could not work. We'd never be able to flee from an angry princess with Lord Barborough on her side. The simple fact that Lord Barborough was advising her should be warning enough that she was not as kind as she seemed. She was greedy for magic, like him. It remained to be seen what lengths she would go to in order to possess it.

"Drowning your sorrows?" came a snide voice that had me whipping around.

Lord Xavier stood there, hand on sword hilt and a smile on his face that I wanted to wipe off. Three guards stood at his back. They wore no livery and sported the battle scars and cold eyes of mercenaries.

I stood, not wanting to be at a disadvantage. Yet if he chose to attack me, there was nothing I could do. I was trapped in a corner with only my knife tucked away in my pocket. There were dozens of witnesses in the taproom, but none would come to the aid of a stranger at the mercy of a heavily armed nobleman.

"What do you want?" I growled.

"To gloat." Lord Xavier's finger tapped on the hilt of his sword as his heated gaze raked over me. "And to see how my prize looks in her sorrow. I don't like puffy eyes and red noses, by the way. I'll have to see that all the tears are beaten out of you before I have you."

"You're revolting."

"Tell me, how does it feel to see your lover in a prison cell knowing he's going to his death in a matter of days."

"Because of *you*. We know what you did. We know you paid witnesses to lie and go into hiding."

He didn't even bother to deny it. His smile stretched, an ugly gash in an ugly face. "Let me guess. You're going to make me pay. I'm quaking with anticipation and fear." He gave a mock shiver, like a big child tormenting a smaller one.

The seed Dane had planted suddenly bloomed, the roots taking hold, bolstering my confidence. I straightened and squared up to Lord Xavier. "Quake no more. There's no need to guess; I'll tell you." My cheerful tone froze his smug smile. "You will tell the magistrate that you killed Jute Weller."

He snorted. "You're deluded as well, I see."

"I don't care what you say, but if I were you, I'd make it appear accidental. Perhaps you came across him in a dark alley and he fell in front of your horse. He might have been drunk or just slipped on a smooth cobblestone. You're a nobleman from Glancia, and if you show contrition and respect, you'll walk free. It was, after all, an accident."

He tipped his head back and laughed, earning stares from the other drinkers in the taproom. "You are quite the storyteller, Josie." He applauded lightly. "But you don't seem to understand. I have no inclination to free the captain. I'm looking forward to the entertainment awaiting us on the scaffold in two days. You can watch with me, if you like. I'll save you a spot near the front where you'll get a good view of your lover twitching at the end of a rope."

My stomach rolled, but I tried to keep my expression composed. "You'll be inclined to free him when you discover I'll give you the gem."

His smile vanished. He stepped forward and wrapped his fingers around my arm. "You said you didn't have it."

"I lied." I wrenched free. "It's hidden, but I can get my hands on it if you do as asked and admit to killing Jute. Only when Dane is free will I hand over the gem."

I did not promise him a wish. He and his mother seemed certain we didn't have both or, as Lady Deerhorn had put it, we would have used a wish by now. It made more sense to let Lord Xavier think we had the gem, but it was useless to us without the wishes.

The problem was, the plan only worked if he could get his hands on those wishes. It wasn't clear from his face if he could. Indeed, his expression had gone quite blank as he thought through the implications. He wasn't as quick witted as his mother.

"It's very simple, my lord. I will give you the gem in exchange for Dane's freedom. If Brant holds the wishes as he says, and you know where to find him, you can buy one from him. Do we have an agreement?"

His finger tapped listlessly on the sword hilt again. "Prove you have it."

"No. I don't trust you not to overpower me when I reveal its hiding place." I nodded at his men. "I'll present it to you once Dane is free and not a moment before."

He clenched his teeth and his lips moved to a muttered curse.

"You have nothing to lose, my lord. The magistrate won't punish you for an accidental death."

"They're punishing the captain for it."

"That's different. Dane struck the man on purpose. Besides, you are a nobleman."

I could see him thinking it through, trying to decide if it was too much of a risk or if I was lying. How he must desperately wish his mother were here to offer counsel.

"I'll think about it." He turned and strode away, his men at his heels.

I sat again and signaled to the serving girl to bring me another drink. My nerves were shredded, my heart racing, and my head spinning. Dane would be furious with me if he knew I'd promised the gem to Lord Xavier after also promising it and a wish to the princess.

But the more I thought about it, the more I saw no additional downside. If we had to flee from Princess Illiriya, we might as well flee from Lord Xavier too. He was already someone we tried to avoid; it would simply become imperative if he accepted my proposal. It remained to be seen if he would follow us to Freed-land, however.

I had to hope he didn't know the direction we were heading.

Not all of the others agreed with my actions when I told them about it the following morning. After they got over their initial shock and anger that Lord Xavier had confronted me, Balthazar, Theodore, Kitty and Meg told me I was foolish for courting even more danger.

"Is it not enough to anger a princess?" Balthazar asked. "Did you have to stir up trouble with a Deerhorn too?"

"I stirred up trouble with the Deerhorns long ago," I said as we all met in the room we women shared.

Theodore clicked his tongue. "You shouldn't have promised him the gem, Josie. What if he mentions it to the princess or Barborough? Then both parties will feel duped."

"Lord Xavier is not a friend to the princess or Barborough. He won't speak to them. Listen. We needed a backup plan in case the princess fails. Dane doesn't think she has enough influence with the king or the lawmakers to succeed."

"We *have* a backup plan," Balthazar said. "Isn't that why we're purchasing herbs and other concoctions today?"

"That's the backup of the backup plan."

I hoped I didn't have to resort to the emetic. I'd asked the inn's cook if I could use a pot of hot water and steep the herbs in the kitchen. He'd been reluctant, but I suspected a few ells would sway him. Getting the prison guards to drink it was another matter.

"Is everything prepared for our hasty departure tomorrow?" I asked to distract them.

"I am hiring horses today," Erik said.

"Make sure they're the swiftest money can buy," Balthazar reminded him.

"I will speak to the cook about provisions," Kitty said. "But I'll be sure to leave space for whatever you buy from the market today."

While I bought the herbs needed to make up the emetic, Meg, Quentin, Max and Theodore would purchase whatever else we needed for our journey. We must travel light with only what we could carry in saddlebags and with only one packhorse in tow.

"And you, Balthazar?" I asked. "What are you doing today?"

"Appealing to the supreme priest again to step in on Dane's behalf."

"Promise him the gem if that doesn't work."

His eyes narrowed. "This is not a joke."

No, it was not, yet I felt more hopeful today than I had the previous night, and that lifted my mood. Having a purpose always made me feel better. It gave me less time for stewing on the dreadful facts.

"I'll go to the prison after my visit," Balthazar said. "Perhaps I will have good news to give Dane."

"Perhaps he will already be free," Quentin said although I could tell he didn't believe it.

"Promise me one thing," I said to them all. "Let me tell Dane about the bargain I struck with Lord Xavier. I want the blame to fall squarely on me, not any of you."

"Good luck," Max muttered. "He won't like it."

"If he's free, he can rant and rave about it all he wants. I'll welcome anything he has to say."

* * *

Dane was not free by the time we visited him after leaving the market. I allowed Max and Quentin to talk to him alone before I replaced them at the cell bars. We hardly spoke. I had little to say that didn't sound as if it were a farewell, and I refused to believe this was the last time I'd see him.

From the sadness in his eyes, I knew he was not as hopeful as me. "Be strong for me, Josie," he said as I was about to leave.

"I am. This will work, Dane. I know it."

"Not that. Not just now." He clutched the bars, suddenly earnest. "Be strong tomorrow and the day after, and the day after that. There's no sense in—"

"Stop it. Do not say another word. This will not end here. Our story isn't finished."

He smiled weakly. "Thank you for believing it enough for us

both. I needed to hear you say it. I need *you*, Josie. You're my anchor."

I laughed, despite the fullness of my heart. "I weigh you down?"

He laughed too. "I mean you keep me from drifting away on a sea of sorrow."

"Very nicely put. Perhaps you were a poet in your past life."

"A poet would not have called the woman he loves an anchor."

My breath hitched. My heart stilled before resuming a rapid, erratic rhythm. I stared at him, and stared and stared.

He turned away. "Sorry. I shouldn't have said that. Not with the way things are with my memory. I didn't think."

I reached through the bars and cupped his jaw, rough with a four day-old beard. My thumb stroked his cheek. "I'm glad you said it," I managed to whisper through my tight throat. "Knowing you love me gives me strength like nothing else."

He swallowed loudly.

"Look at me, Dane."

He peered up through thick lashes.

"I love you too," I said. "And tomorrow, I will hold you in my arms after you walk out of prison a free man."

He did not mention that he might not be free to marry me, for which I was glad. It wasn't something either of us wanted reminding of. This moment of tenderness was for both of us to hold onto as we waited for the pieces of the plans to fall into place.

I left him to rejoin the others waiting outside with our purchases. They stood across the busy courtyard at the public fountain. I headed towards them, giving the half-built gallows a wide berth, only to be stopped by Lord Barborough. I tried to keep the groan out of my voice as I greeted him.

"Have you been waiting for me?" I asked.

He glanced towards my friends, making sure they hadn't yet spotted him and that we had time to talk. "I want to know if you spoke the truth about the gem and wishes when you offered them to the king."

If he was asking me that, it meant he hadn't encountered

Lord Xavier and didn't know I'd also offered him the gem. "I wouldn't lie to your king. That would be foolish."

"I must be absolutely certain. My life depends on this, Miss Cully."

"So does Dane's. You can be assured, I would not risk his life or the lives of any of our friends by lying about something so important."

He tugged on the sleeve of his limp arm. "Then why haven't you used the wishes and gem for yourselves yet?"

"For one thing, how do you know we haven't used one? I only offered you the use of a single wish, not both."

He conceded the point with a nod.

"For another, we are a noble group. Far more honorable than you give us credit for. We struck a bargain that we would only use the wishes on something we all agree is worthwhile. The problem is, we couldn't come to an agreement. Until we do, one person is in charge of the gem, while a different person has the wishes. And no, I will not tell you which of us has what."

His top lip lifted in a sneer. "It will tear your group apart. Greed is always more powerful than honor."

"It won't matter, will it? Not if we give your king the last wish."

"The king doesn't believe in magic and the princess is a woman."

I crossed my arms and arched my brows. "Meaning?"

"She doesn't have any influence in the kingdom. No magistrate will release the captain on her command. Give *me* the wish and the gem and I will have the captain released without question."

"You have the power to get a man pardoned?"

"I do."

I doubted it but did not say so. "My lord, I don't care who frees him or how. The wish and gem will not be handed over until he is with us, safe. If you want to collect the magic for yourself after that point, by all means, do so. Now, if you don't mind, I'm joining my friends, who are currently marching over here with angry looks on their faces and hands on their swords. We know you brought Dane's trial forward."

He glanced behind him to see Max and Quentin advancing quickly. He left without so much as a goodbye.

"What did the sniveling weed want?" Max asked, watching Lord Barborough retreat.

"To betray his king and princess and make promises to me he can't possibly keep. It seems we're not the only ones playing a dangerous game in Merrin Fahl."

* * *

I DIDN'T SLEEP that night and awoke early the following day to the news that Dane's execution had been delayed until the afternoon.

"That's good," Meg said, her arm around my shoulders.

Erik stopped pacing the bedchamber floor and looked at her. "It is still going ahead. That is bad."

"Any delay is a positive sign. It means the princess is getting through to the king. Perhaps he wants time to learn more about magic before committing."

"Meg's right," Max said. "This is good news."

I found it difficult to agree but I made a show of it, for their sakes, and they made a show of it for mine. All but Quentin. He sat on the bed, his knees drawn up, head resting on his folded forearms. During the quiet moments, I could hear him sniffling.

When the others went down to breakfast, I stayed back. I sat beside him and hugged him. He cried into my shoulder until he couldn't cry anymore.

"I'm sorry, Josie," he said when he was finally calm enough to speak. "I wish I could be strong like you."

"I'm not strong, Quentin. I have my doubts too, but I won't let them get the better of me. Not until all hope is gone, and at this moment, we still have reason to hope. The lure of magic is very powerful."

I didn't tell him it was the aftermath of Dane's release that worried me too. If we were caught fleeing, it might not be just Dane condemned to death. It could be all of us.

"If you think so..." he hedged.

"I do. Now come downstairs and eat something. We might not get another chance for some time."

My courage remained with me until the sun hung high in the sky. After that, every ring of the temple bells chipped off another chunk of it until I was left trembling by the time the afternoon shadows grew long in the prison courtyard. The longest, darkest shadow of all was cast by the gallows.

The late hour meant we had reason to hope the king was still considering his options. Executions were usually held in the mornings, according to the gossip of those waiting in the courtyard with us. The gallows had been erected the day before, and guards now stood around the yard's perimeter to keep the restless crowd at bay. The crowd had thinned as the hour grew later, but many lingered, sometimes shouting their frustration with the delay at the prison itself.

With the memory of Mull's riots fresh in my mind, I hoped they wouldn't be too upset if my emetic had the desired effect and the execution was delayed even further. The large number of guards would make escape difficult, but the larger number of onlookers was to our benefit. It would be easier to disappear amongst them.

I touched the knife in my pocket and hoped I wouldn't have to use it on any of the suffering guards. If all went to plan, it would be easy to slip past them as they purged themselves, take the key hanging beside Dane's cell door and unlock it. From there, Dane could overpower a guard, swap clothing with him, and slip out unnoticed.

Theodore emerged from the prison and crossed the courtyard to join us. I waited impatiently for him to reach us, trying to gauge from his face what news he had.

"The execution is still set for sunset," he said gravely.

My heart sank. The princess had not managed to convince her father, and Lord Xavier had not given himself up. My first two plans had failed. It was time to enact the third. We could not wait any longer.

"Did you deliver the barrel of ale?" I asked Theodore.

"I watched on as it was passed around. The guards all drank thirstily. I also found out the latrines are at the back of the cells."

"It won't take long before they're occupied."

Theodore looked to the guards at the prison entrance. One of them already touched his stomach, frowning.

My hand fluttered to my own stomach, tight with anxiety. It had begun. We'd set Dane's escape in motion and couldn't back out now.

"They're such an arrogant lot," Kitty said, looking around at the restless crowd from beneath her hood. She'd wanted to be with us, not Erik and the horses, but we'd insisted she wear a hooded cloak, despite the warmth. With Lord Barborough and Lord Xavier in the city, she couldn't risk being recognized. "Look at them, panting with anticipation to see a foreigner hang. It's disgusting. I'd be ashamed if I were their duchess."

"Glancians are just as bad," Meg pointed out. "Not that we've had many executions in Mull, but I've heard it gets like this in Tilting."

Max emerged through the crowd, breathing heavily. "Any word yet?"

"Still going ahead at sunset," Theodore said.

"Damn. And Josie's emetic? Is it working?"

"Give it time." Just as I spoke, one of the guards at the door raced inside, hand over his mouth. The other looked decidedly uncomfortable. "Very soon now."

Meg followed my gaze. "It'll surely get put off until tomorrow."

I hoped so. It would make our work even easier if Dane was kept inside where the guards were in no condition to stop him walking out with us.

The second guard followed the first inside, clutching his stomach. The third was too distracted by his own cramps to notice. It was almost time.

Balthazar tapped Max's leg with his walking stick. "How are Quentin and Erik?"

"Anxious, but they don't need me." Max rested his hand on his sword hilt. "I have to be here. It's not just getting Dane out, it's the presence of Lord Xavier too. If he sees Josie, he might try to kidnap her to get the gem."

"He won't try anything in public. Not here."

Max suddenly stiffened. I followed his gaze to see someone pushing through the crowd. Someone I hoped never to see again.

Brant.

Why now, of all times? We had to get into the prison as soon as the final guard abandoned his post, and having Brant realize what we were up to would spell disaster.

"What are you doing here?" Max snarled as Kitty touched her hood and lowered her head.

"I want to see the entertainment." Brant rubbed his hands together. "It's going to be a spectacular event. When will it begin?"

"I meant what are you doing in Merrin Fahl."

Brant shrugged. "Just passing through."

"Did you follow us here? Was that you in the forest?"

"I have no idea what you mean." Brant looked past Max to the rest of us. "Where's the Marginer and the sniveler? Couldn't stomach it, eh?"

Theodore joined Max, his hand on his sword hilt too, although if Brant drew first, we all knew Theodore would only be in the way.

Brant snickered. "You're as threatening as a flower."

Theodore shook his head in disappointment. "Dane could have killed you several times over. After Leon died, he could have done it without repercussions. But he chose not to. He chose to protect you instead. You owe your life to him."

Brant spat on the ground near Theodore's feet. "I owe him nothing. Nor do any of you. He could have wished your memories back long ago if he'd given me the gem to use up one of the wishes."

"You know why he did not," Balthazar said. "Now the gem is no longer in his possession so the point is moot."

"Still pretending it was stolen, eh?"

I glanced at the remaining guard on the door. He bent over and vomited onto the cobbles but didn't leave his post. "None of us have it," I said, somewhat absently.

Brant looked like a dog who'd been thrown a bone. "That's not what I hear."

I went very still. Max and Theodore glanced at one another,

but it was Balthazar who spoke. "You think yourself so clever. But that was a very foolish admission. Now we know who you're working for."

Brant went to step towards him, but Max blocked him. Brant had to settle for pointing instead. "I don't work *for* anyone, old man. *I'm* the one with the wishes. *I* have all the power."

"Not without the gem you don't."

Brant bared the gaps between his teeth in a snarl. "I'm going to find myself a nice spot to view the entertainments."

He disappeared into the crowd and I let out a sigh of relief.

Kitty peered out from beneath her hood. "Did he look as though he recognized me?"

"He didn't even look your way," Meg said. "I loathe that man. It should be him on that scaffold after what he did to Leon."

"It's clear!" Max nodded at the prison door, now unattended. The guard must have run off while we were distracted with Brant. "Let's go."

I picked up my medical pack, handed it to Theodore, and pushed through the crowd, not looking behind me to see if the others followed. Only Balthazar was set to leave us and return to Quentin and Erik. In theory, only Theodore and I were necessary to the plan, but the others had insisted on at least coming to the prison entrance. As a doctor and his assistant, we hoped—prayed—we would be allowed inside to attend the ill.

Our entire plan hinged on them believing one of their number had fetched us.

Murmurs rippled through the crowd, growing louder and louder until cheers erupted. The benefit of being Glancian was that I could see over the heads of the shorter Vytillians in front. But it was only a single man that emerged through the prison doors. The gold cloth of his belt was stark against his black robes.

"It's the Glancian high priest," I said, stopping short. "What's he doing here?"

"He must have received Bal's message about Dane and raced here from Tilting," Max said, setting off again. "He has come to help too."

I pushed past Max and cut off the high priest's path. He

gasped then looked relieved when he saw it was me. Relieved but weary, the efforts of traveling at speed from Tilting etched into every shadowy crease around his eyes.

"Josie, I was just coming to find you." Exhaustion made his voice heavy.

No, not exhaustion. It wasn't just tiredness dragging at the high priest. It was something much worse.

I felt sick as dread settled into my bones. Something was very wrong.

He took me by the arms with the intention of speaking earnestly to me, but in truth, his grip was the only thing holding me upright. My legs felt weak, boneless.

"I'm sorry," he said. "I tried to speak to them, to appeal on Dane's behalf. I told them he's a good man, that he couldn't possibly have done it. But the prison warden wouldn't listen."

The prison doors opened again and guards marched out, their systematic steps a dreadful rhythm that pounded in time to my heart.

"They look well," I whispered. "Why do they look well? Why are they not purging?"

He frowned. "The illness is *your* doing?"

He looked to where the first of the prisoners emerged behind the guards. Their hands and feet were shackled to the prisoner behind, forming a human chain. "Not all the guards fell ill," the high priest said.

The prisoners filed out, one by one, shuffling their feet, the shackles restricting their movement. Their heads were bowed, their shoulders stooped.

Except for the prisoner at the end. Dane looked directly at me.

CHAPTER 7

"No!" I screamed. I tried to run towards Dane, but Max hooked me around the waist. "This isn't supposed to happen!"

The high priest looked from my stricken face to Dane as the prisoners mounted the scaffold. "I'm sorry, Miss Cully, I wish I could do more."

I grasped his hands. "Please, tell them this isn't right. Tell them the god wishes him to be free! *Do* something. You have the power."

His eyes softened. "I'm so sorry, but I don't. I tried. Believe me, I tried very hard to convince the magistrate and then the warden. But it was no use."

I let him go, shoving his hands away. "Then why were you looking for me at all?"

"To offer you comfort."

"I don't want comforting, I want justice! Dane didn't kill anyone!"

My words were drowned by the crowd's cheers as the first of the prisoners was lined up beneath the noose. The hangman positioned it around his neck and pulled the lever to open the trapdoor beneath the prisoner's feet. It all happened so quickly that the roar of the crowd took me by surprise.

The next prisoner was unshackled from the remaining two

and brought forward. He began to cry as the first body was taken down.

"Max, give me your sword." I reached for it, but he batted my hand away.

"What are you going to do, Josie?"

"What do you think?" My words were a growl. Like an animal, I was going by pure instinct and my instincts screamed at me to free Dane by any means possible.

He stood with his head bowed, his hands working furiously behind his back, but he couldn't free himself from the shackles. His shirt cuffs were bloody from where the iron bands rubbed against his wrists.

"Max, give me the sword," I said again. "Then go. Collect Bal, Erik and Quentin and leave the city."

Another shout from the crowd erupted as the second man danced the hangman's dance.

"I'm not letting you do this alone," Max said, drawing his sword.

As if he heard the whine of the blade, Dane glanced up. His jaw hardened and he shook his head at Max.

Max looked to Meg. She didn't speak but her face was tight as she tried to hold back her emotions.

I grabbed Max's hand. "I'll do this. You need to protect Meg and the others."

"You *can't* do it," he snapped. "Look at this place! Even if you manage to free him from the chains, you'll never escape the courtyard!"

"He's right," the high priest said. "Josie, please, think of yourself. You can go on. You *will* go on and live a valuable, wonderful life."

He reached out a hand to me but I batted it away. "Don't talk to me about going on. Not without him."

He winced. "It pains me to see you throwing away your life for a man. All it will achieve is your death too. You cannot succeed."

The crowd whooped as the third prisoner twitched and kicked, dying a cruel death before their eyes. I closed mine but the image of him hanging there remained.

I turned in earnest to Meg. "I have to do this. You know I do. Help me."

She threw her arms around me. Our hug was brief but fierce. "Give her the sword, Max."

He hesitated.

"Max!" she shouted. "Give it to her!"

I eyed the scaffold where the third prisoner was being taken down. I glanced at Dane. He shook his head at me and mouthed "Don't."

I held my hand out to Max. He swore then mouthed an apology to Dane before giving me the sword. With one last distraught gaze in Dane's direction, he took Meg's hand and they ran off through the crowd.

"Josie," Theodore pleaded in small voice.

I kissed his cheek. "Take care of Balthazar and Quentin for me."

Kitty burst into tears and buried her face in my shoulder. Theodore had to wrench her free then they left too.

I turned back to the gallows to see the noose being positioned around Dane's neck. The guards stepped back, no longer needed, but did not leave the platform altogether.

Dane's legs were unshackled but his hands were not. One of the guards would have the key. I had to kill the hangman before he opened the trapdoor then kill both guards before they attacked me.

Hailia and Merdu give me strength.

I set off, only to be grabbed by the high priest. "I can't let you sacrifice yourself."

I jerked free.

"He doesn't want you to do this!"

He was right. Dane was shouting at me, his words lost in the roar of the baying crowd. His meaning was clear, however. Go. Leave. Don't try to free him.

I stormed up the scaffold steps and reached the top before one of the guards stepped forward and struck me across the head. If it weren't for the crowd surging up behind me, I would have tumbled down the stairs and landed on the cobbles.

I was jostled and handled, passed from one person to another in a state of shock. My vision blurred, either from tears or the blow to the head, or perhaps both. My ears rang, but a single voice broke through the noise.

"Let me through! Stop the execution! King's orders! Stop the execution!"

I gasped out a cry of relief as the crowd shouted abuse at the newcomer. I didn't dare hope that I'd heard correctly, but I hoped anyway as I saw the sheriff escort another man towards the steps. His authority was enough to forge a path through the throng. The people suddenly quieted and an eerie hush blanketed the courtyard.

The sheriff nodded a greeting when he saw me. "Seems your prayers have been answered. No need to cry now, miss. He's a free man. King's orders."

I tried to find Dane but there were too many people and I couldn't see much through my tears. I clung to the stair railing as I searched for him, hardly believing he was going to be free.

Not daring to believe.

"Josie?" came Max's shout from the base of the steps. "Josie, is it true?"

I nodded even though I couldn't see him. I couldn't see a thing, nor could I catch my breath, I was crying so hard. Next thing I knew a strong set of arms embraced me. Familiar arms.

Dane.

I clutched his face and stroked his hair back, and he did the same to me, as if it were the first and last time we'd ever touched.

The crowd erupted, cheering and whistling, their bloodthirsty lust suppressed by something sweeter. The emotions of a mob could be fickle.

Dane took my hand and led me to Max. "I want a word with you about following orders," Dane growled at his friend.

Max embraced him.

Meg, Theodore and Kitty took it in turns hugging Dane and then me, but my mind already raced ahead to what we had to do next. This wasn't over.

Max's thoughts followed the same path as mine. "We have to

go," he said. "Erik and Quentin are with the horses, Bal should be there now too. Theodore, give Dane his sword."

Theodore unstrapped the sword belt and handed it and the sword to Dane.

I looked around for the high priest, standing on my toes to see over the sea of heads, but he was nowhere in sight.

Dane took my hand and we set off through the lingering crowd. They were not prepared to disperse until the dramatic change in Dane's fortune had been thoroughly discussed.

"Wait!" someone called from behind. "The princess wishes to speak with you. You must come with me. Wait!"

"Damn it," Dane muttered. He stopped.

"We have to keep going." I pushed him. "If she finds out we lied, you'll be right back up on that scaffold."

He indicated the royal guards stationed ahead, and the sheriff and his constables coming up behind. He was right. We couldn't get away. If we tried, it would look suspicious and be a sure sign that we were going to renege on our promise.

"We'll say we lost it," I said quickly.

The royal footman who'd hailed us approached, escorted by armed constables. Dane ordered Max to leave. "Meet us later."

"I'm staying with you," Max said. "You seem to get yourself into trouble without me to back you up."

Meg grabbed his arm. "You are not staying. You're needed elsewhere."

When Theodore took Max's other arm, the sergeant didn't stand a chance. They marched him away just as the footman joined us, panting. Sweat beaded his forehead and dampened the hair near his ears.

"Her Royal Highness Princess Illiriya of Vytill has requested your presence at the castle." It didn't sound like a request.

"Now?" I asked. "Dane has been in prison for days. He's in no state to call on a princess."

Dane rubbed his bearded jaw to drive the point home. "May I take leave to freshen up first?"

"No." The footman strode off towards the waiting carriage, leaving the constables to make sure we followed.

We sat with the footman in the cabin and drove the short

distance to the castle. Dane and I sat opposite one another and didn't speak. I simply gazed at him, my heart full beyond words. Despite the filth of the prison clinging to him, he was the most beautiful sight I'd ever seen. He gazed on me with a small smile too.

As we approached the castle, I leaned forward and pushed up his sleeves. Dried blood covered his wrists, but the wounds were not deep. I would bandage them later when we had a moment.

We were shown into the same chamber where we'd met with the princess the first time. She rose from a chair by the fire and glided smoothly towards us, Lord Barborough at her heels.

"Thank the goddess you're all right," she declared as Dane bowed and I curtseyed. "I was worried we were too late."

Dane rose from his deep bow. "I owe you my life, Your Highness. Thank you for convincing the king."

"You have Lord Barborough to thank for that." She stepped aside to allow her advisor to come forward. "He answered my father's questions in great detail."

"His Majesty is a fast learner," Lord Barborough said. "I think he also wanted to believe in magic, he just needed a little more convincing. Now, Her Highness has fulfilled her part of the bargain. It's time for—"

"You're injured!" The princess took Dane's hands and turned them over, palms up, to reveal the bloodied underside of his wrists. "We must attend to these instantly. Lord Barborough, send someone to fetch warm water, a salve and bandages."

"But—"

"Now!"

Lord Barborough bowed stiffly, his lips pressed together in a rigid line, then strode out of the chamber.

"This is terrible," the princess said, inspecting Dane's wounds. "Just terrible."

"They're not so bad." Dane removed his hands and put them behind his back.

She cocked her head to the side and gave him a stern look. "I'm sure you've suffered worse as a guard in the king's retinue, but you're under my care now, and I don't like it. The shackles were far too tight. I must have a word to the jailors."

"There's no need to trouble yourself, Your Highness."

"There is every need. We are not barbarians in Vytill. Ah, my lord, you have the supplies?"

Lord Barborough entered ahead of three maids, one carrying a silver bowl, the next one with a bottle of salve and a cloth on a silver tray, and the third a roll of bandages and a towel, also carried on a silver tray. He bowed before his mistress, all outward contrition, but I suspected he was seething on the inside. This delay annoyed him, but it must gall him that he had to play lackey to Dane.

The princess indicated Dane should sit and roll up his sleeves then she knelt in front of him, the bowl on the floor beside her. She dipped the cloth in the water, but Dane pulled back before she could dab his wounds.

"Your highness, don't trouble yourself. Josie will do it."

The princess's gaze didn't even flick to me at the mention of my name. It wasn't lost on me that she had barely acknowledged me at all. Indeed, she hadn't addressed me directly once. I was superfluous, unimportant. She only had eyes for Dane.

"The wounds were inflicted by my father's jailors; I must attend to them. It doesn't feel right to allow anyone else to do it. Now, sit still. I'll try to be gentle." She smiled sweetly at him.

Dane glanced at me before extending his wrists. I stood and watched as the elegant princess tenderly wiped the blood away and dried his wrists with the towel. She handed the towel to one of the maids and the second stepped forward as if she'd been given orders to do so. The princess scooped out a few drops of the creamy salve and rubbed it into the wounds. Dane tensed but made no sound.

The princess smiled up at him. "It stings a little."

Of course it stung. If it didn't, it would be useless. Dane was a grown man, not a child, and he knew that. She didn't have to explain it. He sat utterly still, his wide eyes staring at her thumb as it made small circles on one wrist then the other.

"Almost done." She signaled for the bandages and the maid

lowered the tray. The princess gently wrapped each of his wrists. "There."

She made to stand, but Dane shot to his feet and assisted her. "Thank you, Your Highness. The kindness you've shown me today won't be forgotten." He smiled at her and she smiled back.

I looked away, struggling to suppress the wave of jealousy swamping me. I had no right to feel jealous. Dane and I were not lovers, and he had made no promises to me.

But he said he loved me. The small voice reminding me of that moment in the prison had me tilting my chin and looking up once again. The man who'd said those words wasn't fickle.

Anyway, there were more important things to worry about than my jealousy.

Lord Barborough cleared his throat. "His Majesty is engaged on state business this evening, however he has instructed me to obtain the gem from you. Tomorrow you will be presented to him in a private audience and he will tell you what he wants you to wish for on his behalf. So. Where is the gem? Who has the wishes?"

"We don't have the gem with us," Dane said.

"Then take me to it. Is it with your friends?"

"We lost it."

Lord Barborough cocked his head to the side. "Pardon?"

"It's lost. We don't know where it is."

"You promised it when you didn't have it?" Lord Barborough barked at me.

"Josie did have it then, but it has since gone missing," Dane said simply.

"You're lying!" Lord Barborough beckoned the guards standing at the door. "Seize them!"

"No!" the princess snapped. "Stand down."

The guards obeyed.

Lord Barborough rounded on her, his body heaving with his hard, ragged breaths. "Your highness, do not believe them! Either they have it and are lying about losing it, or they never had it. Either way, you cannot let them get away! The king kept his end of the bargain. If they cannot keep theirs, the king has no choice but to send the captain back to prison to await execution."

Princess Illiriya's nostrils flared. Her good mood of earlier was nowhere in sight as a mask of imperial authority descended over her. The steely calm sent a shiver through me. We were utterly at her mercy, and I wasn't entirely sure she possessed any.

I dropped to my knees in front of her. "Please don't send him back to prison, Your Highness. I did have it when I made the bargain, I swear to you, but it was stolen from its hiding place soon after. I should have told you, but I wanted Dane to be freed. I wanted it desperately. Please do not punish him for something that's my fault."

"Josie," Dane warned.

I ignored him and looked up at the princess, staring down her nose at me. Her narrowed gaze drilled into me. I clasped my hands together and was about to beg again when Lord Barborough grabbed me by my hair, wrenching my head back.

"Liar," he snarled, his face an inch from mine.

Dane stepped forward and punched Barborough in the jaw, sending him careening backwards. He fell to the floor with a thud.

Lord Barborough rubbed his jaw and licked his lip, testing for blood. "Arrest him!"

"No!" The princess's order kept her guards back. "That's enough, my lord. You've had your say."

Dane helped me to my feet. I could feel his vibrating anger through the hand he placed at my back. His glare drilled into Lord Barborough, who picked himself up off the floor.

"The king wants the wish he was promised, Highness," Lord Barborough said. "If they cannot fulfill their end of the bargain, the bargain is off. It's what your father—"

"Do not tell me what my own father would want. I know him better than anyone, and I can assure you he doesn't think people should die for magic."

"B—but Your Highness! This is a gross betrayal! Should we not check with him?"

"The king is busy."

"In the morning then."

She paused before giving a shallow nod. She indicated the door. "Please leave us now, my lord."

Lord Barborough bristled, his brow deeply furrowed. I thought he would challenge her order, but he wilted beneath her scowl. "Until tomorrow," he said, bowing.

She watched him retreat. Once the guard shut the door behind him, she let out a breath. She must have been holding it for some time because she seemed to weaken a little.

"I never liked him very much," she said. "My father foisted Barborough upon me when he returned from Glancia, hoping I could make sense of everything he claimed. I admit, his claims about magic were fantastical, but I did come to believe. It took my father much longer, unfortunately."

"We're grateful you managed to convince him in the end." Dane watched her through his lashes. "And grateful for this delay."

"I understand the situation completely," she said quietly. Too quietly for the guards to hear. Her smile turned wistful. "I would have lied about having it too, to get you out."

Neither Dane nor I spoke. I didn't dare, lest she change her mind and order the guards to arrest us. We were so close to freedom that I could smell the fresh air of the countryside, yet I was well aware that it all rested on the benevolence of this woman.

The princess turned a grim smile onto me. "I cannot be angry with you for promising a wish to save his life, Josie, but my father will not be so forgiving, no matter what I just said to Lord Barborough. He won't believe your story that it went missing after you made that promise."

"Why are you risking your father's wrath for us?" Dane asked.

"That is a complicated question with more than one answer, but suffice it to say that my father's plan for my future does not align with my own. Perhaps his plan will come to fruition anyway, but with a magical wish, it will be guaranteed. I'd rather see events play out in a more natural way. At least then I know the outcome was meant to be."

I wasn't sure I believed fate—or the god and goddess—had

our best interests at heart when shaping the future, but now wasn't the time for a philosophical or theological discussion. She had just admitted to treason. Not that her father would punish her the way he would punish a traitor, but it was a monumentally risky thing to say to two people she hardly knew.

So why did she? Why admit that she'd never really wanted her father to have the wish but knew promising it to him was the only way to set Dane free? It made sense that she didn't want her father to sit on the Glancian throne for the simple reason that it upset the power balance of The Fist Peninsula. It limited whom she could marry and would perhaps see her having to search in far-off lands for a suitable husband. But why admit that to us?

Dane eyed her with that careful, assessing way of his. Usually, he summed people up quickly, but I suspected the princess was proving difficult to put into a labeled casket. "The high priest of Glancia believes your father is telling the two Glancian dukes they have more supporters than they realize in the hope it will start a war between them before they're ready."

"I've never met him, but I believe your high priest is very astute," she said.

"I'm surprised you haven't met him," I said. "He's here in the city. We just saw him outside the prison."

"Which duke does he support?"

"No one, publicly," Dane said. He did not add that the high priest privately supported Buxton.

"He should make his opinion known," she said, not caring that he hadn't answered her. "Such a well-respected man will make people stand up and notice. It might help the Glancian nobles decide which duke to favor. Speaking of Glancian nobles, I met one recently," she said. "Lord Xavier Deerhorn. Do you know him from your days at the palace?"

"Never trust a Deerhorn," Dane warned.

She laughed, but it quickly withered when she saw his stern expression. "I'll keep that in mind."

"The Deerhorns are a power-hungry family, and Xavier is cruel. Never be alone with him, Your Highness."

She frowned. "Thank you for the warning. He petitioned my

father a few days ago, asking for support for the duke of Gladstow."

"Considering your father's own plans for the throne, I'm surprised Gladstow is bothering."

"So am I."

"Perhaps Lord Xavier needed an excuse to be here," I said to Dane.

He nodded, understanding my meaning. Lord Xavier had been here to chase us and get the gem for himself. He had to make it look as though he was working on behalf of Gladstow or the duke wouldn't have liked his ally entering enemy territory.

"Be careful, Your Highness," Dane said again. "These are dangerous times."

She smiled. "You are kind to worry about me, but there's no need. I am well versed in the ways of powerful men. Very few can get the better of me."

Dane conceded the point with a bow. "I can believe it."

"For a palace guard, you are quite well versed in the ways of kings and dukes yourself."

"I learned a lot in my days at the palace."

"More than you would want, perhaps."

Dane laughed lightly. "Sometimes."

She grinned, but it was fleeting. She glanced at the door. "We've spoken long enough. Your situation is still perilous. I am sorry to do this to you, but you're going to have to leave the city immediately. Don't return to the inn, don't collect your things or your friends. I don't trust Barborough. While I don't think he'll dare interrupt my father while he hosts friends tonight, he might take matters into his own hands. Please make haste and be careful."

I curtseyed deeply. This woman surprised me at every turn. She was helping us at great personal cost to herself. Her father would be furious with her when Barborough told him she let us go.

She touched my shoulder. "Have courage, Josie. You're going to need it. And please, keep him safe. I suspect this won't be the last time he gets himself into trouble defending a friend."

I looked up from my curtsey to see her smiling at Dane, her

eyes sparkling. She put out her hand to him and he took it and kissed it.

"Thank you, Your Highness," he said levelly. "For everything."

I looked away, too aware of the tightness in my chest.

Dane's hand slipped inside mine. I wrapped my fingers around his and offered him a weak smile that he returned. I wouldn't let jealousy ruin what we had. Whatever that was.

Guards escorted us outside and I jumped at every footfall, every movement. I expected Lord Barborough to appear at any moment and order our arrest.

But nothing happened. We left the castle, passing through each gate unhindered. Even so, when we reached the street, I was happy to run alongside Dane. I couldn't get away from the castle fast enough.

Night had fallen while we were talking to the princess, and the streets looked different with only the occasional welcoming torch flickering at the entrances of taverns. We retraced our steps back to the prison courtyard, now deserted of its bloodthirsty audience. I turned away from the hulking frame of the gallows with a shiver and led the way to the public stables where our friends waited.

Everything inside me remained taut with my heightened sense of awareness for my surroundings. Even here, I expected the king's guards to suddenly appear and arrest us. Or perhaps Lord Barborough would take the risk of delaying us himself, without his king's permission. He was desperate to get his hands on the gem and wishes, enough to take matters into his own hands.

It was this alertness that had me stopping suddenly when the whine of a sword being unsheathed rent the air. Dane heard it too and whipped out his blade. He turned in a slow circle, listening, searching the shadows.

But it was when his back was turned that the attacker made his move. Like all experienced predators, he went for the weakest first.

Me.

CHAPTER 8

The attacker's cloak billowed, and like a bird of prey, he swooped in from the shadows. I barely had time to gasp, but it was all the time I needed to pull out the knife from my pocket when my hand was already clutching it.

I struck upward as I dodged to the side, catching the attacker on the underside of his jaw. He hissed in pain and his sword clanged onto the pavement. Dane finished him off then immediately set himself up for another attack.

It didn't come.

I rolled the cloaked figure over with my boot but didn't recognize him and he wore no identifying livery.

Dane took my hand and we ran. No one followed, but it wasn't until we were almost at the stables that I dared slow down a little and speak.

"How did he know we would come back to the prison courtyard?"

"He might have followed us from the castle," Dane bit off. "I should have been more aware of my surroundings."

"Dane! Josie!" Quentin sprang out of the shadows and threw his arms around Dane then did the same to me. "I'm so glad you're all right."

"There's no time for that now," Dane told him. "Where are the stables?"

Quentin led the way and we received the same enthusiastic greeting from the others in the stable yard. I was just as relieved to see them as they were to see us. It wasn't simply the fact that it was safer in a larger group; it was the fact that I couldn't imagine going anywhere without them. They'd become my family, as important to me as my parents had been. It wouldn't be right leaving them here while we fled the city, as the princess had suggested.

Balthazar was the last to accept our hugs. He embraced me with more ferocity than I thought his old bones capable of. "We were worried you would never leave the castle," he murmured in my ear.

"So were we." My gaze sought out Dane, now issuing instructions to Max, Erik and Quentin while the others listened. "We have to continue with our plan to leave. We'll explain on the way. Are you capable of riding swiftly at night?"

"I am if you are."

The saddlebags were packed and the horses ready for our immediate departure. We rode through the city streets at a steady pace without incident. Even so, I felt as though I couldn't breathe until Merrin Fahl was behind us.

With the moonlit road ahead clear, we were able to ride until we reached a forest sometime in the middle of the night. We did not light a fire or erect tents, but ate rations we'd brought with us and slept on the ground.

We were too tired to talk until the following morning as we ate cold meat for breakfast at dawn and pored over the map.

Balthazar tapped his finger on the peaks known as The Razorbacks. "We can't go that way. It's too dangerous."

One branch of the mountain range separated Vytill's southern border from Freedland's north-east, while another branch cut through Freedland. Each branch had a single pass through it. While the Razorbacks weren't as high as Widowmaker Peaks, they were much steeper.

"The route via the two passes is rarely used," Balthazar said. "My research tells me that most trade enters Freedland via the Upway River, crosses Lake Torment, then travels to Noxford via Blood River. It's too treacherous and difficult to get through the

Razorbacks. We'll go the safer way too, by horse instead of boat. We'll skirt Lake Torment then follow Blood River into the capital, Noxford."

Kitty made a sound of horror. She, Quentin and Meg were packing our things rather than inspecting the map. "Lake Torment, Blood River…it doesn't sound less treacherous to me."

"Who named these places?" Quentin asked.

"The revolutionaries," I said. "The names were changed after they won the Freedland civil war."

"Just because they're revolutionaries, doesn't mean they couldn't have chosen nicer names."

Dane pointed at Merdu's Pass then Hailia's Pass, the two crossings through the two branches of The Razorbacks. "We have to go this way. It'll be fine."

Balthazar arched his brows. "How do you know?"

"The route you pointed out is the best route for *trade*. We're not merchants and we don't have goods to bring into Freedland."

"We have a packhorse," Quentin pointed out.

"The packhorse can traverse through the passes. It'll be cold, some sections may be difficult, but there's a village on the coast between the two branches of the Razorbacks where we can restock our supplies." He indicated Priest's End, a mere speck on the map on the outcrop known as East Knuckle. It was the only speck between the two branches.

"Is it necessary to take the difficult route?" Theodore asked. "No one seems to have followed us. The princess must have believed your story about the gem being stolen."

Dane and I exchanged glances. We'd been in such a hurry to leave the night before, we hadn't told them about the attack.

"It's not the princess we have to worry about," I said. "The greater threat comes from Barborough, either working alone or on behalf of the king, or Lord Xavier and Brant. One of them hired an assassin to try to stop us reaching you last night."

Kitty gasped, and Meg stopped what she was doing to scowl at me, perhaps for not informing them earlier. Not that it would have made a difference. We had moved as quickly as we could.

Dane rolled up the map. "We have to avoid the main route into Freedland. They'll expect us to go that way."

"It's decided," Max said with an emphatic nod. "The captain has made his decision. We travel through the mountains."

"I'm no longer your captain. You're free to debate with me or disregard my orders—my suggestions—altogether, if you wish."

Max's grunt held a hint of humor. "Prison changed you."

Dane laughed and clapped him on the shoulder. There were no more discussions about disregarding orders or taking the easier route into Freedland. We would head for the Razorbacks.

We set off at a good clip through the forest, but not as fast as the previous night. Kitty rode up alongside me and indicated I should fall back a little with her to where Erik and Quentin brought up the rear of our little group.

"Josie, can you ask Dane if we can hire a wagon in the next village?" she said.

"Why can't you ask him?"

"Because he'll dismiss it immediately if it comes from me. But if *you* suggest it, there'll be more chance he'll agree."

"I doubt it."

"We all know he'll do anything for you."

"Not if it's a bad idea, which getting a wagon is. We don't know if we can even take one through the passes. Besides, we have everything we need. A wagon is unnecessary."

"For you perhaps. I'm unused to sleeping on the ground." She scratched her head. "I lay awake last night imagining things crawling into my hair and making a nest."

I kept my gaze studiously on her face, not her hair where two dried leaves poked out of her ragged blonde locks. She hadn't bothered trying to brush it that morning and it looked like an inviting place for a creature to make its home.

"Tell him it's for Balthazar," she whispered.

"I heard that," Balthazar said from where he rode just ahead of us. "Don't use me as your excuse, Kitty."

Kitty sighed. "I miss being a duchess."

"Do not be sad, my duchess," Erik said cheerfully. "I will worship you later."

A secretive smile touched her lips only to quickly fade. "Not without a covered wagon."

"We will go behind a tree."

"I am not rolling around on the ground like a common whore!"

"That is what the tree trunk is for."

Kitty blushed. "Honestly, Erik, you're quite the savage sometimes."

"Only for you, my sweet duchess."

She rolled her eyes but her smile returned.

I rode off to join Dane at the front, riding just ahead of Max and Meg. He kept his gaze on the track but greeted me amiably.

"Let me guess," he said. "Kitty sent you up here to ask me if we can stop in a village along the way to purchase some kind of comfort she's in desperate need of."

"A wagon," I said. "A covered one. Although I think Erik managed to change her mind and accept a more savage existence."

"How intrepid of her."

"Hopefully her adventurous spirit will last until we reach Priest's End."

We rode in comfortable silence together for a while, but I could see he wanted to say something. I waited, my heart full, hoping he would repeat the admission he'd made to me in the prison. His words still raced through my head in quiet moments, and would forever swell my heart.

"Will you take some friendly advice?" he asked.

I sighed. "Are you going to lecture me?"

"It's about your plan to free me from prison."

"You mean the plan that failed? It was a terrible idea in the first place. If the princess hadn't managed to convince her father to pardon you—" I bit down on my trembling lip. I didn't want to be reminded of how close I'd come to losing him.

"It wasn't a terrible plan. But next time, dispatch the guards as soon as they begin throwing up. Don't give any of them an opportunity to fetch reinforcements."

"By dispatch you mean...?"

"Kill."

"I don't like killing people who are merely performing their duties. It's not their fault you were about to hang for a crime you didn't commit."

The gloved hand resting on his thigh curled into a fist. "Then you shouldn't follow me. I can't foresee a future where we won't need to dispatch men performing their duties."

"Dane," I said gently. "You don't have to pretend you don't care. Not with me. I know it troubles you as much as it troubles me."

He shook his head ever so slightly. "The problem is, I don't think it troubles me as much as it should." He shrugged. "I don't know. Perhaps it does. Perhaps..." He shook his head again. "I don't know what I feel about anything lately. Ever since leaving the palace and Mull, I feel...unsettled. Out of place. Like this journey is not only a bad idea but pointless."

"It won't be pointless. Perhaps you're not linked to Freedland, but some of the servants certainly are. Max, for one. And Balthazar too, somehow."

"That's not it. I must be from Freedland. I have a Freedlander's coloring. So shouldn't I feel like I'm going home?"

"Not when it hasn't been your home for some time. You can't remember it, Dane. But you remember Mull. Mull became your home. When your memories return—"

"If."

"*When* your memories return, your sense of belonging will change again." I reached out and touched his arm. "You *will* remember, Dane."

He took my hand in his and stared down at it. "I wish I didn't have to."

"You don't mean that. Not really."

His hand squeezed mine. "You know me better than I know myself." He let me go and returned his hand to his thigh where it once again balled into a fist.

We rode in silence again for some distance before he suddenly turned to me, frowning. "You mentioned Brant earlier. You said the attacker last night could have been hired by Deerhorn, the king, Barborough or Brant. Why him?"

"We saw him yesterday, before your...before you were led out of the prison."

"I should have known he'd break away from the others and

reach Merrin Fahl before them. He never got along with the other servants. What did he want?"

"To goad us. He let slip that he knew we'd used the gem to bargain for your freedom."

"Only the princess or Barborough could have told him about your bargain. The princess wouldn't stoop to dealing with Brant, but Barborough would."

I bit the inside of my cheek, considering the best way to admit what I'd done. "It might not have been either of them who told him."

"Go on," he said when I hesitated.

"You gave me the idea actually."

His frown deepened. "What idea?"

"You suggested it would have been a better idea to use the gem to entice Lord Xavier into admitting he killed Jute. I even told him how to word it for the authorities so that it would seem like an accident. It was quite a good idea."

"No, it was not," he growled. "I'm sure I didn't say it was a *better* idea. I do recall saying it was dangerous to strike any kind of bargain with the Deerhorns. Are you telling me you spoke to Lord Xavier?"

"He visited me at the inn."

He glanced over his shoulder to Max.

"I was alone at the time," I said. "Drowning my sorrows." I cleared my throat as my attempted lightness fell flat. Dane's face turned thunderous. "Anyway, Lord Xavier didn't want to make that admission to the magistrate, but it seems he did tell Brant that I'd offered him the gem. It wouldn't surprise me if either of them was behind the attack last night."

Dane looked directly ahead, his body rigid. He was furious with me.

"At least now we know who Brant's working for," I said. "He probably promised the Deerhorns a wish if they helped him retrieve the gem." Dane kept his gaze dead ahead. "It *must* be Lord Xavier who told him we had it, not Barborough. You see, Brant mentioned that he'd heard we have the gem, not the gem *and* the wishes. I promised the princess both gem and wishes, but just the gem to Lord Xavier, since I was quite sure he believed Brant had the wishes. So now we know they've struck a deal. That's a benefit to come out of this."

His gaze slid sideways to me. "There is no benefit to having Brant, the Deerhorns and Barborough all after us."

"Don't forget King Phillip."

His eyes narrowed to slits before he looked forward again, presenting me with his shoulder. He quickened his horse's pace.

I followed and drew alongside him again, only to have to fall back when the track narrowed.

"Do not ignore me," I snapped. "I did it for you, to get you out of prison, in case the princess couldn't. It could have worked."

"But it didn't."

"I'd bargain with the Deerhorns, Brant and the sorcerer itself if I had to, Dane."

He said nothing.

"Stop behaving as if you wouldn't have done it too if the situation was reversed."

"I wouldn't." It was a half-hearted protest with not a hint of conviction.

"I know you better than you know yourself, remember."

He grunted and directed his horse to the side to allow me space to move up. "I hate arguing with you."

"I hate it too," I said with a sigh.

His eyes flashed with mischief. "No, I mean I hate arguing with you because you always win."

I reached across the gap and thumped him in the arm.

He laughed. "That was pathetic."

"Oh, you want me to punch you hard? Gladly. You deserve it."

I went to smack his arm again but he rode off.

He looked back over his shoulder. "Try and catch me. I'll go slow."

The wretch. He knew I'd never catch him. I managed to urge my horse to speed up, but the close trees made me too nervous to make her go faster. She seemed to sense my hesitation and deliberately kept a more sedate pace than Dane's energetic horse.

I finally caught up to him at a deep pool. He'd stripped off entirely and was swimming away from me with smooth strokes. He reached the rocks on the other side where he set about pulling out river grass from the shallows. It was good for cleansing and healing, and had a delicious sweet smell.

He washed off the prison grime then swam back as the others arrived. He stopped when he got close enough to stand and walked until the water was waist deep. Droplets streamed from those wonderfully broad shoulders and chest, and dripped off his hair. He didn't care about modesty so I didn't bother to turn away. I stood and admired.

"Oh my," came Meg's soft protest behind me. "I can see why you like to look upon him."

"From a purely professional perspective, of course," I said, smiling at Dane. He was looking back at me with a quizzical raise of his eyebrows since he couldn't hear our conversation.

"Naturally," Meg said, laughing. "Oh!"

I turned to see what had startled her only to be almost barreled over by a naked Erik sprinting past, whooping. He ran into the water and dove into the depths before surfacing on the other side. He flicked his hair back, spraying drops of water in an arc, and grinned.

"Come in, Kitty!" he called out.

"I prefer my baths warm, thank you," she said, taking up a position beside me. "Besides, I can see better from here."

"In case one of them drowns?" Balthazar asked from where Theodore was helping him down from his horse.

"Precisely."

Erik beckoned Max and Quentin but both shook their heads.

"Go on," Meg urged. "It looks like fun."

"It looks cold and wet," Quentin grumbled.

Max hesitated before removing his doublet and jerkin. "Turn away," he said before removing his breeches. "Don't look until I'm in the water."

Kitty and I dutifully turned away while Meg covered her eyes with her hands.

"No peeking," he told her.

I heard his footsteps on the leaf matter as he ran past and the loud splash of water followed by Dane swearing. I turned back to see him fishing Max out of the deeper section and dragging him back to the shallows. Max's face was red from coughing.

"So he lived in a landlocked village," Balthazar said mildly.

Meg removed her boots and waded into the shallows. "Are you all right?"

Now safely in shallow waters, Max nodded. "Fine. Thanks, Captain."

"My pleasure, Sergeant."

Dane swam off to join Erik, who promptly tried to draw Dane into a race. Dane refused and they fell into a playful argument. I'd never seen Dane like this with his men before, and I wondered if it was new to them too, or if he'd always been more friendly during their quieter moments at the palace.

Going by the smile on Max's face and Quentin's admiration as they watched on, I would guess it was a new and welcome development. Despite what Dane said about not feeling at home here, he was certainly relaxed.

Balthazar tapped Theodore with his walking stick. "Quentin, Theo, let's set up a camp in that clearing through there. It's growing dark and my body aches. I won't be able to get back on that beast today."

Quentin stroked the horse's nose. "Your horse isn't a beast; he's a good, calm fellow. Aren't you, Boy?" Mere months ago, he'd sat awkwardly on his horse and fallen off so many times that he was the butt of the other guards' jokes. He'd come a long way since I'd first met him. He was now as capable on horseback as most of the other palace guards.

"You go," Theo said from where he sat on a large rock. "I'm enjoying the, er…"

"View?" I offered.

"Company."

I sat on the rock beside him. "Me too."

Erik finally coerced Dane into a swimming race, which Dane won. He won the second and third too, but not the fourth. Erik cheated by getting out of the water on the far bank and sprinting to the end.

Kitty squealed with laughter and clapped her hands. "We can see all of you, Erik!"

He bowed in our direction. "You are welcome, ladies! And Theodore too. I hope you enjoyed the show."

Max rolled his eyes. "We should have left him in Merrin."

Meg joined me on the rock, grinning from ear to ear. "Kitty has quite the roguish streak."

I watched Kitty as she openly admired Erik performing all sorts of, er, interesting moves with his pelvis on the other side of the stream. "I think she's more of a village girl at heart than she likes to admit."

"You do village girls a disservice," Theodore said. "Most ladies at the palace privately engaged in exhibitions far bawdier than this. Village girls are well behaved by comparison."

Meg and I both stared at him. I couldn't imagine Kitty doing this sort of thing when she was a duchess, and I certainly couldn't imagine Miranda and her mother doing it either. They were both genteel and proper to their core. Lady Violette Morgrave and Lady Deerhorn, however, were another breed entirely.

Dane called my name from where he stood beside Max in the shallows. I tried very hard to only look at his face but found my gaze wandering over his chest, down to his abdomen and the V of muscle disappearing into the water.

Dane cleared his throat. "Josie, there are some clean clothes in my saddlebags."

"Are there?"

"Can I have them, please?"

"Of course."

He waited. "Can I have them now?"

"Right. Just going to get them." I got up and slowly walked to his horse, backwards.

He smirked and crossed his arms, making the muscles on his chest and arms bulge. "I could freeze out here."

"You'll be fine. I've got medical training. I know the signs of freezing and you're not exhibiting any yet."

Erik swam across the stream, got out and walked straight up to his horse. He didn't bother to fish out clean clothes from his saddlebags but walked the horse off through the trees to the clearing where Quentin and Balthazar had begun setting up a camp.

"Erik!" Quentin cried. "Put that away. Nobody wants to see it."

"The ladies do," Erik said.

Kitty picked up her skirts and followed. "I'd better help set up. Balthazar should be resting."

Theodore followed her and Meg got to her feet. "Come on, Josie. Kitty's right, and we should help. Besides, Max's extremities are starting to turn blue."

Max looked down at himself then dipped both hands under the water to cover his nether regions.

I allowed myself to be dragged away by Meg, walking backwards until I stumbled over a stick. My clumsiness earned me a smug smile and a wave from Dane.

* * *

THE FOLLOWING morning brought a new day that was entirely different from the one before. Not only was our pace slower, but everyone was snippy and cross. Perhaps it was the lack of sleep or drizzling rain that dampened our mood, or perhaps it was the jagged, sharp mountains rising from the flat plains ahead like dragon's teeth. Whatever it was, Kitty snapped at Erik and he snapped back, Meg and Max hardly acknowledged each other, and Theodore had fallen into morose silence. Quentin tried to tell jokes to lift everyone's spirits until Balthazar told him to be quiet.

Dane was back to ignoring me, and by midday, I was tired of it. "Do we need to find another pond?" I asked, joining him at the front of our little group.

"Pardon?"

"So you can wash away your sour mood."

"Sorry," he said simply.

I waited for more but he sat in the saddle, his body moving effortlessly with the horse's steps, a hand resting on his thigh. We traveled at a walking pace today. With the twin cities well behind us, escape no longer felt urgent, and those of us unused to riding were suffering from long hours in the saddle.

"I don't want an apology," I told him. "I want things to return to the way they were between us."

"It can't."

"Why not?"

"You know why. It's best this way until I learn about my past."

"You didn't think that way yesterday. You enjoyed yourself."

"Yesterday I let my guard down. I shouldn't have. It was wrong of me and unfair to you."

So we had circled back to that point in our relationship. It felt like a backwards step. Or a step in the wrong direction. "Can I not have your friendship, at least?"

"Of course. You'll always have that, Josie. Always."

"It doesn't feel like it sometimes."

He blinked rapidly as he stared at the snow-capped peaks ahead. "I'm sorry."

My heart sank. His apology was all I would get from him for now.

I eased back and let him go on ahead. Meg joined me as Max moved up alongside Dane.

"Let me guess," she said. "He told you he can't be with you because he doesn't know if he has a wife."

I sighed. "And Max?"

"We're not at the same place in our relationship as you and Dane, but I suspect that's because he doesn't want to get too close for the same reason." We watched the men speak quietly to one another for a few moments. "I feel like I'm just waiting," Meg went on. "Waiting for their memories to return, waiting for them to find out if they are free, and to learn about themselves. Waiting, waiting, waiting."

"Freedland will produce answers."

"Some, perhaps, but not all. They'll never know everything until they get their memories back, and that won't happen without magical intervention. We don't have the wishes or the gem, Josie, and we're running away from the person we're quite sure has the former."

"We'll see Brant again."

"When? We could be in Freedland for some time."

I frowned at her. "It's not like you to be this impatient, Meg. Are you missing home? Do you want to return to Mull and your family?"

"It's not that." She nodded at Max.

I smiled wryly. "I understand you completely."

"Riders!" Quentin shouted from the back of our group. "Coming up fast!"

Dane peeled away from the front and rode back. He stopped a short distance away and returned. "There are about ten of them. I saw flashes of purple and gold."

"Royal guards," Theodore said.

"Sweet Hailia," Kitty whispered. "They'll easily catch us."

"Head for Merdu's Pass." Dane pointed to a low point between two peaks. "Ride as fast as you can and find somewhere to hide. Max, Erik, Quentin, with me."

"You can't hold off ten of them!" I cried.

"Go!" He wheeled his horse around and rode towards the royal guards.

Erik followed without hesitation. Quentin gulped, gave me a grim smile, then he rode off too. Max nodded at Meg, and she nodded back before he followed Dane, Erik and Quentin.

"Josie! Meg!" Kitty cried from some distance away. "Hurry!"

I rode at the back of our fractured group with Balthazar. He looked uncomfortable, but he didn't utter a sound of complaint. He kept his gaze on the mountain range.

The landscape became steeper, the valley narrowing. The stream that fed the River Mer flowed swiftly, crashing over rocks and trapped debris. We followed it into the densely forested foothills where the track thinned, almost disappearing in places, as it headed up the steep inclines. It would only get steeper from here, and the trees would thin out as we climbed before disappearing altogether.

"If we're going to hide, it has to be here," I called to the others.

Meg, Balthazar and Theodore stopped to survey the area.

Kitty kept going until she realized we weren't following and turned back.

"We should keep moving until we reach Freedland," she said. "If the men can't hold them off then we won't be able to."

"We can't outrun them," Theodore said. "Dane knew that, which is why he told us to hide."

Kitty looked at Balthazar and her shoulders slumped as she gave in. "Very well. But where?"

"Somewhere off the track," I said. "And I think we should go separately so as to do as little damage to the underbrush as possible."

"You mean to confuse their trackers if they have them?" Meg asked.

"A good idea," Balthazar said, setting off through the trees to the left. "Everyone find somewhere well away from the path. Don't get lost."

Kitty looked around, her brow crumpling. "But I have a terrible sense of direction. I'll never find my way back."

For some reason, that made me smile. "Can you see the sun?" I asked.

She squinted up at the tree canopy where dappled light filtered through to the leaf matter on the ground. "Yes."

"Head that way and keep the sun over your left shoulder. When you return, it will be on your right."

"But the sun moves," she whined.

"It will only move further to your left."

"Don't you mean my right?"

"Kitty!" Meg snapped. "Just go. We'll whistle for you when all is clear. Just follow the sound."

Kitty blinked back tears. "Why didn't you just say that in the first place?" She headed off into the underbrush, ducking under a low tree branch.

"I'll stay here near the track," Theodore said. "Someone has to meet Dane and the others if they return."

"*When* they return," Meg said.

He dismounted and handed me the reins. "Take my horse. I'll hide up there behind that bush. I'll have a good view of anyone approaching."

I shook my head and dismounted too. "I'll stay. You have to take my horse, Theo. I can't control both if they get startled."

He looked doubtful, so I thrust the reins into his hand, giving him no choice. They headed into the forest and I made my way up the slope to the bush Theodore had pointed out. It did have a view of the track in both directions, but the track was winding, the forest thick, so the view wasn't far reaching. I wouldn't know who approached until they were almost upon me.

It seemed to take forever before the thunder of hooves in the distance reached my ears. It was impossible to tell how many riders there were, but it was more than one.

Dear Hailia, let all four of our men return safely.

I rested a hand on the damp earth, ready to spring out at the first sight of them. The vibrations increased, the rumble of hooves drew closer. I rose up from a crouching position to hail them, expecting to see Erik, the best horseman, leading.

But it was not Erik. It was two riders dressed in purple with gold braiding on their uniforms. And they came to a stop right in front of me.

If they were here and Dane was not…

I felt sick.

They dismounted and inspected the ground, churned up by our horses. One pointed out the paths each of us had taken into the forest. He followed one set of prints to the edge of the track and shook his head. The prints disappeared on the leaf matter. My friends were safe as long as they stayed hidden.

But I was not safe. One of the riders indicated my lone footsteps. His gaze followed them to where I was hiding behind the bush.

"One is there," he said. "Going by the size of the boots it's the old man or a woman. And they're alone."

His companion adjusted his grip around his sword. The blade was bloody. "I'm going to enjoy this." He plunged up the slope towards me, a gruesome grin splitting his face.

CHAPTER 9

I dipped my hand into my pocket and pulled out the small surgical knife. My other hand scooped up a small rock.

I watched the first guard through the leaves and branches of the bush, advancing steadily up the slope. He looked eager to claim his prize, either the "old man or a woman." Easy prey.

Or so he thought.

"Come out, come out," he sang off key. He came right up to my hiding place and stood on his toes to peer over the bush.

I threw the rock away to my left. It made a small sound, just enough to make him think I was hiding over there. He looked towards it.

I struck upwards with the knife as I rose, stabbing the guard through the throat to kill him instantly. This was no time for merely inflicting a minor wound. Not when there was another behind him and I was alone. Blood gushed from the wound as he slumped forward over the bush. I removed my knife and plucked his sword from limp fingers. The longer blade was necessary if I was going to defeat the second man.

He advanced up the slope, sword drawn and ready to swing. I emerged from behind the bush and clutched the hilt with both hands, my knife once again tucked into my pocket. With my height and the benefit of the slope, I had the strategic advantage.

But he was a skilled swordsman, and I'd barely even held one before. Any advantage would be almost useless.

"You Glancians are all the same," he snarled. "You're animals. You fuck animals like that Marginer. I'm going to enjoy fucking you all the way back to Merrin."

He lunged at me and I just managed to get the sword up in time to parry the strike. The blow jarred my wrists and arms, but I had no time to shake off the pain. The blade descended again, swiping in an arc at my head.

I flattened myself to the ground and rolled out of the way, thrusting the sword upwards. The tip struck him across the underside of his jaw, not enough to kill him, only anger him further.

With a roar, he grabbed his sword in both hands and struck down. I rolled to the side then rolled back as the sword plunged again. I had no time to lift my own sword to either strike or parry. All my efforts went into dodging each fierce blow.

Dirt and leaves flicked onto my face, in my eyes. I blinked them clear just in time to see the sword descending towards my head yet again. There was no time to raise my sword, no time to move, just squeeze my eyes shut and pray for a swift death.

It didn't come.

I opened my eyes to see the guard falling forwards. He landed beside me with a thud, his dead eyes staring at me. A knife protruded from his back.

I scrambled away, half sliding, half running down the slope and hugged Balthazar as he stood in the middle of the track. "You saved my life."

He patted my shoulder. "It would seem so."

I drew away and wiped my tears on my sleeve. "I didn't know you could do that."

"The warrior priests in Tilting told me I was a good knife thrower. Apparently I trained with the other priests in my younger years, but I had no aptitude for swordsmanship or horsemanship. The only skill I learned with any success was knife throwing. I've kept one on my person ever since I learned about it." He looked at the dead guard. "It seems the priests weren't merely flattering me after all."

"Where is your horse?"

"Tied to a tree through there." He indicated the forest behind him then gazed along the track in the direction the guards had come. It was silent.

"I have to go back," I said, heading up the slope again. "I have to see for myself if..." The words stuck in my throat along with my tears.

"Let me fetch the horse. We'll go together." He headed into the forest, whistling.

I retrieved both swords and Balthazar's knife from the bodies then returned to the track. By the time I reached it, Meg, Kitty and Theodore had returned. There were no congratulatory hugs, no smiles, just a weighty silence.

We mounted and rode back the way we'd come. As the best rider, Kitty was in the lead, but she suddenly stopped up ahead. She put up her hand to urge us to halt.

That's when I heard it too. Hooves thundering towards us.

Merdu, not again. I couldn't fight off more guards. My arm and shoulder ached, my heart too. I just wanted to find Dane and the others. I needed to know what happened to them.

Theodore and I dismounted and moved to the front, swords raised. Neither of us was skilled enough to fight while mounted. Balthazar remained behind, knife in hand, ready to throw it again.

The hoofbeats drew closer. I adjusted my grip and stance on one side of the road while Theodore took up position on the other, sword raised to strike.

Because of his location on the track's shoulder, he had the first view of the riders. He lowered his sword and broke into a grin. "Erik!"

Erik rounded the corner at speed and pulled his horse to a stop. Kitty dismounted and ran to him and he scooped her up with one arm, sat her on the horse sideways in front of him, and hugged her. She didn't care that he was covered in blood.

"Erik?" I asked, my voice weak. "The others?"

Even as I said it, I heard more hooves. I raced along the track until I saw them. First Dane then Max with Quentin some way behind, leading the packhorse. I let the sword go and started to cry.

He was alive. They all were.

Dane's hug started fiercely, his arms tight as they wrapped around me. But it soon became tender, as he kissed my forehead, my damp cheeks, and finally my mouth.

"I thought you were surely all dead," he said when he pulled away to search my face.

"And I you."

"Did you see the two guards?"

I nodded, my lip wobbling again as fresh tears threatened.

His thumbs stroked my cheeks and he peered into my eyes. "And?"

"I dispatched one. Bal got the other."

He took in the discarded sword, the blood on my clothes, and Balthazar clutching a bloodied knife. "Bal?"

"You first." Balthazar nodded in the direction they'd just come. "What happened?"

"We should keep going," Max urged. "That could have been an advance party."

Dane agreed. "We'll tell you our story as we move. I want to get as far as we can before nightfall."

We mounted and set off again, riding single file because of the narrow track. Dane, Erik, Quentin and Max eyed the two bodies as we passed them.

"They escaped while we were engaged with the others," Dane told us. "I saw them go but couldn't stop them."

"He had two guards on him," Max said. "So did Erik."

"Three," Quentin piped up. "You should have seen Erik. One time he stood on the saddle to get a good angle to strike, all while the horse was going full tilt. Another time he fell to the side to escape the guard's blade. I thought he'd fallen off but he righted himself when the danger passed. It all happened so quick, I hardly had time to blink."

"You should have been concentrating on your opponent," Max chided him, without any heat in his voice. "Not watching Erik."

"It is good that he watches me." Erik tapped his chest. "So he can learn from the best rider, the best fighter."

"The best fighter *on a horse*," Quentin pointed out.

Erik beamed. "I am good on a horse, it is true."

The people of the Margin were known for their horsemanship, but it only just dawned on me that they weren't simply good riders, but good fighters on horseback too.

"I wonder what else the Margin folk do on horseback," Kitty said, quite innocently.

Erik's grin widened. "We will see, later."

Max groaned.

We told them about Balthazar's secret skill of knife throwing, which led to me describing how I'd fought off the first guard. Dane remained silent throughout the retelling.

We made camp as dusk fell in a cave we stumbled across half way up the mountain. I patched up the men's cuts by torchlight at the back of the cave with Kitty and Meg assisting, but immediately extinguished the torch afterwards. We made no fire and ate the cold salted pork we'd brought with us.

The day had been long, and I was so tired that I felt drowsy soon after eating. I lay down but my arm ached, so I sat up again and rubbed my shoulder.

Dane sat beside me. "You have something for that in your medical pack."

"How do you know what I have in my medical pack?"

"Because you're well prepared and carry everything we could possibly need." He reached for the pack and rummaged through it. It was too dark to see inside, but he pulled out a jar he'd found by touch. "What about this?"

I could just make out the distinctive shape of the promfrey sap jar in the moonlight. "That's for burns."

He returned it and pulled out another. "This one?"

I laughed softly and took the jar and pack off him. "It'll take you all night." I found the jar of tumini spice mixed with the pulp of overripe blackberries. The heat of the spice was good for muscular aches, and massage helped too.

I removed my doublet and jerkin and unlaced my bodice. I paused but when Dane didn't avert his gaze, I continued until I could pull the bodice down to reveal my bare shoulder. I removed the jar stopper, but Dane took the jar from me.

"I'll do it." His voice was all thick velvet, deep and rich. He scooped out some salve and rubbed it on my shoulder in slow, gentle circles.

I leaned into his touch. "What happened to keeping your distance?"

"I'm weak." His whisper brushed my hair and warmed my neck.

I lifted my gaze to his. "You're the strongest person I know."

"Not when it comes to avoiding you." His eyes gleamed, two bright orbs in the dark. They drew closer until they filled my vision.

The kiss was tender but no less powerful for it. It wasn't a hungry kiss, a kiss between lovers held apart too long. It was sweet and sad, intensifying the dull ache that lodged in my heart months ago into a piercing pain.

A movement at the cave entrance startled us apart, but it was only Theodore joining Quentin on the first watch. With a shuddery sigh, Dane put his arm around me and drew me down with him. We lay together, my body nestled against his, my head on his chest, until I fell asleep.

* * *

No one followed us the next day. It would seem the group of royal guards that attacked us had not been an advance party for a larger group. By the time Lord Barborough realized they weren't returning, we would be in Freedland. It wouldn't be worth sending another party over The Razorbacks to retrieve us.

The steeper we climbed, the more difficult the terrain became. The forest thinned then stopped altogether and the trees were replaced with low shrubs and fallen rocks. A cold wind whipped across the barren landscape, but the sunshine and exercise kept us warm.

All but Erik and Balthazar dismounted and led the horses single-file. In the rear, the packhorse was tied to Dane's horse, which in turn was tied to Erik's. Dane led Balthazar's mount carefully, talking to it in soothing tones whenever the loose stones beneath its hooves shifted.

It was slow going and by nightfall we'd progressed half way up the mountain. The saddle of Merdu's Pass was in sight, but it was another day's ride away.

We camped among the shrubs that offered some protection from the wind once we lay down. Erik built a small rocky wall to protect our campfire and we dined on our first cooked meal since leaving Merrin Fahl. The two rabbits we'd caught during the day offered little sustenance, however, and we all went to bed hungry.

I huddled with Kitty and Meg for warmth and suffered through Kitty's complaints about the cold until Erik joined her. Her contented sigh made me long for Dane's warm arms around me, but I didn't ask him to lie with me. The previous night's tenderness had been an admission of our love, but an unspoken agreement had passed between us. It could not happen again.

Not yet.

Somehow, I managed to get some sleep but awoke to dampness. A misty rain fell all morning, making the rocky path slippery. We trudged carefully forwards, always heading up, not uttering a word to the person before or aft. No one was in the mood for jokes or casual conversation. We were focused on the pass as if it would be the end of our arduous journey.

But it was not the end, merely the mid-point. We reached the flat saddle of Merdu's Pass just before darkness fell and made camp beneath a rocky outcrop. The rain had ended some time before, thank Merdu, but we couldn't make a campfire without dry wood, so we ate what we could find in the saddlebags. A hot meal would have been welcome, but the god of weather did not smile on us.

The wind was stronger through the pass between the mountain peaks, and as the night wore on, the air grew colder. We huddled together, cloaks wrapped around us, hands tucked into pockets, and tried to sleep.

Sleep did not come for me, but Quentin snored softly, and Meg's breathing became heavy as did her body against mine. I tried to control my shivers so as not to wake her. The moon and stars stayed hidden so there was no light to see Dane by. If he slept, I couldn't tell.

Dawn's glow revealed a light dusting of snow covering the track. Deeper drifts collected in dips and between boulders. I'd never seen snow before and couldn't believe how white it was, how pristine, until it melted and turned the path to mud.

Kitty blinked hard at it, as if she couldn't quite work out what she was seeing. Then she promptly burst into tears. "I hate this. My body aches, I'm freezing and hungry, and I want to go home."

Meg put an arm around her shoulders. "Come on. The sooner we leave, the sooner we'll get out of this cold and into an inn."

Erik patted the saddle in front of him. "Ride with me, my duchess. I will keep you warm."

She stepped towards him but stopped herself and shook her head. "I am not a duchess now. I'll walk. You have the horses to manage."

I took Kitty's hand. "You're coping very well."

"No, I'm not." She sniffed. "You and Meg haven't complained once. Nor have the men."

"Meg and I are hardy village girls." I nudged her with my elbow. "Meg's right. The sooner we move, the sooner we'll reach Priest's End. I don't know about you, but the only thing keeping my legs moving is the prospect of a hot meal."

Kitty accepted her horse's reins from Theodore. "I don't know what I'll do first," she said. "A hot bath? A warm meal? Or just sit by a fire with a cup of tea in hand."

"Mulled wine," Meg said dreamily. "That's what I want. I haven't had mulled wine since last winter."

"What's mulled wine?" Max asked.

Meg looked surprised by the question at first but then she recalled his memory loss. "It's spicy and warm. The perfect accompaniment for winter feasts."

Quentin handed me the reins to my horse. "I'm going to buy myself a sheepskin coat and wrap myself in it," he said. "Then I'm going to ask the innkeeper to cook me a feast fit for a king and I'm going to gorge myself." His stomach audibly growled and we laughed.

Dane clapped him on the back. "I'd settle for bread and cheese right now."

"Ooh yes," Theodore cooed. "I miss the smell of freshly baked bread."

I groaned. "Enough talk of food. My stomach feels hollow. Anyway, I've decided I'm going to eat whatever is available upon our arrival."

"I'm going to eat whatever is available while soaking in a hot bath." Kitty dug a hand through her tangled locks, abandoning her attempt at brushing it when her fingers got caught. "And there'll be a maid to wash my hair and another to wash my clothes."

Quentin sighed deeply.

I walked alongside Balthazar, hunched into his cloak to his eyes. "Bal? Are you all right?"

"I'll manage," he said stiffly.

I touched his arm. Even through the clothing, I could feel him shivering. I removed my cloak to give to him, but Dane put a hand on my shoulder from behind. He shook his head and removed his own cloak then gently wrapped it around Balthazar, ignoring the old man's protests.

We did not stop all day, but our descent was just as slow as the ascent. The treachery of loose, slippery rocks meant we had to tread cautiously, and we spent another night on the slopes in the cold. At least the snow and rain had stopped, and the wind seemed to weaken too. We managed to get a small fire started with some dry wood we found beneath a cluster of bushes, and we all huddled around it, worshipping the flames.

I was so exhausted I fell asleep sitting up, my back against Meg's. Sometime during the night I must have lain down, and I awoke in her arms. Dane was awake too and I joined him where he stood with the horses, looking down at the valley below and at the second branch of the Razorbacks looming in the distance.

"Freedland," I said, pulling my cloak tightly around me. "It looks peaceful, empty."

He pointed at the hazy horizon to the south. "That's the sea. Priest's End is there somewhere."

"I know it's only a small village with a reputation for being rough, but right now, it seems as wonderful as Leon's palace to me."

"To me too." He lifted the collar of my cloak to cover the back of my neck. His thumb stroked the patch of skin beneath my ear before he withdrew. "Let's head off before one of us goes mad from hunger and decides Quentin looks the tastiest."

"Oi!" Quentin had come up behind us, unbeknown to me but not Dane.

Dane laughed and ruffled the youth's hair. "The faster you move, the less appealing you'll seem as we get closer to Priest's End and proper food."

We reached the valley by the time the sun was on its descent. The grassy plain wedged between the mountain ridges seemed devoid of life at first, but closer inspection revealed rabbits and other small creatures scuttling here and there.

That night's supper was a feast in comparison to the last few. The weather in the valley was warmer and we all slept peacefully under the open sky. Not even Kitty complained about the lack of privacy as Meg and I held up our cloaks to create a screen for her to do her business behind.

The next day, the sun shone. We could have traveled faster but kept the pace slow in deference to Balthazar. He didn't complain, but I could tell from his crooked back and pinched face that the ride had been too much for him. That night I made a soothing tisane from the herbs I'd brought with me to ease his aches. I was glad I'd packed them. The Freedland plants growing on the plain were not familiar, and the ones I needed didn't grow in grasslands anyway.

The following morning dawned grayer, and the clouds darkened as the day wore on. The rain began when Priest's End came into view, and by the time we reached the village, late in the afternoon, we were thoroughly wet.

I'd heard Priest's End referred to as Arse End and when we entered the tiny village, I could see why. The cluster of buildings squatting at the bay's edge were squeezed between two high cliffs that must keep the village and dock in shadow for much of the day. The houses were small and most looked to be in need of repairs. Some seemed abandoned altogether, their roofs caved in, their walls falling down and doors broken.

For a village with so few buildings, the main street was unusually busy. Dozens of men lolled about in doorways and against the tavern walls, sometimes alone but often with a woman. Their grunts left no doubt as to what they were doing. Several drunkards slept in gutters, oblivious to the stagnant pools of muddy water they were lying in. Going by the smell, I suspected it wasn't always mud mixed with the water, either. I also suspected some of the bodies were dead. Those who were not dead, or dead drunk, scowled at us as we passed. I'd never felt more of an outsider.

"Keep together," Dane warned. "Don't show aggression, don't look as though you're going for your weapon, but be prepared to draw at the first sign of trouble."

Kitty covered her nose. "This place smells like a cesspit."

"It is a cesspit," Theodore muttered. "A human one."

We passed a man pissing against a bollard, and another lounging in a doorway, picking his teeth with the point of a long, curved knife. Dark eyes peered back at us through his greasy black hair. He had a short, stocky build and an olive complexion, much like Max.

A woman leaning over a railing beckoned Dane with the crook of her finger. Her large breasts somehow managed not to fall out of her loose bodice, despite leaning forward. "Looking for a good time, handsome?"

"We're looking for an inn," he said. "Is there one nearby?"

"A respectable inn," Theodore added.

She wiped her nose with the back of her hand. "Respectable? Nope, not here. If you want a bed for the night then try The Golden Trident." She chuckled, revealing broken teeth and swollen red gums. "Can't promise the bed won't be full of lice and the bread free of maggots, but The Three Tentacles is full on account of there being two ships docked. Not that it's much better."

We continued on in the direction she indicated until we reached one of the few double story buildings in the village's main—and only—street. It was as ramshackle as the rest, however, with grimy windows through which dim light could be seen. The sign of a trident stabbing an octopus swung from one hinge. It couldn't be considered golden by any stretch of the imagination.

Kitty pulled her cloak tighter. "I don't like this place."

"It's either this or we continue on and camp outside the village," Dane said.

She hesitated.

"We need supplies," Meg said. "We haven't got enough food for a decent supper. We have to stop here."

The decision made, we passed beneath the archway to the inn's stable yard. A stable hand lay sprawled on a bale of hay, a hand down his breeches, snoring. We stabled the horses ourselves, fed and watered them, then stowed the saddles and tack. We carried our packs with us into the inn.

The chatter slowly died and faces turned towards us. Someone at the back belched, and a woman spat on the floor at Erik's feet. Our usually jovial Marginer glared back at her. This was one woman he wouldn't flirt with.

Dane approached the innkeeper and was given two keys when he handed over coins. "The last rooms," he told us. "The women can have the pick of the two."

There was no decision to make, however. The rooms were identical in every way. There was only a single bed, a dirty, chipped basin, and a small table. We three women could make do, but the six men couldn't fit in one room.

Erik, Max and Quentin decided to sleep in the stables, while Dane offered Balthazar the bed. He and Theodore would find space on the floor.

Balthazar inspected the mattress with its straw innards poking through holes. "I think the floor is a safer option. These holes were made by something with small teeth."

Kitty made a choking sound and clutched her throat. "I never thought I'd say this, but I'd rather be camping out. Somehow the ground feels cleaner than this place."

In our own room, Meg picked up the blanket between thumb and forefinger. It was stained yellow in places and a patch had been cut out of the middle. "I'll be using my cloak again tonight."

Kitty sighed. "There goes my dream of a comfortable bed and washed clothes."

"You can also kiss your dream of a warm bath goodbye." I pointed at the wash basin. "I'm not sure I want to use that. It has a yellow rim."

Meg picked up the empty basin. "I'll clean it in the stable yard. I saw a well out there."

I rummaged through my pack and handed her a pouch of herbs. "Use these. They have cleansing properties. Don't go alone."

Kitty nudged the bedpan out from under the bed with the toe of her boot. "Take this with you and give it a good scrub."

Meg arched her brows. "I thought you were trying not to be a duchess. You wanted to be just like us village girls."

"Cleaning that is a step too far."

Meg eyed the filthy bedpan. "It might be for me too."

I handed her the blanket. "Use this to carry it. Try to avoid the stains."

"Soak your hands in Josie's herbs afterwards," Kitty called out as Meg left with the basin and bedpan wrapped in the blanket.

When Meg returned some time later with the clean bedpan tucked under her arm and the basin full of water, I knew the herbs had been a success. She placed the basin on the table and directed Kitty to go first.

"I'll wash your hair while you wash yourself," she said.

Kitty pulled her hair back and held it out of the way. It had long since come loose from its arrangement. "I think you'll need to replenish the water after each of us is done." She leaned over the basin to wash her face and gasped at her reflection. She pawed at her hair, trying to smooth out the tangles. "Why didn't you tell me I looked like a slum dwelling whore?"

Meg tipped her head back and laughed so hard she cried. I laughed too, partly at her reaction and partly at Kitty's.

Kitty began to cry, but not from laughter. "There are leaves in my hair, and who knows what else." She scratched her head. "Do I have lice? Meg, check if there's something crawling in my hair. I can feel scurrying little feet."

"Do lice have feet?" Meg asked. "Or do they have paws? Or tiny claws perhaps?"

"Just check!"

Meg dutifully checked Kitty's hair while I helped her undress. After we all washed and put on clean underclothes from our packs, I scooped up our dirty clothing and headed to the men's chamber. Dane and Theodore joined me, also clutching piles of clothes. Their hair was damp and their skin clean. Theodore seemed to be in the best spirits he'd been in for days, his step once again sprightly. Being dirty was as horrifying to him as it was to Kitty.

It was already dark in the stable yard, nightfall having arrived early thanks to the high cliffs casting their long shadows. Quentin joined us at the well with clothing bundled under his arm. His hair was wet too, but he seemed cheerful.

"How are the stables?" I asked.

"Filthy. Erik spent this entire time mucking them out. He says the horses shouldn't have to live like that."

He dumped his clothes on the ground just as the door to the inn opened and two sailors spilled out. One leaned a hand on the wall and vomited. The other walked off, singing loudly.

"Disgusting," Theodore muttered. "The sooner we leave tomorrow, the better."

"I want to ask around about missing persons first," Dane said.

Theodore indicated the drunk now sitting in his own vomit. "I think most of these people are missing from somewhere on purpose. It wouldn't surprise me if half of them are running from the authorities in some city or other."

"It's certainly a good place to get lost," Dane muttered as he pulled up the pail full of water. "Not a single person has asked us why we're here or where we came from."

Quentin watched as Dane poured water into my basin and I tipped some herbs in. "Have you noticed that a lot of them look like Max?" he asked. "Short with dark hair and tanned skin. I think Max is a Freedlander and maybe I am too. The captain is definitely only half."

"A number of the palace servants are Freedlanders," I said. "I'd say it was the dominant birthplace among you."

Theodore accepted the pouch of herbs from me. "This country will deliver answers. I'm sure of it."

* * *

WITH OUR BELLIES full and our bodies clean, spirits were high the following day, despite the uncomfortable sleep most of us had. None had wanted to risk the mattresses, not even Balthazar.

We headed to the market together, if the four women selling produce from wheelbarrows could be called that. The dock itself was busy with sailors preparing to set sail on high tide. Most looked a little worse for wear after a night spent on dry land at the taverns and whorehouses, but somehow they managed to perform their duties without throwing up or falling asleep.

"There isn't much here," Meg whispered to me after inspecting the barrows.

She was right. The lettuces were limp, the tomatoes soft, and the apples rotten. The root vegetables were in better condition, and we bought up most of the stock sold by the toothless woman with the wild gray hair. I also bought dried herbs and spices to replenish my supplies and asked the woman about the ones I didn't recognize. I left her stall with more herbs and spices than I'd meant to buy, eager to try her recipes for new remedies.

At each barrow, Dane asked the seller if she knew of any missing persons. None did. He also made sure to parade each of the men past each barrow, but the women didn't show any signs they recognized them.

"We'll ask at the ships," Dane said. "Then head back to the inns and taverns and make inquiries."

With the first ship preparing to sail shortly, we had a difficult time getting the attention of the sailors. They answered our questions about missing people readily enough, but getting them to look up from their tasks at the faces of our men was another matter. Dane resorted to asking outright if they recognized any.

All answered in the negative.

With the morning slipping past, it became obvious that another night would need to be spent in Priest's End. There were too many people to ask and no one wanted to leave until we'd exhausted all avenues. Freedland simply felt too promising to do a half-hearted attempt.

We trudged back to the inn with our packs full of supplies. Two sailors emerged from one of the taverns and stepped in front of Quentin and Dane. One stroked his full black beard as he sized Dane up. The other pinched Quentin's cheek.

"Who's a pretty boy then, eh?" he sneered. "What's a little lad like you doing in a place like this?"

Quentin stiffened and stepped back. His tormenter went to follow, but Dane intercepted him.

"Let us go on our way," he said. "We don't want trouble."

"Hear that, Darry?" The bearded one nudged his friend in the ribs. "They don't want trouble."

"You're in the wrong place then," Darry told Dane. "Priest's End is where folk come looking for trouble." He nodded at me. "I like your women. How much for that one?"

Dane grabbed the man's doublet and shoved him to the ground. "Get out of my sight before I slit your throat."

The bearded one drew his sword. "You shouldn't have done that."

Dane, Max, Quentin and Erik drew their weapons.

The bearded man swallowed.

Darry got to his feet, his eyes bulging as he stared at Max. "Well fuck me. I thought you were dead."

CHAPTER 10

*A*le was a good lubricant for keeping loose tongues talking so we headed into the tavern the men had emerged from and bought a round of drinks. Their tongues didn't just require ale to be loosened, however. Dane had to pass over some ells.

"What do you mean, you don't remember?" asked the bearded sailor named Gerald when Max explained he'd lost his memory.

"I must have been hit on the head," Max said. "I can't remember anything before waking up as a guard in King Leon's palace."

"Who's King Leon?"

"King of Glancia, idiot," said Darry.

"Not anymore," Max said. "He died. I left the palace and came here, thinking I must be from Freedland. I want to find out more about myself, maybe find my family." His gaze flicked to Meg then back to the sailors.

Gerald snorted. "A royal guard? You? Merdu, they must have been desperate to hire you."

Max stiffened. "Why? I'm a good fighter, I can use a sword and ride."

"Aye, but you're a thief."

"He don't know that," Darry said. "He forgot, remember?"

"Thief?" Max tilted his head to the side. "What did I steal?"

"Anything that weren't nailed down." Darry snickered into his tankard. "Couldn't trust you with nothing. I reckon you'd steal a drunk's gold teeth right out of his mouth while he slept."

Max's fingers gripped his tankard hard. "I think you have the wrong man."

"Nope." Darry shook his head. "I spent two weeks on a ship with you. I don't forget a face."

"Nor me," Gerald said. "You're the man who stole my boots one night. Right here in Priest's End, we were, at the end of our voyage. You got me real drunk and when I woke up the next morning, my boots were gone." He held out his palm. "You owe me for the new pair I had to buy."

Darry pushed Gerald's hand away. "Don't mind him, Max. It's his own fault for flashing them around, telling everyone how much he paid for them in Noxford. If you hadn't taken them, someone else would. Maybe even me." He chuckled into his ale.

Max swallowed. "I'm a thief," he said dully.

Meg covered his hand with her own, but he pulled away. Her fingers curled up before retreating to her lap.

"You said you thought he was dead," Dane pointed out. "Why?"

"I heard he got caught for stealing a horse and got sent to a prison mine near Gull's Wing," Darry said.

Gerald waved his tankard around, sloshing ale over the sides. "That ain't why he got sent to prison. You don't go to a prison mine for stealing a horse."

"It was a minister's horse," his friend said.

Gerald shook his head. "Prison mines are for the worst offenders. I heard he started a fire. People died."

Max pushed back his chair and strode out. Theodore went to follow him, but Meg caught his hand.

"Give him some time alone," she said.

"It might not be true," Theodore told her. "I don't trust their memories any more than I trust ours."

"Oi." Darry looked offended. "We got perfec'ly good memories." He tapped the middle of his forehead, leaving a red mark. "And I remember Max good and proper."

"What was he like?" Meg asked.

Darry and Gerald looked at each other and shrugged. "Like anyone else," Darry said. "Always on the look for the next soft mark, the next meal, the next ship, the next game to play. Gotta fill in time before Merdu takes us." He swiped up his tankard, a thoughtful frown on his face.

"That doesn't sound like Max," Quentin said.

"What do you know of his past?" Meg asked the men. "Did he have a family?"

"Don't know, don't care," Gerald said.

"Is he from near here?" Dane asked.

"He didn't say, but he got on the ship at Noxford. He wasn't a real sailor. I reckon it was his first voyage."

"I reckon he ain't never seen the sea neither," Darry said. "He looked scared to get too close to the edge of the deck."

Max couldn't swim. So why did he get on a boat in the first place if he couldn't swim?

Like Meg, I couldn't believe that he'd been a thief, let alone started a fire deliberately. The men must be mistaken.

Dane studied the door through which Max had gone with his arms crossed over his chest and a frown. He looked as though he doubted the picture these men had painted of Max too.

Balthazar leaned forward, engaging the men for the first time since meeting them. His quiet authority had them eyeing him with caution. "I hear those prison mines are harsh places. I hear prisoners die there all the time and have no hope of release."

"Aye, all true," Darry said with a serious nod. "But that ain't why I thought he was dead. He hadn't been in prison long enough to wither away in there. I heard he went to the prison mine near Gull's Wing. You ain't from around here, so you wouldn't have heard, but there was an escape from that prison."

"How many prisoners escaped?" Dane asked.

"All."

"All?" I exchanged a glance with Dane. "How many is that?"

Darry shrugged. "Hundreds. Maybe a thousand."

There'd been just under a thousand palace servants.

My heartbeat quickened and my mind raced, all the way back to a conversation I'd had with my father after first meeting

Dane, Max and Quentin on Lookout Hill near Mull. He'd been worried about me talking to strangers, reminding me of the prison escape that had occurred some months earlier. We'd heard about it from the sailors entering the harbor, and he'd been worried the prisoners would come to Mull to disappear. I'd dismissed his concerns. Dane and his men had worn palace uniforms, and I'd not known about their memory loss or magic at the time.

But he might have been right. The servants could quite possibly be the prison escapees.

Quentin pushed back his chair and lowered his head into his hands. "Merdu and Hailia. Prison."

Dane put a hand on his shoulder to quieten him. The last thing we wanted was to let anyone know they were *all* escaped prisoners.

Theodore left the taproom and came back with Max. "He needs to hear this," he told us as he resumed his seat.

"Tell us about the escape," Dane said to Darry.

Darry and Gerald exchanged glances, having sensed our keen interest. They sat back in their chairs and regarded Dane. "We want extra. Four more ells."

Dane handed it over without question. Going by Darry's disappointment, I suspected he wished he'd asked for more. Max's fist thumping down on the table put an end to his hesitation, however.

"You've got your money, now talk," Max snapped. "Tell us about the escape."

Darry shrugged. "I don't know how it happened. I was on a ship at the time. It weren't until we docked in Noxford that we heard about it. Apparently there was a riot, and the guards were killed with mining tools."

"Not mining tools," Gerald cut in. "Their own weapons, that's what I heard."

"Were any of the prisoners recaptured?" Dane asked.

"That's what we've been telling you. All of them were and all of them were executed for murdering the guards."

"Executed," Dane said flatly.

"Aye," Darry said.

"All of them?" Balthazar asked.

"Aye. Except Max, it seems." Darry lifted his tankard in salute for Max.

"He's not the man you think he is," Dane said quickly. "His name's not Max, for starters."

Gerald frowned. "But you called him Max."

"It's a nickname. His real name is Mark but there was already a Mark in the palace guards so I changed his name to avoid confusion."

"But he looks like the Max who stole my boots."

Dane slid another four ells across the table. "No, he doesn't."

Darry pocketed two of the coins and Gerald the other two. "Aye, he doesn't," Darry agreed.

The two men left but we remained behind. No one spoke and soon the silence thickened so much I couldn't stand it.

"Meg, Kitty, do you both remember hearing about the escape?" I asked.

Meg nodded but Kitty shook her head.

Meg looked to Max. He'd lowered his head and was studying the ale in his tankard with intensity. "I didn't hear about their recapture and execution, however."

"Nor did I," I said. "That part never reached Mull."

"It's a long way from Freedland to Mull," Theodore muttered.

Another silence blanketed us. I tried to catch Dane's attention, but like the others, he was lost in his own thoughts. Meg nudged my foot to get my attention. She mouthed, "Say something."

"It doesn't mean you're all criminals," I said. "People are wrongfully jailed all the time."

"Josie," Meg chided. "It doesn't even mean they are the escaped prisoners from the mine near Gull's Wing at all. It could be a coincidence."

"They recognized me," Max said, snatching up his tankard. "They're sure I was sent to that prison." He tapped his chest with his thumb. "I'm a thief, arsonist and murderer."

"Not a murderer," Balthazar said. "If you murdered in cold blood, you'd have been hanged, not sent to the mine. It's more likely the fire was started accidentally and people unfortunately perished."

Max sneered at him. "Well that's a comfort. I'm just a killer, not a murderer."

Meg placed her hand on his arm. "You're neither."

He jerked away without meeting her gaze.

"You're a good man," she went on. "You're all good men. Learning this doesn't change that."

"It changes much," Erik said heavily.

"It explains much," Balthazar countered. "The lashes on your backs, for one. The undernourished bodies but big muscles of most of the servants when we first arrived at the palace."

Theodore nodded. "The rough look to many, and the filth." He stared at his hands. "I remember waking up wondering how I could possibly have dirt ingrained in every crease. My finger-nails were in a terrible state too."

"We all smelled bad," Erik agreed. "And I was so hungry, I ate until I threw up that first day."

They fell into silence, no doubt remembering their confusion upon waking in the palace, the horror of their memory loss, the strangeness of their new situation. In their wildest dreams, had anyone considered they were all prisoners together? I doubted these men had. None were thieves or thugs by nature. It remained to be seen what circumstances had sent them down that path and landed them in one of the worst prisons on The Fist Peninsula.

"So…were we executed?" Quentin asked in a small voice.

Balthazar pinched the back of Quentin's hand.

"Ow!" Quentin cried. "What was that for?"

"To see if you are dead or not," Balthazar said. "I'm assuming not, if you felt that."

"No need for sarcasm."

"We were not executed," Theodore explained more gently. "It's more likely we were whisked away by the sorcerer and sent to work in the palace. Perhaps the sorcerer made it appear as though we were executed."

"Or the authorities could have simply put the word out that we were recaptured and executed," Dane said. "It would quell any panic that might arise from knowing a thousand prisoners were wandering around. In time, when the prisoners didn't cause any problems, the authorities must have thanked the god and goddess for their good fortune."

It made sense, and I could well believe the authorities manipulating the story to suit them.

Theodore suddenly sat up straight. "That's why there were so few reports of missing persons in all the cities and villages we've passed through. We weren't missing. We were in prison. Our friends and families knew that."

"Most knew," Dane corrected him. "Yen, Paddy and Percy's families didn't. Balthazar, too. The priests in Merdu's Guards thought he left Tilting for a reason, they just didn't know what it was. He must have been arrested after his departure."

"Paddy and Percy were in trouble with the law in Tilting," I pointed out. "It seems it caught up with them, unbeknown to their friends and family in the slum."

"Do we write to them?" Quentin asked. "Should we tell the others about this?"

Dane shook his head. "Not yet. I want to find out more, first."

"So we head to the prison near Gull's Wing," Balthazar said, pushing to his feet.

"But all the guards died," Kitty said. "No one left alive will know what happened."

"Someone must." Dane sounded hollow, as if the light inside him had been extinguished.

He strode out of the tavern and led the way alongside Max towards The Golden Trident. They streaked ahead, while Quentin and Erik lagged behind, carrying our packs full of produce from the market. Their pace was slow, as if every step took effort. Behind them, Balthazar and Theodore talked quietly.

"Have we lost them?" Meg asked. She stared at Max's rigid back while I stared at Dane's. He hadn't looked at me since finding out about the prison.

"Of course not," I said, trying to keep her spirits up as well as my own. I hooked my arm with hers and my other with Kitty's. "They just need to get over this shock and learn more about themselves. Their *true* selves. They need to know they're good people."

Kitty dabbed at the corners of her eyes with her pinky finger. "What if they learn they're not? What if the crime they committed is unforgiveable?"

I refused to believe that. I refused to even think about it. Getting *them* to believe it was going to take time, however.

* * *

It was a gloomy party that departed from Priest's End the following morning. I was glad to leave the village behind, although the prospect of crossing the western branch of The Razorbacks appealed to me less and less the closer we got to the mountains.

"Finally, some fresh air," Kitty said, breathing deeply. "It's no wonder the priest threw himself off the cliffs when he reached that revolting village. He wanted to get away from the putridity."

"Is that how the village got its name?" Quentin asked.

"According to legend."

"What was the village called before it was named Priest's End?"

"Does it matter?" Max snapped.

"I was just wondering," Quentin muttered.

"Do it quietly. No one wants to listen to your prattling."

Quentin pouted.

"At least he's trying to make an effort to fill the silence instead of wallowing in it," Theodore said.

Max stiffened. "Is that aimed at me?"

"Mostly, but there are others here who took the news of our pasts just as badly." He glared at Dane's back, as rigid as a pole.

Like Max, he'd hardly spoken since learning the news about the prison except to bark orders. It reminded me of when he was under pressure as captain. Brant's misdeeds brought this cool, steely side out of him, as did the grim days following the fire in Mull. I wish I could go to him, but my advances would be met with brusque indifference, even if he did want them.

"There's a lot for them to think about," Meg said. "We must be understanding."

"We are all in the same situation," Theodore pointed out. "We are all escaped prisoners. We all committed crimes that put us in prison in the first place. That doesn't mean we're bad people."

Max wheeled his horse about and rounded on him. I'd never seen his jaw set so hard, his eyes flashing with anger. He'd always been so agreeable and considerate towards his fellow guards and the villagers. "You think that because you haven't seen the sort of people who end up in prison. I've seen the evil residing in the palace cells."

"So have I," Theodore said.

"Not like we have. You don't know half of what they did. The captain kept the worst from you to protect you."

"Precisely. He protected us because he's a good man. As are you, Max. If you were inherently evil, *you* would have ended up in those cells too."

Max's response was to snarl and turn away. He rode off, streaking ahead of Dane. Meg started to go after him but changed her mind. She watched him with tears in her eyes, her teeth nibbling her lower lip.

Theodore pushed forward too but stopped in front of Dane, blocking the road. "Listen to me, all of you. We are not evil. The friends we left behind are not evil. Whatever crimes we committed that landed us in prison will be a result of our circumstance—poverty and lack of opportunity leading to desperation. Not acts of evil."

"Hear, hear," Kitty said.

We all agreed. All except Dane and Balthazar.

Dane still had his back to me as we set off again, so I rode up to Balthazar instead. "You have something to say?" I asked, perhaps a little too harshly. "You don't agree with Theodore?"

"I do not," he said. "Because I choose not to believe those drunkards in Priest's End until we know for certain."

Quentin frowned at him. "Their story explains a lot, Bal. You said so yourself. The scars on our backs, our hunger when we woke up in the palace."

Erik agreed. "Even the king was thin and dirty. He was a prisoner too." He grunted. "Probably for lying."

"No one is sent to prison for lying," Theodore said. "Especially not a prison mine."

Leon's dying words came back to me. They had haunted me for some time, and now they finally made sense. "He said he saved you."

Up ahead, Dane half turned, listening.

"He said the magic was the only way to save you from a slow and painful death," I went on.

"Do you think he meant from the execution?" Quentin asked.

"I doubt it. If the escape was orchestrated by the sorcerer, you were never in danger afterwards. I think Leon meant he saved you from the prison mine itself."

"No one survives in there for long," Meg added.

"Let's not jump to conclusions," Balthazar said. "Not until we know each and every servant's story."

Theodore shook his head. "You need to get used to the idea you did something illegal, Bal. I'd hate for the truth to come as a shock to you."

"I am prepared for any eventuality. I'm under no illusions that I have lived a blameless life."

Theodore looked to Max up ahead and sighed. "Do you want to speak to him, Meg, or shall I?"

"You go," she said. "You're his friend. I'm nothing to him."

"If you believe that, you're as deluded as Balthazar." He rode off so did not hear Balthazar tell him he wasn't deluded.

"I simply choose not to jump to conclusions," he said to us.

Hailia's Pass was not as far from Priest's End as Merdu's Pass had been, and we reached the foothills by late afternoon and camped on the treed slopes beside a stream. I made a calming tea while the men hunted for our supper, but it didn't seem to soothe tempers. It certainly didn't break the dark silences.

I lay awake, thinking about the prison mine and what my friends must have endured there. It would have been an arduous existence. The prisoners would have hauled rocks all day, pushed heavily laden carts, and lived like rats in the tunnels. They would have been given just enough food and water to

survive, and would have been kept in line with harsh punishments. Evidence of those punishments were still visible on their
backs.

Quentin would have found it difficult with his small stature;
Theodore too, with his delicate nature. I couldn't fathom how
Balthazar had survived more than a day, and I dared not
imagine Dane subjected to the horrors of the mines. I couldn't
begin to know how he reacted.

I did know that he wasn't an evil man, and I waited until he
took over the watch from Erik before joining him and telling him
so. "Theodore's right." I sat on the rock beside him at the edge of
the clearing, very aware that he didn't want me giving him a
lecture. Too bad, because he needed to hear what I had to say.
"Circumstances beyond your control forced you to turn your
hand to crime. I won't let you think of yourself as a criminal,
Dane."

He remained unmoved, his gaze on the dark plain below. "I
agree that poverty and lack of opportunity are valid reasons for
resorting to crime. But I'm educated, Josie, as are Theodore and
Balthazar; Quentin, too. Educated men can easily find work.
They are not poor."

"Then perhaps Balthazar is right, and those men were wrong
about the prison escape, or about recognizing Max. They were
very drunk."

He didn't respond, and I knew he didn't agree. He believed
those men. As did I.

"Don't do this, Dane. Don't shut me out because you think
your past is one of evil and cruelty. Don't you dare believe that
of yourself, because I don't. No one does."

He stood, still staring ahead. "I was known as Hammer.
There must be a reason for that." He walked to the edge of the
clearing and crossed his arms. I was dismissed.

If I'd known how to get through to him, I would not have
left. But my advances wouldn't be welcome, nor my words, so I
returned to the patch of earth between Meg and Kitty and lay
down again. Meg took my hand, and I clutched hers in return
until I drifted to sleep.

* * *

THE FOLLOWING afternoon we traveled over Hailia's Pass. The western branch of The Razorbacks was not as high as the eastern, and the pass named after the gentle goddess was easier than the one named after the formidable, warlike god.

Quentin tried to cheer us up, but after a snappy retort from Max, he fell into silence. Not even Theodore seemed interested in trying to talk them out of their glum mood. Of all the men, Erik seemed the least perturbed by the news that he'd been in a Freedlandian prison mine. Perhaps because he already knew after Merrin that he was a thief and he'd come to terms with it. Although he wasn't morose like the others, he was certainly more contemplative than usual, but he did manage smiles for Kitty. I even caught them kissing during a quick midday stop.

I rode at the back of the group with Balthazar but could think of no way to start a conversation. Should I mention the prison or not? Should we talk about something else entirely?

It was he who broke the silence eventually. "If we really are from this prison, then there's something I don't understand. Most of the servants are clearly from Freedland, but many are not. So why were they all in a Freedlandian prison?"

"Freedland's prison mines are not just for Freedlandians," I said. "Prisoners from all over the Fist are sent to them for punishment. Freedland takes money for them, of course."

"They're *paid* to accept the criminals from other countries?"

I nodded. "Only the worst ones."

"The ones they don't want back," Balthazar mumbled. "The ones they hope will die in the mines."

"You sound as though you now accept what those drunks told us."

He lifted his chin. "I am considering all possibilities. So these prisons take money to accept foreign prisoners and get free labor in their mines. What a nice arrangement," he bit off.

I'd never given the prison mines much thought before. I knew they existed but no one from Mull had ever been sent to one, and my entire life had centered around my village. It made sense that the prison mines were located in the country that the rest of the Fist seemed to have forgotten. Freedland was so far away from Glancia, its people and political situation so different, that it was as foreign to me as Zemaya. Indeed, I'd met more Zemayans than Freedlandians before the palace servants came into my life.

I'd certainly never expected to meet anyone who'd been imprisoned in one of the mines, let alone fall in love with a former prisoner. A prisoner who had not completed his sentence.

* * *

THE DESERT SANDS of southern Freedland were punctured by rocky hills and little else. Tufts of hardy bushes clumped together in dips where water must pool after rain, but going by the dryness, there'd not been any rain for some time.

The endlessness of the desert took me by surprise. I knew Freedland was largely empty, but I'd still expected a village here and there, a small creek or the occasional tree. But there was a lot of nothing. The wind blew across the wasteland, whipping up the sand and throwing it in our faces, as if to say "you dare to come here, now suffer for it." It was abundantly clear why travelers took the route along the northern border, following Blood River from Lake Torment to Noxford. Only those who didn't want to be found tackled the Razorbacks and the desert.

It took us five days to reach the village of Gull's Wing on Freedland's south west coast. Five days of spitting sand out of my mouth every time I opened it. Five days of squinting at the horizon, searching for a building or tree, anything to offer relief from the burning sun. Five days of wondering what we'd learn at the prison mine.

We ran out of supplies on the third day. Despite the men hunting in the early evenings and mornings, they found little to eat except for some desert rats that Kitty and I refused to eat. Thankfully our water lasted until the fourth day, but only because we rationed it.

The one good thing about being hungry, thirsty, exhausted, and miserable was that no one felt like talking. The tension that had been simmering within the group since leaving Priest's End didn't boil over, but it didn't disappear, either.

I didn't try to comfort Dane again, and Meg hardly spoke to Max at all. I caught him looking at her on more than one occasion, however. His torment was written into every groove of his face.

Gull's Wing was a beautiful sight when it came into view on the fifth afternoon. Like Priest's End, it nestled in a small bay between two cliffs. It was larger than Priest's End, however, and was not as remote. While the desert spread to its east, fertile farmland to the north supplied the village with an abundance of produce.

We dined heartily at a good inn that night, and Kitty finally got her bath, although she wasn't quite as interested in it being warm as she had been when we were high up in the freezing Razorbacks. I felt much better after washing the sand out of my hair, nose and ears, and even felt like trying to coax Dane out of his grim mood.

I found him in the taproom with Max, questioning the innkeeper and his wife.

"It was located to the north east of here." The innkeeper waved a hand in what I assumed was the direction of the prison mine.

"Was?" Dane asked.

"It was abandoned after the escape. The High Minister did the right thing for once and kept it closed. It didn't feel right to re-open it. Not after all those deaths."

"The executions of the escapees were carried out there?"

The innkeeper gave Dane an odd look. "I meant the death of the guards. Ain't no one cares about them prisoners. They can all rot in Merdu's Pit. They were the Fist's filth. No murderers, mind, but rapists, kidnappers, torturers, thieves, pirates—you name it, they all ended up there or at one of the other two prison mines in Freedland."

Max dragged a hand over his cleanly shaved jaw. "I need another drink."

The innkeeper's wife took his tankard and refilled it from a barrel. "Why are you so interested in that mine anyway?"

Max drank deeply, leaving Dane to answer. "We were passing through and heard the story of the escape."

The innkeeper snorted. "Passing through Gull's Wing? No one passes through Gull's Wing."

"Noxford, not Gull's Wing. It's fascinating, so we decided to come and see the mine for ourselves. So there's nothing to see?"

The innkeeper polished the counter top with a rag. "Afraid not. Just some rocks the prisoners were in the middle of crushing when they rioted, some carts and barrows abandoned in the tunnels."

"Everything was left just as it was," the innkeeper's wife added as she dried a tankard with a cloth. "They say it looks as if the prisoners stepped away for a break. Not that they got breaks, mind. Some of the guards used to come in here on their days off, and they told me the prisoners started before dawn and finished well after dusk. They wouldn't know what time it was down in the mines, would they, so what did it matter."

"They got no breaks in that whole time?" I asked. "What about food or water?"

"Criminals like that don't deserve food or water. They deserve to die down there."

I pressed a hand to my mouth as bitter bile surged up my throat.

The innkeeper's wife shook her cloth at me. "Girls like you should thank the magistrates for putting away men like that."

"The prisoners didn't survive long, I take it," Dane said.

"Not more than a few months, so they say," the innkeeper said with a shrug as if all those lives didn't matter.

Dane ordered a drink for me and another for himself. Max drained his tankard and also asked for a refill. "Do you know everyone in this village?" Max asked.

"Every soul," the innkeeper said proudly. "About three hundred live in Gull's Wing. Used to be more, when the guards and their families lived here. After they died, the families moved away, mostly back to Noxford. Why do you ask?"

"Have you seen anyone looking like me pass through?"

The innkeeper looked at his wife. She studied Max then shook her head. "Why?"

"My brother's missing. We look alike. I thought he might have been in the village."

"Sorry, son," the innkeeper said. "I haven't seen your face or one similar around here."

"My husband's real good with faces, so if he says he hasn't seen him then he never came in here." The innkeeper's wife patted Max's arm. "I'm sure your brother will turn up. Where are you from?"

"Near Noxford."

"There you are then. He probably went looking for adventure in the city. Have you searched there?"

Max merely shrugged and stared into his tankard, abandoning his story. He'd been trying to find out if he was local to Gull's Wing. Perhaps he'd hoped he lived here instead of being a prisoner, resulting in some confusion for the drunkards in Priest's End. It would seem not.

"Do you know someone who can escort us to the mine tomorrow?" Dane asked. "We'd like to see it."

The innkeeper's wife stamped a hand on her ample hip. "What is it with all you travelers wanting to see the mine?"

"It's only natural," her husband chided. "People got an interest in grim history."

"It ain't history yet. Not for some."

He rolled his eyes. "Don't mind her. All this interest is good for business. Things were a bit slow after the escape, but it's picked up lately on account of people like you coming to see where it all happened. Not that we've had travelers from as far as Glancia before." He jutted his chin in my direction. "I reckon the mayor should start charging a fee." He chuckled. The deaths of the guards hadn't affected him too greatly then.

"Sander too," his wife said. "He could do well out of all the travelers we send his way."

"Sander?" Dane asked.

"Your guide. He lives not far from here. He'll take you tomorrow, if he's not out fishing."

"He'll make time for you," the innkeeper said. "He likes taking people to the mine. He says it's good for him, helps him remember his friends who died. He says he doesn't want to forget them or it'll be like they never existed."

Max arched a brow. "I thought all the prisoners were caught and executed."

"Sander wasn't a prisoner. He was a guard. He wasn't on duty at the time of the escape so he wasn't killed. Only the night shift was murdered by the escapees. All the guards on the day shift were lucky, but Sander's the only one who stayed in Gull's Wing. He decided to retire here by the sea. The rest left to find work elsewhere. You can ask him all about the guards tomorrow. He's got a very good memory. He can remember all their names, their children's names, where they came from, and what they looked like."

The innkeeper's wife agreed. "Sander doesn't forget a thing. You just ask him a question about any one of his friends at the prison and he'll tell you everything about them."

I knew she was referring to Sander's fellow guards, but I couldn't help wondering if his memory extended to the prisoners as well. If so, then we couldn't go to see him. If he recognized Dane and the others as prisoners, he'd set the authorities onto them.

CHAPTER 11

"**A**bsolutely not," Max said, slicing his hand through the air to underline his point. "It's too dangerous."

"How will it be dangerous?" Meg asked with a determination that matched Max's. They kept their voices low, however, to avoid being overheard by other patrons in the taproom. "We are simply three women with an interest in seeing the mine."

"Without husbands or fathers to escort you?" Max shook his head.

"Max is right," Dane said. "If nothing else, the guard will be suspicious."

The others nodded, including Kitty. I glared at her and she gave me a small shrug.

There had to be a way. We couldn't allow the guard to see the men but we couldn't visit him alone either. As much as I hated to admit it, Dane and Max were right. It would be very strange for three Glancian women to make inquiries about prisoners.

It was Balthazar who came up with an idea. "You can be widows. Your husbands were sent to the prison mine and you wish to see where they lived and died and hopefully hear stories about your loved ones from a man who knew them during their incarceration."

Kitty's eyes lit up. "What an excellent idea. We can tell the guard our husbands were wrongly accused. He wouldn't believe women like us would be married to criminals anyway."

The idea was a good one, and I nodded along with her. "That way we can also use their names. Dane, Max and Erik."

"Not Erik," Dane said. "It's too much of a stretch to believe Kitty married a Marginer. Say it's Theodore. Max can also go, but under an assumed name. He has already told the innkeeper that his brother is missing, so he can simply extend his story and say his brother was arrested and sent to the mine. Josie can be my widow, and Meg can be Quentin's."

Erik snorted. "No one will believe she married him."

Quentin stiffened. "You saying I ain't worthy of her?"

"You're not," Max growled.

Erik slapped Max's shoulder with the back of his hand. "I mean he is just a boy."

"Then I'll say he's my brother." Meg sized up Quentin, perhaps looking for a resemblance of some kind to reinforce her story. They were not alike in any way.

"Half-brother?" I suggested.

It was decided. The men felt better with Max escorting us, and we three women had solid stories to tell. I wanted to go immediately but we would have to wait for the morning. It would be another restless night tonight with answers so close yet not in our grasp. It must be even more excruciating for the men. Perhaps that explained why none made a move to retire for the evening, despite long days in the saddle.

Dane signaled to the serving girl to bring more ales then paid her when she carried over the tray laden with tankards. Quentin's jaw dropped when he saw how many ells it cost.

"Bloody hell, that's expensive," he said. "They got gold in their ales here?"

"It's the taxes," Balthazar said. "Everything is taxed in Freed-land, including the ale."

Max stared into his tankard and sipped instead of taking a deep drink like he usually did. "Taxing ale ain't right. What's a man supposed to drink after a hard day's work?"

"Wine?" Theodore suggested.

"Also taxed," Balthazar said.

"Really?" Theodore also stared into his tankard. "I don't remember the prices being high in Priest's End."

"I suspect Priest's End gets most of its supplies from smugglers. Smuggled goods avoid the middleman—namely the tax collector."

Theodore looked around at the small groups talking in earnest nearby. "It's surprising anyone drinks in Freedland at all."

"I can't believe everyone just accepts it without complaint," Quentin said.

"Who says they're not complaining?" Dane asked. "From what I can tell, almost everyone in here is talking about the upcoming elections and what it means for them, including the suggested changes to the taxation system."

"Election?" Quentin echoed.

Balthazar smirked at Dane. "You've been listening in to conversations again. Sometimes I think your job at the palace encompassed more eavesdropping than fighting."

"I rarely eavesdropped." Dane sounded offended.

Max winked at Balthazar. "He mostly coerced information out of folk."

"Is someone going to answer me?" Quentin asked. "What's an election?"

"Exactly what it sounds like," Theodore said. "The leader of Freedland is chosen, not born."

"By who?"

Theodore looked to Balthazar. "The people," Balthazar said. "If you listen in to the conversations around you, like Dane, you'll hear them talking about the pros and cons of the candidates."

We fell silent. The conversations at the other tables were quiet but earnest, going by the occasional stabbing of a finger into the table to make a point.

That changed by the time we finished our ales and prepared to retire. The drink must have taken hold of the other patrons, and those who'd only spoken quietly before, now voiced their opinions of the high minister in loud protest.

"He's got to go!" someone shouted.

"Aye!" cheered the others around him.

"But the other candidates are no better," said one brave soul seated on a stool near the window. "No one's going to lower taxes."

"They might *reform* them," said another. "Whatever that means."

"Bloody ministers," said another, closer to us. "I bet the taxes line their pockets and pay for their nice houses."

"Aye," several chimed in.

"Where's the money going? That's what I want to know!"

The innkeeper's wife marched up to him and swatted him with her cloth. "Pipe down! This ain't no place for a political rally."

The instigator muttered an apology into his tankard. The room quieted somewhat, although the conversations remained more animated than they had been earlier in the evening.

It was time to retire before we found ourselves embroiled in something that didn't concern us.

* * *

SANDER, the retired guard, was not what I expected. He was a broad man of about sixty who was tall compared to Max but not as tall as we women. He may have once been muscular, but it had run to fat, and not just in his body. His face was a series of thick bulges marred by scars, symbols of a rough past. I wondered how many had been inflicted by prisoners.

His formidable appearance was softened when he smiled in greeting, revealing more gaps than teeth. "Come in, come in. I've been expecting you. Shall we have some tea before we head off? My wife's brew is delicious."

The innkeeper had written ahead to notify Sander of our interest in seeing the mine. Even so, this warmth was more than I was expecting.

"My wife's at the market," Sander said as he poured tea from the pot into cups. "She sells the fish I catch."

"You're a fisherman now?" I asked.

"Sure am. I gave up being a guard after the escape. It's a job for younger men, not old dogs like me." He paused as he passed around the cups. While his lips stretched into a flat smile, his eyes were dull. He must be remembering his fellow guards who'd died that day at the sorcerer's hand. "I like it here in Gull's Wing, and the fishing's good," he went on. "I've got myself a small boat that I take out to my secret places." He tapped the side of his nose with his finger. "My wife sells what I catch, and that's enough for us to live on. It's a simple life and we ain't going to get rich, but it's a better life than being a guard, especially down at them prison mines."

"Why are you shaking your head?" I asked.

"They're brutal places. It takes a lot out of a bloke to see his fellow man treated like that. And women too."

Meg looked to Max, but Max just sat there, cradling his cup, his expression blank. After introducing himself as Mark then the rest of us as his friends, he'd fallen silent. It must feel strange for him to drink tea with a man who would have been his enemy. Sander might even have been the one who whipped him.

"Didn't the prisoners deserve their fate?" Meg asked. "That's what we were told."

"Some did, aye," Sander said. "I won't deny that there were prisoners with hearts blacker than the deepest sea. But not all."

Meg gave Max an arched look. "I imagine some committed crimes simply because they were poor or desperate," she said.

"True enough, but we guards weren't to know who was real evil and who was just a poor bloke down on his luck that got caught thieving, or whoring in the case of the women. Not when they arrived. Everyone was the same to us at first."

"What was the prison like for them?" Meg asked.

"I don't like to say, miss. It's not nice for ladies like yourselves to hear."

"We want to know."

He shifted his weight and glanced at Max, but Max didn't look up from his cup. "Well, you got to understand that the mines were dark places and the prisoners were down in them tunnels all their waking day. They were hungry, tired, hot and thirsty. They knew they wouldn't survive long, and if a man knows he ain't got long to live, he doesn't care no more. They were already in Merdu's Pit. They might as well have already been dead. I don't blame them for rising up. Not really. I just wish they hadn't killed all my friends. Some were good men. Some were bad, and just as cruel as the prisoners, but most were good." He lifted his cup, saluting his lost colleagues.

I swallowed and lifted my own cup but didn't drink. I suddenly didn't have the thirst.

"You ladies look sick." Sander swirled the liquid in his cup. "Is it the tea?"

"It's the thought of how those prisoners lived." I looked to Kitty and she nodded, urging me to continue, as did Meg. Max sat morosely opposite and didn't look my way. "You see, our loved ones were prisoners in that mine."

Sander sat back heavily as if the stuffing had been knocked out of him. "Well. That explains why he looks familiar."

Max suddenly looked up. "You recognize me?"

"Aye, and I thought it was from the prison, but I knew it couldn't be." Sander frowned. "Are you telling me you were once a prisoner there and survived the execution?"

"My brother was a prisoner," Max said quickly. "Twin. His name was Max. Do you remember him?"

"A little. I'm good with faces, and yours is familiar. A twin, eh?" He smiled. "How about that."

"What was he imprisoned for?" Meg asked. "Do you remember?"

Sander shook his head. "We weren't told what crimes they committed, but some told us anyway or I overheard them talking to the other prisoners. Conversation weren't banned altogether, just seditious talk."

Max returned to clutching his cup and staring into the tea. Meg rested a hand on his arm, but he jerked away.

"Can't say I remember your brother much at all," Sander went on. "Sorry. So you don't know what he was arrested for?"

Max shook his head.

When he didn't go on, Meg added, "He left home without informing his family where he was going. Mark later found out he was arrested and sent to the prison mine."

"The authorities wouldn't tell you what he did?" Sander

asked. He was right to seem incredulous. It didn't make sense that we'd know the punishment but not the crime.

"Is there any way we can find out?" I asked. "What happened to the prison records after the escape?"

"All destroyed in the riot. The warden's office was burned to the ground."

The sorcerer had been thorough in obliterating all records of the servants' pasts. It was a grim reminder of how powerful it was.

Sander drained his cup then waved it at the door. "Ready to go?"

"In a moment," I said. "We have some other questions about our husbands and brothers."

Sander frowned. "Husbands?"

"Kitty and I are widows whose husbands were sent here. Meg's brother was too."

Sander's frown deepened. He crossed his arms and regarded us from beneath the shelf of his protuberant brow. "But you seem so nice and normal. Not wives and sisters of thieves, rapists and the like."

"They were wrongly convicted," Meg said. "We traveled from Glancia to see where they lived their final days. We hope it will help our grieving."

"It will help us close that chapter of our lives," Kitty added, sounding pleased with her analogy.

Sander grunted. "I'm not sure I can help you. There were a lot of prisoners and I didn't talk to many. I knew a lot by sight, like his brother." He nodded at Max. "But that's all."

Kitty shuffled her chair closer to Sander. He leaned forward too, suddenly interested in what she had to say. "My husband's name was Theodore." She waited, but Sander didn't respond. "He was about thirty years old and from Dreen."

"Full Dreenian or half?"

"Full."

Sander stroked his grizzly gray beard. "Well, there weren't many full Dreens but I definitely remember one clearly on account of his unusual crime."

"I thought you didn't know what crimes they'd committed,"

Max said. Like us, he'd also suddenly become interested in what Sander had to say. He set aside his cup and moroseness and rested his folded arms on the table, listening.

"I remember this one. Theodore you say." Sander nodded slowly. "He might have been called Theo, now that I think about it. Slim fellow, quiet, delicate."

"That's him!" Kitty clapped her hands. "Do go on, Mr. Sander. Tell us everything you remember about him."

Sander hesitated, but couldn't take his eyes off her. He reminded me of a stunned rat, enthralled by a bright light.

"Go on," I said. "Please, tell us about him. Nothing you say will shock us. Kitty knows her husband well, but we simply want to make sure we're talking about the same man."

Sander nodded slowly. "I see what you're implying, ma'am."

Kitty blinked innocently at me. Unlike the others, she didn't have an inkling as to Theodore's nature. If our ruse was to work, she needed to.

"You know," I said to her with an exaggerated wink. I dropped my voice to a whisper. "How he prefers men."

Her eyes bulged. "Oh!"

"Forgive her," Meg said to Sander. "It's an embarrassing subject for her, you understand."

Sander's face flushed scarlet. "Seems we are talking about the same man. The Dreenian was the talk of the prison when he came in. None of us guards thought he'd last more than three days. Some even put wagers on it."

"Wagers!" Max bellowed.

Sander put up his hands. "Not me. Some of the others made wagers from time to time about the prisoners. The prison brought out the worst in some, and not just the prisoners."

"What did he go to jail for?" I asked. At Sander's glance in Kitty's direction, I added, "Just so we know we're discussing the right man. Whatever you say cannot cause further embarrassment."

Sander screwed up his nose and I thought I'd have to prompt him again, but in the end, he blurted it out. "Sodomy."

It came as no surprise to any of us, but it didn't quite make sense to me. "I don't know about Freedland, but in Glancia, the criminal act is largely ignored. Dreen too, I believe."

"And Freedland. That's why it caused a stir when he arrived. He told one of the guards why he'd been arrested and word quickly spread. None of us had ever seen a prisoner jailed for sodomy, let alone sent to a prison mine. Everyone was real curious about it and eventually one of the prisoners asked. Theo said he was arrested in his homeland and given a harsh sentence on account of his lover's father was a real important man in Dreen. He reckoned the father put pressure on the magistrate to give a harsh sentence, that's why Theo ended up here."

"Who was the lover's father?" Kitty asked.

"You don't know?"

"No."

Sander shrugged. "Me neither. Your husband didn't tell a soul. He said he'd take the name to his grave." His gaze turned distant before snapping back to Kitty. "So why does a beautiful Glancian woman marry a Dreenian who likes men?"

Kitty waved off his question. "It's complicated."

"How long was Theo in the prison before the escape?" I asked.

"A month."

"That long? So he was stronger than you thought."

"It weren't easy for him. He wasn't built for hard labor and those early days, he wanted to give up. But some took pity on him."

"Some guards?" I asked.

"Other prisoners. There was a small group that took up together, they protected each other and the weak, the ones who maybe shouldn't have been in there, now that I think about it."

Max and Meg shared a glance. "Was I— Was my brother one of those protectors?"

Sander shrugged. "I don't recall. Maybe. Maybe that's why I remember his face."

Max swallowed and rubbed his jaw. His haunted gaze once again connected with Meg's, and I could see the moment her heart cracked at seeing him so anxious and eager at the same time. I remember when I'd first met the palace guards in the forest outside Mull, and how their eyes had sported the same look.

"What do you mean they shouldn't have been in there?" Meg asked in a small voice.

"I mean they were different to the other prisoners. They didn't seem like bad folk to me. Some were even educated. They were kind and shared their bread, sometimes going without if the other was in a real bad way. If one fell, they picked him up, and some of the bigger prisoners helped push the carts of the smaller ones." He shrugged again. "They were friends, I suppose, although I don't reckon they all deserved that friendship. I remember this one fellow, a weak man, always whining about how unfair his imprisonment was, how he shouldn't have been there. Liked the sound of his own voice, that one."

"Do you know his name?" I asked.

He shook his head. "He was part Glancian, I think."

I straightened. "Tall and dark?"

"Not tall, but a bit fairer, like a Glancian."

I blew out a breath. It wasn't Dane, thank Hailia. It certainly didn't sound like him. A whining man who liked the sound of his own voice... Merdu! "Was his name Leon?" I blurted out.

Meg, Max and Kitty suddenly focused on Sander. He didn't appear to notice the extra attention, however. He clicked his fingers. "Aye, it was. I remember on account of some of the other prisoners used to tell him to be quiet all the time. 'Shut your hole, Leon,' they'd say." He chuckled. "Did you know him too?"

"Not really," I said. "Do you know why he went to jail?"

"I do, because he made sure everyone knew how unfair it was. He was jailed for impersonating the king of Vytill."

A small bubble of laughter escaped Kitty's lips. "It does seem unfair to be arrested for that, particularly considering he was an actor."

"Was he? Huh. Well, he shouldn't have lampooned the king. Not in Merrin, outside the king's own castle, no less. Seems to me he was asking for trouble."

It sounded exactly like something the foolish, ridiculous Leon would have done. He often acted rashly, without considering the consequences.

"The king of Vytill must have made sure he was sent here," Sander said. "Everyone agreed it was unfair, but no one cared too much on account of Leon being so annoying. Prison was hard on him. More so than on your husband, ma'am," he said to Kitty.

"Why is that?" Kitty asked.

"Well, ain't no one liked Leon much. The group I told you about before, the one your brother might have been a part of, Mark, they protected the weaker ones, but some wouldn't protect him. They just didn't like him. Only one helped him when his cart was too heavy or when the guards tried to whip him for not working hard enough."

My mouth went dry and my throat tightened. He *must* be referring to Dane.

"And who was that?" Max asked. Like me, he seemed to have stopped breathing as he waited for Sander to speak.

"That's the thing," Sander said. "This fellow was the most memorable, but I don't recall his name."

"Why was he memorable?"

"He was educated, well-mannered, even to some of us guards who didn't treat him too bad. He was strong as an ox and a good fighter, and took it on himself to protect the weak when some of the other prisoners or guards tormented them. Even Leon. That made them all like him more, especially when he took their whippings on his own back."

"He took their beatings?" I murmured.

"He knew some wouldn't survive if they were whipped, so he volunteered himself in their place. I reckon it almost killed him once, but he recovered and carried on. Six months he was in the mine, I reckon it was. Six months before the escape." He scrubbed a hand over his beard, shaking his head. "I reckoned he was the one who organized it, but there ain't no way of knowing. Maybe the authorities got it out of him when they caught them, but they didn't tell us nothing."

"Is that because he was a natural leader?" Kitty asked.

"Aye, and because he's the only one capable of killing the guards in cold blood."

All the air left my body. I felt limp and loose-limbed, hardly able to hold myself up. How could he think such a thing of Dane? He must be wrong. He must be thinking of someone else.

"Are you sure you don't remember his name?" Meg asked, her thoughts following the same path as mine.

"I remember what he was called, but it weren't his real name. His nickname was Hammer."

CHAPTER 12

I pressed a hand to my rolling stomach. There had to be some mistake. The Dane I knew couldn't kill all the guards in cold blood, like Sander claimed. But why did Sander think him guilty of such a heinous crime?

"Why did they call him Hammer?" Max asked. His reticence of earlier had disappeared. Like the rest of us, he was absorbed in Sander's story.

"It's the name the guards gave him after he attacked one of us." Sander spoke matter-of-factly, as if it had just been another day, another brutal event in the mine. "He bashed Carlos with the hammer he was using to break rocks. He was one of the few allowed to use tools on account of him being a good prisoner. But he proved us all wrong when he smashed it into Carlos's head."

I covered my mouth as bile surged.

"Why did he attack him?" Meg pressed. "Surely he had a reason."

"Hammer didn't say. I still remember Carlos's cry of agony. Hammer was pulled off him by the other guards, but if he hadn't been, it could have been worse."

"Was he punished?" Max asked.

"Aye, he was put in the disused well for a week with no food and just a little water. When he came out, he carried on as if nothing happened."

"You put him in a *well*?" I cried.

He put up his hands. "It weren't me that put him there, it was my superiors. They didn't like Hammer, but I did. Not then, mind, but later, he became one of my favorites. Sometimes we'd talk, just about politics and the like, nothing personal. I started to think maybe he was jailed by mistake. But then I'd remember the way he attacked Carlos with that hammer. It was a good reminder not to trust any of them."

"Why wasn't he executed for murder then and there?" Meg asked.

"Carlos survived, so it weren't a hanging offense."

Max gave me a grim smile, as if he were trying to cheer me up but didn't have the heart for it. "What did the other prisoners think of Hammer after that incident?" he asked.

"Few lived as long as Hammer, so the incident was forgotten by most prisoners after a while. Except maybe the Marginer. He was in the mine longer than Hammer. The incident with Carlos happened before your husband got there, ma'am," he said to Kitty. "Before Leon, too. I'd say some of the prisoners were happy to see a guard attacked. Others didn't care. We weren't too popular with the prisoners, it's safe to say." He huffed a humorless laugh. He didn't seem cruel and was probably not the one inflicting the whippings on the prisoners. He had simply been doing a job he disliked, and that made him no different to many.

"What was Hammer imprisoned for?" I asked.

"I don't know. He never said and the warden never told us guards. He reckoned it was none of our business. Maybe he was worried we'd treat some of them kinder if we thought they didn't deserve their fate."

He stood and collected the cups, turning away to rinse them in a tub of water. The rest of us exchanged glances behind his back, and Meg reached for Max's hand. Instead of pulling away, he drew it to his lips and kissed it. He let go as Sander turned back to us.

"Ready to go to the mine now?" he asked cheerfully.

We followed him out to the two-horse cart we'd hired for the day. Max drove with Sander beside him while we women sat on the back and listened to the former prison guard try to strike up a conversation.

"You from Noxford?" he asked.

"Nearby," Max said.

"What's it like in the capital these days?"

"The same."

"I mean with the elections coming up. Are folk as restless there as they are here?"

Max nodded.

Sander turned a little so we women could hear him better over the rumble of the wheels. "The election is all everyone can talk about here in Gull's Wing. Who do the folk in Noxford think will win?"

"Hard to say," Max said.

"Same here. Ain't no one likes any of the candidates much. Only one has promised to fix the tax system, but I got my doubts the reforms will be better. They're all corrupt, I reckon." He shook his head. "It's a shame. If General Nox knew that only forty years after his revolution that the country he fought so hard to free would end up in the hands of corrupt ministers, he'd be disappointed." When no one responded, he tapped Max on the shoulder. "Don't you agree?"

"Aye," Max said. "It's a real shame."

"Forgive me for asking," Meg said. "I don't know much about Freedland's history, but I do know the former monarchy was unpopular. Do the people regret the revolution now that the current ministers are just as bad?"

Sander swung round to face us fully. "Just as bad? No, miss, this is a song and dance compared to them days. I'm old enough to remember what it was like to have a king, and I don't want to ever go back to that. The king wasn't just corrupt, he was a tyrant. He executed anyone who spoke out against him, even if there was no evidence, just rumor. He gave lands and trade rights to his favorites, which led to more corruption. It drove the country into the ground, and when that happens, its the poor who suffer most. The king didn't care about regular folk. The poor were as good as slaves to him; cheap labor that never seemed to dry up, no matter how many died from exhaustion and starvation. It was bad back then. Real bad. General Nox did this country a service when he killed the king."

"Do most people agree with you?" Meg asked.

"Aye, but there are some descendants of the old noble families who want to see the monarchy restored. Problem is, there ain't no one to put on the throne. None from the royal line, anyway. They were all executed."

"Did the king have children?" Kitty asked.

"Two sons and a daughter, none of age. General Nox executed them all, and the queen too."

"How awful."

"He had to do it or they'd always be a beacon for monarchists. As long as a member of the royal family lived, they had someone to put back on the throne. It would have led to more wars. But without a descendant, there was no one to rally behind. He did the right thing, General Nox. I know it sounds cruel to you, ma'am, on account of you being from a country that still has a monarchy and you also being a woman, but sometimes difficult decisions have to be made for the greater good. Freedland's been peaceful since the revolution. We've still got our problems, but at least we've got our freedom."

It was a sobering thought and not one I wanted to contemplate. The killing of innocent children for the "greater good" seemed just as tyrannical as the king's actions. But Sander would never believe it.

He must have sensed our discomfort, because he assured us the executions had been done kindly and swiftly. "They were beheaded at the same time so the queen never witnessed her own children's deaths. He was a fair man, General Nox."

"He was a ruthless revolutionary," Meg shot back.

"No, ma'am, he was not. He was a reluctant revolutionary. He didn't want to rise up against the king, but with the people growing restless, he knew he had to take command or there'd be a massacre of poor folk, with his men carrying out the massacring. He was the only one capable of stepping in and taking charge. He did a fine job too. He's remembered fondly here in Freedland, ain't he, Mark? Shame the current high minister and the other candidates can't be more like him. They could learn a lot from General Nox's legacy about fairness and standing up for the weak and downtrodden. He'd be shocked by the high taxes we have to pay now. He'd be investigating where our taxes go, that's for sure. We could do with another leader like him."

Kitty looked unconvinced by Sander's enthusiasm for the man who'd overthrown the monarchist system, but Meg listened intently. Of the three of us, she was the most revolutionary minded. She believed in fairness for all. I would remain neutral. For one thing, Freedlandian politics was none of my concern, and for another, history wasn't always remembered with accuracy even by those who'd lived through it. General Nox may have been a wonderful man, or he could have made sure he was remembered that way by ordinary folk like Sander. Blood River and Lake Torment did not receive their new names because the revolution had been without loss.

It took some time to reach the mine but not as long as I expected. "It's closer to Gull's Wing than I thought it would be," I said to Sander as he assisted me down from the back of the cart.

"It allowed the guards to live in the village. We didn't need separate housing at the mine." He indicated the burnt bricks of a chimney and fireplace at the edge of a grassy area at the foot of the hill. Blackened bricks marked the outer wall's foundations. It had been a sizeable structure. "That's all that's left of our dining hall, weapons room, and the warden's office. It was destroyed in the fires set by the prisoners."

He went on to explain that the grassy area where we now stood had once been barren wasteland. The constant back and forth of prisoners pushing their carts between the mine's mouth in the side of the hill to the spoil heap some distance away had removed all vegetation, but it was now regenerating. He looked pleased as he surveyed the area with his hands on his hips, like a farmer surveying his crops.

"And where did the prisoners sleep?" Kitty asked, looking around.

"In a barn over there." Sander pointed to a burnt patch on the earth. There was no brick fireplace or foundations, no rubble or any sign that a building had once occupied the space except for the scorched ground.

"All of them?" Meg asked. "Men and women together?"

"Aye. It weren't a good idea but there was no money to build a second building."

"Have the bricks been removed?"

"What bricks?"

"From the fireplace." Meg indicated the surviving structure from the guards' building.

Sander's face pinched. "I'm sorry to say, ma'am, but there was no fire for the prisoners."

"Not even in winter?"

He shook his head.

"That is outrageous!"

"It was a prison mine, ma'am." Sander sounded pained.

"Dogs are treated better than that."

"You've got to remember, they were sent here to die. Many of them were the worst criminals. They offended over and over. They thieved and raided; they raped and bashed. Some, like your husband, might have been here on account of an unfair trial, but mostly they were here because the regular prisons weren't punishment enough."

Kitty folded her arms as if she'd felt a sudden chill. "A swift execution would have been kinder."

Meg looked to Max who was regarding the mine entrance. "But it wouldn't have given them hope," she said. "Where there is life, there is hope of survival, of freedom."

I took her hand and squeezed.

Sander lit the torch he'd brought with him and led us into the yawning hole cut into the side of the hill. The wheel ruts from the carts were clearly visible in the earth, as were the pick marks from the tools used to carve out the tunnel from the rocks.

"Only prisoners who could be trusted were given tools," Sander explained. "But even then, they were not positioned close together and there was one guard for every three prisoners. It's why I can't understand what happened that night. How did the prisoners get the better of the guards?"

"They outnumbered you," I pointed out. "And they were desperate."

"Aye, but they were exhausted and weak from hard work and lack of food, and there were always a lot of guards on duty. If a prisoner struck a guard, he would have been easily caught before he could hit another. Like that Hammer fellow I told you about. He never got a chance to attack again after he bashed Carlos."

Max glared at Sander. "Maybe that's because he only wanted to hurt Carlos, no one else. Carlos must have done something to make him mad. He must have deserved the bashing."

"We'll never know for sure why Hammer did what he did, and we'll never know how the prisoners managed to escape. At least they were all caught and executed. It would be a real worry if they were still out there somewhere."

Max rested a hand on his sword hilt and continued to glare at Sander's back as the former guard moved further into the tunnel. Meg clutched Max's arm as if afraid if she let him go he might attack Sander.

I watched Sander with less animosity than Max. The guard surprised me with his kind attitude towards some of the prisoners. But what surprised me even more was the doubt in his voice as he talked about the escape. He suspected something was amiss.

"Did the women do the same work as the men down here?" Kitty asked.

"The stronger ones did." Sander indicated the walls of the tunnel on either side and above. Wooden supports had been put in place in some parts but it was mostly just bare rock on all sides including the ceiling and floor. "Some picked at the rocks, some hauled it into carts or pushed the carts out." He pointed at the rectangle of light at the tunnel's entrance. "But many women did other chores."

Kitty looked at the rocks at her feet. "Like cleaning?"

"Some cooked meals for the guards. We ate in the hall. They all wanted that work on account of getting access to food."

I ran my hand along the wall, feeling the divots and gouges from the picks. It must have been back breaking work. I wouldn't have lasted long in here, nor would many of the female palace servants. While some were quite robust, many were not. That meant quite a few had been cooks. Surely too many for the number of guards stationed at the mine. They must have performed other duties.

"What about the other women?" I asked.

Sander forged deeper into the tunnel and we had to hurry to catch up. Meg slipped on a rock in the dark and Max caught her before she fell.

"Slow down," he growled at Sander. "You're the only one with light."

Sander stopped. "Sorry. Forgot I had women with me this time. Usually it's just men who want to come in here."

"Speaking of women," I said. "You avoided my question. What did the other women do who weren't cooks but were not strong enough to work in the mine?"

Sander studied the rocks above his head and sighed deeply. "You don't want to know, ma'am."

"I do."

"No, you don't. Besides, I don't want to tell. That's a chapter best left untold."

He moved off again, slower, but we did not immediately follow. Sander might not like telling us about that chapter, but we could all guess what the remaining female prisoners did. They'd been used by the guards as whores.

Kitty suddenly sat on a boulder, as if her legs could no longer hold her. "I've seen enough."

Meg sat with her but shot to her feet again when Max fell back against the wall, bent over from the waist. His breaths came hard and fast as if he couldn't breathe. Yet the air in the tunnel wasn't too stale this close to the entrance.

She put her arm around him and appealed to me. "Josie? What's wrong with him?"

"The maids..." Max managed to whisper.

He didn't need to say more. We understood. He'd become friends to many of the servant women. Thinking of them here, forced to pleasure their captors...it was abhorrent.

"He needs air," Sander said with authority. "It happens to

some who aren't used to it." He led the way back outside. "I reckon we rest for a bit then go back in. You haven't seen the end yet."

"We'd like to leave," I told him.

"You don't want to see where your husband worked, ma'am?" he said to Kitty. To Max, he added, "Or your brother?"

"No thank you," Kitty said with a shudder.

"Did they work near each other?" I asked.

"Aye, along with Hammer and the prisoners he became friends with. I remember Leon used to follow Hammer around like a dog. Wherever Hammer went, Leon went. I reckon he was too scared of the other prisoners to leave the side of the one man who protected him. Same with another fellow whose name I can't recall now. Scrawny lad, couldn't have been more than eighteen. He cried day and night when he first came. Hammer took him under his wing and made sure he got through the nights. Soon enough, he was put on the tools too. They all were, except Hammer was never given a pick or hammer again after the incident with Carlos. He had to work with his bare hands or push the carts. The warden no longer trusted him with tools."

The scrawny lad must be Quentin. Sander had mentioned almost all the men in our little group, as well as Leon. They must have all kept together in the mine, keeping close to Dane for protection and assistance. The only one Sander hadn't mentioned was Balthazar.

"The elderly prisoners must not have lasted very long in the mine," I said.

"Few old folk were sent here," Sander said. "Dangerous crimes are a young man's game." He wagged a finger at me. "There was one who lived and survived here for some time, but that's only because he was treated better than the regular prisoners."

"Why is that?" I asked, although I suspected his answer would be because Balthazar was a priest.

"He was made assistant to the warden. He kept the accounts, wrote reports, that sort of thing. He worked in the warden's office and ate the same as the guards. He even slept in the warden's office when it was too cold to join the other prisoners. He did important work and wasn't a threat."

"What did he do to get himself imprisoned here?" Kitty asked.

"Don't know. He had a blunt tongue and he wasn't afraid to tell folk what he thought of them. I reckon he offended the wrong person. A powerful person. Someone who wanted to shut him up good and proper. This place is effective for taking a man's voice away."

We emerged into the sunshine, blinking and shielding our eyes from the harsher light. It was a welcome sight nevertheless. The tunnel walls had begun to feel too close. At least *we* could enjoy the sunshine. The prisoners would rarely have seen it. Only those pushing out the rubble in barrows came outside. The rest spent their waking hours in the mine, the darkness kept at bay only by torches. Not even rats lived in such degradation.

Sander extinguished the torch in the dirt and looked back at the mine's entrance. He sighed and shook his head before turning away. "I still don't understand how it happened."

We followed him to the cart without responding. It was not a conversation any of us wanted to engage in.

"The escape," Sander said, as if someone had asked. "It was real strange. Not just how it could have happened with so many guards on duty, but where they went. Gull's Wing is the closest village to the mine, but there are others not far away and farms too. But there wasn't a single sighting of the prisoners."

"Perhaps because they were caught quickly," Kitty said as she accepted Sander's help onto the back of the cart.

Sander went to help Meg, but Max wedged himself between them and put his hands to her waist to lift her up. He did the same for me too, before giving Sander another glare.

Sander didn't seem to notice. He was already heading back to the driver's seat. "That's the thing. They weren't caught immediately. It was weeks later when the village crier read out a declaration from the justice minister that all prisoners had been captured and executed. It didn't say where they were found."

"Perhaps in a cave?" Kitty said.

"There ain't no caves and no hiding places that weren't

searched in the weeks following the escape. The authorities combed the woods, farmlands, desert and mountains, and found no sign of them. Not even a footprint." Sander turned to Max. "Not until much later, when they all *should* have died from starvation anyway. Yet they were all alive enough to be executed. Don't you think that strange?"

Max shrugged one shoulder and urged the horses forward.

Sander grunted. "Well I think it's strange. So do many others. The rumors got us all thinking."

"What rumors?" I asked. At Meg's glare I put up a finger to ask her to trust me. I suspected Sander might lead us somewhere we wanted to go.

"Now, I'm not saying I believe in it," Sander said. "It's just something to consider. I trust our authorities told the truth. Don't go thinking I don't trust the official word, because I do."

"But?" I prompted.

He sighed and swiveled on the seat to look at me. "But it's real unlikely that they survived that long, and left no evidence of where they hid. It's no wonder there were rumors that magic helped them escape."

"Magic?" I echoed, doing my best to sound surprised. I laughed for good measure.

Sander laughed too. "It's silly, I know. Magic ain't real. Some still believe it though. Zemayans and some of the fools in the village, mostly. Course, some of us wondered if magic was involved at first. It was a real popular theory there for a while."

"Why not anymore?"

He shrugged. "It's not something most folk think about now. It happened months ago."

"Yes, but it was quite a major event in your lives. Particularly yours, Sander. You clearly still think about it."

"Every day," he murmured.

I inched my way up the cart to sit near him. "Do you have reason to believe magic could have been involved? Is there some evidence of it?"

He huffed a laugh. "Magic doesn't leave evidence or it wouldn't be magic, would it? No, I don't believe. Like I said, some do. Idiots and Zemayans."

It was the second mention of Zemayans in regards to magic. Freedland was so far from that foreign land that it was a surprise he knew magic was akin to Zemaya's religion. "Have any Zemayans been here to look at the site?"

His face lit up with enthusiasm, as if he'd been waiting for me to ask. "Just one. He asked all sorts of questions, even asking me what the prisoners dug up the day they disappeared."

My breath hitched. The Zemayan knew about the gem. "And what did they dig up?"

"Just the same thing they always dig up. Rocks."

"What else did the Zemayan ask?"

"Nothing. He wanted to look at the mine. He went all the way, deep into the tunnels. Real superstitious, he was." Sander indicated his chest area. "He wore dozens of necklaces with colored beads on them and teeth hanging off them. I reckon they were charms to ward off evil spirits on account of the way he clutched them the further in we went."

"Did he do anything in the mine? Did he perform a ritual or some such thing?"

"He just looked around, real careful, pushing over rocks and checking underneath. He asked me how so many prisoners could just disappear without a trace, but I couldn't give him an answer. Later, I heard he'd been asking questions around the village too."

"I know a Zemayan," Max said. "Back in Noxford, there's one. Killen, his name is. Was that him?"

Sander stroked his beard. "He was from Noxford, that part I remember, but I don't think his name was Killen. It started with a T." He continued to stroke his beard then suddenly clicked his fingers. "Taaj. That's it. His name was Taaj."

* * *

TELLING the others what we'd learned from Sander was the most difficult conversation I'd ever had. I thought we should do it separately, but Max wanted to do it with all of us present.

"We're in this predicament together," he'd said as we drove to the inn after taking Sander home. "We should face the truth together too."

Quentin, Theodore and Erik met us in the inn's stable yard. They'd seen our approach and couldn't wait any longer to speak to us. Max assured them they'd get answers inside.

"Where are Dane and Balthazar?" I asked.

"Securing a table in the corner of the taproom," Theodore said. "I should warn you, Dane's in a foul mood. He doesn't like being left out of information gathering adventures."

"It was fortunate he was left out of this one. Sander would have recognized him. The rest of you, too," I added as Theodore fell into step alongside me. "You must avoid him at all costs while we're here."

Dane's gaze lifted from his tankard upon our entry and connected with mine. I shook off my reservations and forged ahead. As difficult as this was going to be, it had to be done.

"Well?" Quentin asked before we'd even sat down. "What did he say?"

We left Max to do the talking. It felt right coming from him.

"He didn't know why most of us were imprisoned," he began. "The guards were never informed."

Quentin's shoulders slumped and he hunched over his tankard. "What a waste of time then."

"He made some guesses, though, and some of us confided in him."

"Confided in a guard?" Balthazar sounded skeptical.

"He was probably one of the better ones," I said. "He claims he even became friendly with Dane, in a way."

Dane blinked rapidly. "Why me?"

"You were one of the longest serving prisoners so he got to know you. He saw something in you that he connected with. You discussed politics together. You were kind to the other prisoners, protecting many of the weaker ones." I told them how he'd taken Quentin, Leon and Theodore under his wing and how the other prisoners respected him because of it. "There was a group of you who became known as the protectors. Because of you, Dane."

Dane's jaw hardened. "He couldn't possibly remember all of us. He was just telling you what you wanted to hear."

We all protested, but it was Max whose voice they listened to. "He remembered, all right. I reckon it was our willingness to protect the weak that made us stick in his mind. His descriptions of us, not just physical but of our characters too, were right. He remembered Leon as an arrogant little turd with a big mouth."

"Did he remember him finding the gem?" Balthazar asked.

Max shook his head. "According to Sander, Leon claimed he was jailed because he lampooned King Phillip, on the castle doorstep, no less."

Theodore flattened his palms on the table. "That's all? It's hardly an offense that warrants such a harsh punishment."

"Never embarrass a king," Balthazar warned. "If we learn nothing else, that is a good lesson to take away from all this."

Max cleared his throat. "Speaking of embarrassing those in power." He coughed again and kept his gaze on his tankard.

"Go on," Balthazar said. "We need to know."

"Right." Max lifted his gaze to Theodore's. "You were jailed because your lover was the son of a powerful Dreenian."

Theodore's eyes widened. Then the color rushed to his cheeks. He swallowed hard and focused on his tankard, cupped between both hands.

"And you, Bal," Max quickly went on. "Sander didn't know why you were imprisoned, but he reckons you gave a harsh opinion of someone important."

Quentin snickered. "That ain't a surprise."

Erik thumped him. "It ain't amusing. He was put in a prison mine."

"Sorry, Bal."

"What about you?" Dane asked Max.

"Sander didn't know," Max said. "Nor did he know why you were there, or Erik, but like I said, he remembered us all, which is why we've got to lay low in Gull's Wing. I reckon we should leave at first light."

"Agreed," Dane said.

Erik, Theodore and Quentin hunkered lower, keeping their faces averted from the other patrons in the taproom.

Balthazar wasn't quite so concerned. "Sander can point at us and shout his suspicions across the village, but it won't matter. According to the official stance, we were executed. We are dead. For the authorities to admit that we're the escaped prisoners would be to admit they lied about capturing all of us."

I didn't particularly agree. While his theory was logical, there was always the chance the authorities would say they mistakenly missed some. It was entirely believable that they miscounted when there were nearly a thousand prisoners.

Dane agreed with me. "We're going to remain in the inn for the rest of today and leave at first light. There's nothing more we can learn here and we'll be more able to disappear in a city the size of Noxford."

We were heading to Noxford anyway. With Balthazar's journey to Freedland our only certainty, it made sense that he traveled directly to the country's capital and its religious temples. We hadn't yet decided if we should make inquiries about him there, however. If Balthazar had kept his reason for coming to Freedland a secret, perhaps it was wise to continue to do so.

"Speaking of Noxford," I said. "Sander mentioned a Zemayan from the capital who visited the mine after the escape became public. This Zemayan wanted to know if the prisoners found something in the mine."

"The gem!" Quentin said.

Erik jabbed his elbow into Quentin's side. Quentin grunted and rubbed his ribs.

"Taaj the Zemayan believed magic set the prisoners free," I added. "He admitted as much to Sander."

"Do you think he knows something?" Theodore asked.

Quentin sat forward. "Maybe he knows the sorcerer."

It was a hopeful note on which to end the evening. We agreed to retire early and stay out of sight, just in case Sander decided to join us for a drink. Besides, we wanted to leave early in the morning.

I couldn't rest, however. Not until I'd spoken to Dane. I took his hand before he entered the room he shared with Balthazar and Theodore.

But he extracted his hand from mine. "Is there something else you need to tell me?" The hard planes of his face left me in no doubt he didn't want to talk to me.

I wasn't giving up, however. "Sander told us how you got the name Hammer."

His gaze darted to mine. "It's bad, isn't it?"

"He made sure to tell us you were a good man. You protected the others and were a leader to many. The prisoners looked up to you."

"Don't avoid it, Josie. What did I do?"

I sucked in a breath and let it out slowly. "You hit a guard with your hammer."

He leaned back against the closed door and dragged both hands over his face. "I killed a man in cold blood."

"He didn't die. That's the only reason you weren't hanged." I didn't tell him about his subsequent punishment in the disused well. It would be akin to rubbing salt in the wound. "Sander didn't know why you attacked the guard. You wouldn't tell anyone. But you must have had a reason."

"Did I?" he bit off. "Or was I just angry and lashed out at the nearest guard?"

He turned to go, but I grabbed his arm. "You could have attacked any of the guards or your fellow prisoners, but you did not. Only that one. Sander said he liked you and—"

"Don't, Josie." Her jerked free. "Don't pretend I was noble and just. I know I wasn't. Not after hearing that."

"I'm not pretending," I hissed. "Nor am I so blindly, foolishly in love with you that I can't see your faults. You're stubborn, overbearing, have a quick temper, and can be arrogant."

"Arrogant?"

"Yes. You let the adulation of Quentin and the others go to your head at times."

"I do not."

I gave him an arched look. "See, stubborn and arrogant."

He crossed his arms. "Your point?"

"My point is that I see your faults and can list them to your face, so believe me when I say cruelty and unwarranted violence are not among them. If they were, I wouldn't care for you like I do."

"I appreciate what you're trying to do, Josie. I do. But I think we both know you're biased, and if that's me being arrogant, then so be it."

"I am not biased! I am quite capable of stepping back and seeing the real you."

"You only *think* you can. But the truth is, you've only known me a few months, and in a time when I am not myself. Until I find out who I am, you can't truly know me. No one can." He jerked open the door and closed it in my face before I had a chance to think of a retort.

I stood there, hands on hips, and glared at the door. I should open it and continue the argument inside. I should tell him he was wrong, that I did know him.

But it would get us nowhere except angry with one another, and he didn't need that. He needed to be shown how good a man he could be. If he didn't believe me or the others, then there was only one solution. Find people who'd known him before he lost his memory and prove it.

Hopefully Noxford would provide answers to his past as well as the reason for Balthazar's visit to Freedland. If it didn't, I was at a loss for where to turn next.

CHAPTER 13

Noxford was a similar size to Tilting and both cities were located on rivers, but otherwise there was little outward similarity between the two capitals. The sheriff's office, courts, and other official buildings clustered around the main square were not old. They'd replaced the ones destroyed during the revolution forty years ago. A bronze statue of General Noxford on a rearing horse stood atop a plinth in the middle of the paved square. The structure was the height of at least four men.

We passed the ancient castle, perched on a hill. According to Balthazar, who'd read up on the history of the city, the former king's residence was now used as offices for the ministers and the private home of the high minister. Scars in the thick outer walls were the only visible reminder of the repairs carried out after the revolution.

The nation's high temple stood on the hill opposite the castle. Like Tilting's high temple, it was a magnificent tribute to the god with an impressive tower shooting into the sky. We passed smaller temples, dedicated to both Merdu and Hailia, as well as the bustling market. The streets radiating from the market were filled with shops selling all kinds of goods, many of which must have been imported from other countries. Freedland wasn't known for its luxurious textiles or precious metals.

Kitty squealed with delight upon seeing the silks on display in the cloth merchant's shop. "Civilization at long last."

"We cannot afford to buy frivolous things," Meg told her. "We must save what little money we have left."

"I have the necklace I was wearing when we falsified my death." Kitty patted her chest where the pendant nestled beneath her clothes. "I can sell it."

"Save it for necessities."

Kitty gazed longingly at the silks until they disappeared from sight. "Lovely clothes *are* a necessity."

"So are lovely women," Erik piped up.

I thought he was referring to Kitty, but he smiled and bowed at two women of middle age with baskets over their arms. Their lips parted with their gasps before they hurried away. I eyed Kitty warily, but she laughed.

"You are naughty," she chided.

He grinned at her and winked, earning a laugh from Kitty in response.

Meg caught my eye and raised a brow. I merely shrugged. Their relationship was a mystery to me as well.

We found the inn that had been recommended to us by the Tilting warrior priests and settled in for the night. We ate heartily but I instantly regretted it when Dane carefully counted out the ells to pay the serving girl.

"Funds are tight," he told us. "We can't spend any more than necessary here or we'll all need to find work."

Kitty pulled a face. "Work?"

"Aye," Quentin said. "It's that thing people do to earn money to pay for food, shelter, clothing." He winked at Meg.

Meg took up the teasing. "But since you're not qualified or experienced, Kitty, you'll have to do something menial."

"You could be a washer woman," Theodore said with mock seriousness.

Kitty pouted. "I've never washed clothes before. I wouldn't know what to do. What about being a ladies' maid? I know what they do, and I'm sure I'd be a better one than Prudence, the trout-faced cow."

"Can you do hair?" Meg asked.

Kitty sighed.

"What about a shop assistant? You could sell things, surely."

Kitty's face lit up. "I could work in that draper's shop we passed before. I'd make an excellent seller of silks and other luxuries." She suddenly clasped Dane's hand. "Do let me know if I must contribute, Dane. I would like to help in any way I can, as long as it doesn't involve washing clothes, doing hair, or anything where I have to touch dirt. Or prepare food. I don't think I'd be very good at that. I like to eat it, not touch it." She wrinkled her nose.

I bit my lip to stop my smirk from breaking free. Meg wasn't so restrained, and a small snicker escaped. Kitty didn't seem to notice. She was caught up in her enthusiasm for enterprise.

We bade one another goodnight after supper, but I bailed Dane up outside his room, as I had done on our last night in Gull's Wing. He'd been quiet for most of the journey to Noxford, but it was more contemplative than morose. It was a good sign that he wouldn't let the story of how he earned the name Hammer effect him too much.

I nodded at the bedchamber door behind him. "Are you going to close the door in my face again?"

He folded his arms over his chest. "Are you going to call me arrogant again?"

"Probably. If not tonight then another day."

He narrowed his gaze. "You test me, do you know that?"

I smiled. "That's because I don't think you should get everything handed to you. You are, after all, handsome, intelligent, athletic, good with a sword, on horseback, with your fists, with women, and sometimes you're even witty."

"Only sometimes?"

"You have an unfair proportion of good traits. Somebody has to remind you of your bad ones once in a while or you'll become unbearable."

He laughed. It was all the more special because of its rarity, and I smiled too. "You know I wasn't mad at you, don't you?" he asked.

I looked away and gave a small shrug.

He settled his hands on my shoulders. "Josie," he murmured,

"I'm sorry I took my frustration and worries out on you. You don't deserve it."

"You didn't take them out on me, you were sharing them with me. That's why I'm here. To share the burden with you. You don't have to bear it alone, Dane. I'm here for you to lean on, confide in, and just generally support you on this mad journey."

He stroked the underside of my jaw with his thumb. "You're already doing all that for me. In fact, the others should thank you. If you weren't here, I'd be impossible." He leaned forward and touched his forehead to mine. "Thank you."

I wanted to kiss him. It would have been so easy to do. I wouldn't even have to move much. But it was best if I didn't make life any more complicated for him. By the time I'd thought it through, he'd put some distance between us anyway.

"Goodnight," he said.

I nodded and smiled but left without responding. My throat was too tight to squeeze words through.

I returned to the room I shared with Meg and Kitty to find them lying side by side on the small bed, staring up at the ceiling, chatting about men. Or, rather, one man.

"Erik is a dalliance," Kitty said. "Nothing more. There can never be anything permanent between us. I'm a noblewoman of Glancia, after all. When Gladstow dies, I'll resume my position as duchess and find myself a worthy husband."

"Erik *is* worthy," Meg said.

"He is a Marginer."

"That doesn't make him less worthy."

"Perhaps worthy was the wrong word. Being a Marginer makes him less *acceptable* as the husband of a duchess. There. Now do you understand?"

"No!" Meg turned to face Kitty and propped herself up on her elbow. "He adores you, Kitty."

Kitty laughed. "He adores all women. I'm not special to him."

Meg appealed to me. "Help me, Josie. Explain to her that she shouldn't treat Erik as if he were a mere dalliance."

I settled on the foot of the bed and unlaced my gown. "Sorry, Meg, I agree with Kitty. While I don't think Erik would make an unacceptable husband for a duchess, if Kitty merely sees him as a dalliance that is the end of it. Besides, he clearly thinks of her the same way, going by his interest in all women."

"See," Kitty said, without a hint of disappointment. "Erik is a flirt with a roaming eye. He has no interest in settling for one woman. He'd grow bored in a marriage. And while I adore him, and will always think fondly of him, he is not what I want in a husband. In fact, I don't know if I ever want to marry again."

Meg sat up and I stopped unlacing my gown. "Why not?" we both asked.

"What is the point in marrying if I cannot bear children?" She swallowed heavily, but there were no tears in her eyes or tremble in her voice. She was beginning to come to terms with it.

"Companionship," Meg pointed out.

"I have that in both of you." She clasped Meg's hand. "And in Miranda."

I waggled my eyebrows. "What about sexual companionship?"

Kitty giggled. "I can get that from dalliances. Perhaps Erik will be the first of many. I do hope so."

Meg fell back onto the bed, chuckling. "Who would have thought you'd be the most daring of the three of us."

"There's no point dreaming about it yet," Kitty warned her. "Gladstow could live to be a hundred. By then, I shall be..." She tried calculating with her fingers but gave up. "Also old."

I nudged her with my knee. "Old women can have dalliances too. I'm quite sure Erik would volunteer his services."

That had us all rolling around on the bed with laughter.

* * *

Since we knew Max had taken a ship from Noxford and traveled to Priest's End before his imprisonment, we decided to head to the riverside docks to see if someone recognized him. Balthazar was convinced we didn't need to worry about the authorities re-arresting them, but I vehemently disagreed. As did Dane. He wore a cloaked hood, as did Quentin, Theodore and Erik, but Max wanted his face seen. Balthazar didn't come with us. The long journey had taken its toll on his frail body and he elected to stay at the inn.

Being visible in the city was one thing, but actually getting people to look at Max's face was another. We had to engage them in conversation, and I had the perfect idea how to do it.

"Do you know any Zemayans in the city?" I asked a dock worker dumping a sack of grain onto a cart.

He looked at us, shook his head, and kept working. We moved on.

Kitty and Meg took up the questioning too. "Do you know of a Zemayan by the name of Taaj?"

"We're looking for a man with Zemayan coloring. Do you know any?"

Our inquiries bore fruit very quickly when a Zemayan sailor overheard us and directed us to the shop of a spice merchant where he'd just come from delivering cargo. "His name's Taaj," he said. "And he's the only Zemayan living in the city, so he says. Don't know how he can live all the way out here in this country of sand and sweat." He wiped his brow on the back of his sleeve and gave us directions to Taaj's shop before heading off towards a ship flying the Zemayan flag.

"Should we go to see Taaj now?" Quentin asked.

Theodore squinted up at the sun. "It is warm out here."

"I want to look around some more," Max said. "Taaj can wait."

A man who'd been walking past stopped suddenly and frowned at Max. He cocked his head to the side, eyed Max up and down, and grunted. "Well fuck. It *is* you."

The blood drained from Max's face and he looked as though he might faint. He opened and closed his mouth, but no words came out.

The man laughed and clapped Max on the shoulder. "What are you, a fish?" He threw his arms around Max and slapped him on the back. "I can't believe you're alive! Why didn't you come home?" He pulled away, suddenly serious. "You're in hiding, aren't you?" His gaze darted around the docks.

"You recognize him?" Dane asked when Max remained silent.

"Recognize my own brother? Sure do. Who're you?"

"What's his name?" Dane asked.

"It's Max," the man said, as if Dane were an idiot.

Max blew out a breath. "Brothers?" he said weakly.

The man winked at him. "Sure."

Max frowned. "Are we or are we not brothers?"

The newcomer's smile faded. "Not really," he said carefully. "But you know that."

"I've lost my memory," Max told him. "Can we go somewhere to talk? I need to learn more about my past."

The man stared at him, his mouth ajar, then he stared at each of us in turn. He balked when he noticed the dot tattoos on Erik's forehead beneath the hood. "Max, what in the god's name are you doing with a Marginer? Did you lose your mind as well as your memory?" He laughed and punched Max in the shoulder.

Max merely glared at him. "What's your name?"

"Drew."

"Take me somewhere we can talk, Drew. Preferably to the house of my family."

Drew blinked hard. "You really have lost your memory."

"I got hit on the head."

Drew looked at each of us again. "And who are these people?"

"Friends who helped bring me here. We reckoned I was from Freedland, so we came here to find my family."

"Where have you been if not in Freedland?"

"Like I said, I lost my memory."

Drew ran his tongue over his top teeth beneath his lip. He made a smacking sound when he opened his mouth. "I can take you, but not them. They can't come."

"Why not?" Max asked.

"Can't tell you."

Max huffed. "Do I have a family or not?"

"Sort of."

"Then why can't I take friends to see them?"

Drew looked around and hunkered down. "How can I be sure they won't take the authorities to them?"

"Huh?"

"Look, I know you wouldn't lead the constables there on purpose, but maybe they're watching you. Maybe the reason they let you go is because they think you'll lead them straight to us. Vance would skin me alive if I was responsible for taking constables to our lair."

"Lair?" Quentin echoed. "Are you a pack of wolves?"

Drew pulled himself up to his full height which was only a little taller than Max, and eyed Quentin up and down. "I know *you* ain't a constable. They don't take skinny little turds, not even if they're desperate."

Max grabbed Drew by the front of his jerkin and shook him. "Do not insult my friends." He let him go, shoving him for good measure. "Now take me and all my friends to this lair, or to my family, or whoever they are. Just take me somewhere where someone knows who I am!"

Drew put up his hands in surrender. "Fine, fine. Come with me. It's not far." He led us away from the docks, past warehouses, grain stores, shipyards, and the customs house, to a series of small streets. I would have become hopelessly lost without a guide to navigate through them. The streets were not laid out in an orderly pattern. Some were curved, only to end in almost the same place they started. Some stopped at a dead end, while others diverted around buildings that looked as though they'd been dropped by the god's hand from above after a drunken night.

As he walked, Drew snuck glances at Max, and sometimes the rest of us, but he no longer seemed worried. His earlier reluctance was replaced by curiosity. Curiosity soon turned to wariness, however, as his pace slowed and he looked up and down the street. He finally stopped at a nondescript door in the middle of a row of tightly packed cottages.

He knocked four times in rapid succession and once more after a brief hesitation. The door opened immediately and an eye peered through the crack. The eye quickly scanned Drew then fell on the rest of us.

"What're you doing bringing strangers here?" the voice belonging to the eye asked.

Drew shoved Max forward.

"Merdu!" The door swung open and a man barreled out. He embraced Max in a fierce hug, thumping him on the back and shoulders with bruising rhythm. The last thump was so hearty it made Max cough.

The man drew back and regarded him. Then he punched his arm, hard. "You prick! Where in the god's name have you been? And why didn't you tell us you weren't dead?"

"Let us in," Drew said, pushing past the man.

The man gave Max a little shove towards the door then stood in front of it to block us, arms crossed over an enormous chest. He wasn't a tall man, but the muscles of his shoulders were so thick they swallowed his neck. His head looked like a pea on an inverted mountain.

"You can't come in," he said.

"They're my friends," Max told him. "They're coming in or you have to come out if you want to speak to me."

The doorman sized up Erik and Dane. "Vance won't like it."

Drew rested a hand on the doorman's arm. "Vance'll be so happy to see Max he won't care if he brings a whole army."

Kitty stepped forward. "You will let us in or I will personally see to it that Max tells you nothing about where he has been these last few months. Is that clear?"

The doorman studied her from head to toe. A slow smile spread over his lips. "Vance is gonna like you."

"Then you'd best let us in. All of us."

He hesitated before giving a nod. "Remove your weapons," he ordered the men. "You can collect them on your way out."

Dane hesitated, but Erik, Quentin and Theodore handed over their swords. Finally, Dane did too. The doorman didn't ask me or the other women, nor did he check the men to see if they carried knives. He wasn't a very good guard.

The doorman stepped aside and we moved past him. Erik slapped the doorman on the back. "Kitty is a beauty, this is true. Your leader will adore her as much as I do."

Kitty looped her arm through Erik's. "Thank you, Erik dearest. That's rather sweet of you."

The doorman gave a short, shrill whistle but didn't follow us to the spacious kitchen beyond. The whistle had alerted those inside that visitors were arriving so they were all looking up when we entered. The two men and one woman sprang to their feet when they spied Max.

The small woman rushed forward, her dark hair streaming behind her, and leapt onto Max, wrapping her arms and legs around him. He staggered but managed not to fall.

"I can't believe it!" she cried. "You're alive! Thank the goddess, you're alive!" With her ankles hooked behind his back, she cupped his face and kissed his forehead, cheeks, ears, and nose.

Max glanced at Meg. Meg studied the stone floor, her face tilted in an effort to hide her birthmark.

Max tried prying the woman off, but she stuck to him like a limpet to a boat hull. "Excuse me, if you don't mind getting off now."

The woman blinked at him. "'Excuse me?'" she mocked. "'If you don't mind?' Were you kidnapped by royalists who forced you to speak like you got a pole up your arse?" She laughed as she settled her feet on the floor. She was a little wiry thing of about my age with hair to her waist and big dark eyes that drank in the sight of Max. Her smile soon vanished and her eyes turned dreamy as she squeezed his hands. "You've been missed, Max. We've been mad with worry."

"Speak for yourself," said one of the men with a broad grin. He must be related to the woman. They had the same eyes and build, and the front teeth of both were angled inwards. He embraced a bemused Max too before stepping back and frowning. "Aren't you happy to be home?"

Max's mouth opened and shut again. He looked to Dane.

It was Drew who answered. "Max reckons he lost his memory. He was wandering around at the docks, hoping someone would recognize him."

The woman barked a laugh. "Is this a joke?"

"No," Max said. "I really have lost my memory. I don't know any of you."

The man who hadn't moved since our arrival finally stepped into the rectangle of light streaming through the high window. He was taller than all of the others with a solid frame. A small scar marked his cheek and another sliced through the black stubble on his chin. His heavy lidded gaze made him seem lazy, disinterested, but a closer inspection showed his eyes to be quick, his gaze assessing. Not only did he take in Max, but also Dane, Erik and the other men.

"Drew," he snapped. "Tell me why you thought it was a good idea to bring strangers here."

Drew nibbled his lower lip. "Max insisted."

"I see no evidence that he insisted." He indicated Drew's face with a wave of his hand. The rings on each of his fingers flashed gold in the beam of sunlight. "You're no uglier than usual."

"He didn't hit me! Come on, Vance, it's Max."

Vance didn't seem to have heard him. "Did he threaten you?"

"No."

"Then why did you bring them?"

Drew pouted and his shoulders rounded in a stoop. He reminded me of Quentin when one of his superiors scolded him. "Because he's still second-in-command, and I still take orders from him. That ain't changed. You never told us Max wasn't your second no more."

"I didn't think I had to, considering he was dead." There was no heat in Vance's voice, just wonder. He suddenly threw his arms around Max. When he stepped back, he sported a smile as broad and genuine as the others.

"It's good to see you, even if you don't remember us." He indicated Dane and Erik with a flip of his ringed fingers. "Any friends of yours can be trusted. You were always a good judge of character. Come in. Sit."

Vance's invitation seemed to relax his friends. They blew out deep breaths and exchanged relieved glances with one another.

"Jenny, get Max and his friends a drink." Vance pulled out a chair from the central table for Max. "Sit with me. Tell me every-thing about your adventures. Tell us how you escaped execution."

The room reminded me of the palace garrison with its stark-ness. The few pieces of furniture were functional rather than decorative, and the only wall hanging was a map of the city. Pins had been thrust through it to mark points of interest.

Vance caught me staring at it. He nodded at Drew then

nodded at the map. Drew removed the pins while Vance sat and Jenny poured ales from a jug.

"Do you have tea?" Kitty asked, eyeing the pot warming over the low fire.

"No," Jenny said, setting a cup in front of Max.

Kitty pointed at the pot. "Isn't there tea in there?"

"It's a special tea. You won't like it."

"I might."

"That tea ain't for you." Jenny thumped another cup down on the table in front of Theodore. "Do you want the ale or not, duchess?"

Kitty gasped. "How did—? Ow!" She glared at me. My kick would have hurt but at least she got the message and didn't complete her question. "I won't have anything, thank you."

"Well?" Vance asked Max. "Where've you been?"

"King Leon's palace in Glancia," Max said. "I found work as a palace guard."

Vance stared at him then burst out laughing. His friends too. Drew laughed so hard that he had to wipe away tears. The other man clutched his belly.

"Forgive us," Jenny said as she placed a cup in front of Quentin. "If you really have lost your memory then you won't know why that's so funny."

"I have lost my memory," Max said through a clenched jaw. "Would you like to tell me why it's a joke to you?"

Vance leaned forward, still chuckling. "Because you're second-in-command of our little enterprise." He twirled his fingers to indicate the room and his friends.

"So?"

"How shall I put this?" Vance stretched out his legs under the table and crossed them at the ankles. "We're not the sort who become guards."

Max just stared at him.

"What he means," Dane said, "is that they're thieves. Thieves and guards are not usually friends."

Vance wagged a finger at Dane. "This one's clever. Are you also a guard?"

"I was, but not anymore. So now you know where Max has

been, you can tell him about his past. He can't remember it, and naturally he's curious."

Jenny thrust her hand on her hip. "You can't remember a thing?"

"No," Max said.

"Is that so? In that case…" She wedged herself onto his lap and circled her arms around his neck. Before Max could react, she planted a kiss on his lips.

Max sprang up, dislodging her. He wiped his mouth with the back of his hand as his face lost all color. Meg shifted in her chair. She stared down at her hands, clasped in her lap, so did not see Max's forlorn look in her direction.

Drew slapped Jenny's arm with the back of his hand and Jenny rocked back on her heels, laughing. "She was joking," Drew told Max. "You two ain't lovers. You never were."

"Sit down," Vance snarled at Jenny. "Don't tease a man like that."

Jenny sat, still chuckling. "It was just a bit of fun."

Max tugged on his jerkin hem and sat again. "Glad this is amusing to you," he muttered. "But it's no fun for me. I don't recognize any of you. I don't know my family, or where I lived. I don't even know my last name."

"It's Bullitt," said the man who looked like Jenny. He thrust out his hand to Max. "My name's Gillon."

Max shook his hand. "Nice to meet you, Gillon."

Jenny introduced herself too, all evidence of mirth wiped from her face. Vance followed suit, and added, "I'm the leader and you're my second. We've known each other since we were babes."

Max introduced the rest of us using just first names then asked for some details about himself.

Vance twisted the gold ring on his middle finger. "Like I said, we've known each other forever. Our mothers were friends. We got into all sorts of trouble as boys." His gaze became distant, his smile wistful.

"What sort of trouble?" Max asked.

"Fighting with the other boys, nicking things, playing tricks on the shop keepers. We were a bit wild. The constables hated us. We earned a reputation that only got worse as we grew up. It got so bad that the sheriff blamed us for crimes we didn't commit."

"Were we ever arrested for these crimes?"

"Frequently." Vance's wide grin revealed a gold tooth left of center. "We were never put away for long stretches. We mostly did petty things, thieving, defacing property…"

"Being a public nuisance," Jenny added with a chuckle.

"Did we hurt people?" Max asked.

Vance lifted a shoulder in a shrug. "Not when our mothers were alive."

Max's face sagged. "My mother is dead?"

"Aye. Dropped dead from hard work, I expect. Same with my mother. They cleaned houses for rich folk."

"And our fathers?"

"I never met mine. Yours died when you were little. I don't remember him."

"Brothers? Sisters?"

Vance shook his head.

Gillon leaned across the table and tapped his cup against Max's. "We're your family. We have been for a long time."

Vance nodded. "You and me might not share blood, but we're as close as two brothers could get." He clasped Max's shoulder, but Max instinctively jerked away. Vance's hand hung in the air for a moment before the fingers curled and he lowered it.

Gillon and Jenny exchanged worried glances.

Drew seemed oblivious to the snub. "So how'd you get to be a guard at the Glancian king's palace?"

"I don't know," Max said. "I can't remember anything before my time there."

"Did he crack his head on something?" Vance asked Dane. "Get in a fight?"

"Not that we are aware," Dane said.

Vance frowned. "You must have noticed something."

Dane shook his head.

"How'd he get work as a palace guard?" Vance asked.

"He was good with his fists and a sword," Dane said. "And we needed more capable men like him."

Gillon smirked. "Guess you lied about your past, eh, Max?"

Max remained silent and didn't meet anyone's gaze.

"Does the fact that you're here mean you aren't guards anymore?" Jenny asked.

"We weren't needed," Dane said. "The king is dead and the dukes are in charge of Glancia."

Her eyes brightened. "The palace is empty?"

"Mostly."

Vance leaned forward. "No one's guarding it?"

Dane's lips flattened. "The remaining guards and servants are more than capable of fending off burglars. Besides, by the time you reach Mull, the next king might be chosen and the palace occupied again."

Vance's grunt was half-amusement, half-respect for Dane.

Max hadn't been listening to this exchange. His gaze had been focused on his cup until now. He suddenly looked up. "What was I like?"

"Huh?" Drew asked.

"My character? What was I like?"

"Serious," Gillon said.

"Sweet," Jenny added.

"Loyal," Vance said, once again leaning towards Max. He looked as though he was going to clasp his shoulder again, but refrained.

"You're an honorable man," Drew said quietly.

Max shot to his feet, his lips twisted with a sneer. "How can I be honorable when I was a thief?"

"Not that kind of honorable," Jenny muttered. "The other kind."

"What other kind? There is no other kind! Either I respected people's property and person or I did not. It seems to be the latter."

Theodore rose too and said, "You had a difficult childhood. You were poor and grew up without a good role model. It's only natural you turned to theft to survive. Don't be so hard on yourself."

"Don't make excuses for me," Max spat. "Or for them."

Vance watched the exchange with apparent indifference. But

his heavy-lidded gaze hid only so much from the world. The twitch of muscle in his jaw told a different story. Max's disgust bothered him.

"Tell me." Max's voice was a strained, strangled rasp. "Did we ever hurt anyone in the process of stealing from them?"

Vance looked away.

Max's nostrils flared. "Did we beat people up?"

Dillon and Drew swallowed heavily and they too looked away.

Max's face paled and he closed his hands into fists at his sides, as if stealing himself for what was to come. "Did I kill anyone?"

CHAPTER 14

*T*he resulting silence was broken by the chair Max had vacated crashing onto the stone floor. Jenny had kicked it. She stood and jabbed her finger at him. "Listen to yourself. You've turned into a self-righteous, do-gooding snob, and I *hate* you!"

"Jenny!" Vance barked.

She glared at Max, her face flushed and her eyes flashing. "We thought you were dead. We mourned you. We had a ceremony to say goodbye, for Merdu's sake! Then you suddenly turn up with a bunch of new friends and start acting all superior. The way you look at us is the same way rich folk look at us. Like we don't matter. Like we're scum. How do you think we feel seeing the man we thought of as our brother, who we assumed was executed for escaping prison, turn up in our lair and treat us like we're nothing to him?" She kicked his chair again, sending it skidding across the floor. "You didn't trust us enough to come here and ask for our help after your escape, and I *hate* you for that. I hate you for leaving us without a word. But I hate you more for coming back and looking down your nose at us."

"That's enough, Jenny!" Vance picked up the chair and righted it. "Max is our brother. No matter what has happened, he always will be. Everything will be fine when he remembers his past."

"And when will that be?"

"Perhaps it will come to him with a little more information," Dane said. "You say you thought he escaped from prison. Are you referring to the escape from the prison mine near Gull's Wing?" Dane's pretense of ignorance was a signal for the rest of us to follow suit. We would not reveal everything to these people, only as much as necessary.

"You know of it?" Vance asked.

"News of the escape reached Mull, but not the subsequent execution. Weren't all the escapees caught again and executed for murdering the guards?"

"So the ministers say."

"You have reason to doubt them?"

Vance indicated Max. "No reason except that he's standing here now."

"Why was he thrown into a prison mine this time?" Dane asked. "What was his crime?"

"A witness saw him leaving the scene of a fire where two bodies were found."

So the drunkards in Priests End were telling the truth.

Max sat heavily on the chair with a groan. "I killed them," he muttered. "I'm a murderer."

"No," Theodore said earnestly. "If you were a murderer, they would have executed you. But you were imprisoned."

Max made no indication he'd heard him. Meg blinked hard, her teeth nibbling her lower lip. I wished she'd go to him, comfort him. It might help them both.

"What was he doing in the building in the first place?" Dane asked Vance.

"He went into the goldsmith's shop to…relieve the shopkeeper of some items that hadn't sold in a while. He insisted on going alone. He'd been watching it for weeks and knew every movement the goldsmith and his wife made. He was confident of a particular time when they wouldn't be home. That's when he broke in. None of us know what happened after that. There was a fire, the bodies of the goldsmith and his wife were retrieved from the burning building, and Max just disappeared. Some weeks later we heard from an acquaintance that he'd been seen down at the docks, trying to get on a ship. We asked around and a sailor told us he'd worked with a man matching Max's description."

"We didn't believe him at first," Drew said to Max. "You hate the water. You can't swim."

"I know," Max said drily. "I found out the hard way."

Gillon whooped with laughter, and Drew soon joined in. Quentin, Kitty and Theodore chuckled too. Meg eyed Max carefully, but when he smiled, she returned it with a measure of relief.

"The sailor told us that Max got as far as Gull's Wing where he was forcibly removed from the ship by constables," Vance went on. "He was arrested for causing the fire, but not the murders of the goldsmith and his wife. They were killed before the fire the sheriff reckoned. He couldn't prove you'd killed them."

"Their throats had been cut," Gillon said. "You wouldn't do that, Max. "

"See," Meg suddenly blurted out. "It wasn't you." Realizing everyone's attention had turned to her, she shrank back into herself and tilted her head again to hide her birthmark.

"When you were arrested, you told the sheriff you'd seen someone leaving the building before you entered. The magistrate believed you."

"You learned all this from the Noxford sheriff?" Max asked. "I thought he hated you."

Vance shook his head. "I went to Gull's Wing where your trial was carried out. It was there that I learned you'd been sentenced to the prison mine for arson as well as all your other crimes over the years. But not the murders. The Noxford sheriff communicated with the Gull's Wing authorities, but it was the Gull's Wing sheriff I spoke to. He didn't know me."

"The Noxford sheriff's been looking for all of us for years," Gillon said. "That's why we didn't want to bring any newcomers here." He nodded at us. "We've got to be careful. If we're not, we could end up in one of them prison mines too."

Jenny shuddered. "I hear what they do to the women there. It's cruel."

"When we heard about the escape, we were relieved," Vance said. "Don't listen to Jenny. We hoped you wouldn't come back here to Noxford. It was too dangerous for you. Glancia was probably the best place for you to go."

"We're real glad you got away," Drew said quietly. "Real glad."

Jenny swallowed heavily. Tears filled her eyes, threatening to overflow. She sniffed and looked down at her feet.

"You have to leave the city again," Vance said. "I know you want to stay to find out more about yourself, but it's too dangerous here. If the sheriff hears you're back, he might come for you again and re-arrest you."

Jenny sniffed again and wiped her nose with the back of her hand. "But the official word is that all escapees were rounded up and executed. They won't like admitting they missed one. They'll just let him go and pretend he doesn't exist."

"It's not worth taking that risk." Vance blew out a measured breath then held out his hand to Max. "At least this time I get to say goodbye. But just for a short while. Maybe I'll come looking for you in Glancia, one day. Mull, did you say?"

Max nodded. He blinked rapidly as he shook Vance's hand, then Drew's and Gillon's. When it came time to shake Jenny's, she folded her arms and looked away. So Max leaned down and hugged her where she sat.

She burst into tears and threw her arms around him. "You big, stupid fool. I'm going to miss you the most."

"I may have only known you all for a short while, but I'm going to miss you too." He pulled away and smiled gently at her. "I'm going to miss my family."

Jenny's lower lip wobbled. Gillon rested a hand on her shoulder and she turned into his chest. He kissed the top of her head as she cried.

Vance walked us to the door where Max shook the doorman's hand. Vance ordered him to return our weapons then check outside. "You'll leave Noxford immediately, won't you?" This he addressed to Dane.

Dane slid his sword into the scabbard. "First thing in the morning."

I stiffened but did not admonish him in front of the others. I waited until the lair was well behind us. "We can't leave until we've learned more about your past, Dane."

"I might not even be from here," he said.

"What about Balthazar? Something important drove him to leave Tilting and come to Freedland without informing anyone. We should find out what that is."

He hesitated before saying, "It's too dangerous for Max in Noxford, and probably for the rest of us too. Vance is right. If we're recognized by the wrong people, the authorities might come looking for us. They lied to the citizens about rounding up and executing the prisoners, and they won't want that lie exposed. Our appearance undermines their authority."

As one, all the men flipped up their hoods. I cast wary glances up and down the street, alert for constables. While Dane was right, and the city could prove dangerous, if he left now, he might never learn the answers he sought.

We had to rely on their memories returning to find out more about his past and that of the others. But without the gem or wishes, none of them would ever remember anything from before their time at the palace.

* * *

We collected Balthazar from the inn before heading out again to find the Zemayan named Taaj. Quentin filled him in on Max's news as we walked, making sure to remind Balthazar why he needed to keep his hood up and his face averted. By the time he finished the tale, Balthazar was aware of Max's past, the reason for his arrest, and Quentin's opinion of each of Max's friends.

Balthazar said nothing, however. He merely plodded along, carefully placing the end of his walking stick between each cobblestone for added stability. It seemed to be taking all of his concentration, until finally he broke the silence.

"I should not have come with you this afternoon," he finally said.

"Why not?" I asked. "You want to speak to Taaj."

"You're all capable of doing that without me, and I am a

195

liability. If we're recognized as escapees from the prison mine, I can't run."

"That's why you're wearing hoods."

"Promise me you will all run off if it comes to that."

When no one answered, he poked Dane in the back with the end of his walking stick. "Promise me."

"No one will recognize us," Dane said over his shoulder.

Theodore hooked his arm through Balthazar's. "No one will be left behind."

Balthazar appealed to me. "Josie, talk some sense into them."

I put my hands up in surrender and continued on.

"Meg, you're the sensible one," Balthazar said. "You understand the need for them to escape."

Meg merely shrugged.

Kitty was the only one to respond. "*She's* the sensible one? Well, I am rather offended, Bal. I'm quite sensible too."

Quentin scoffed. "You wanted to waste money on a sedan chair this morning."

Kitty made a miffed sound through her nose. "You're impertinent."

"This is true," Erik said with a serious nod.

"You don't even know what impertinent means," Quentin said.

"Do you?"

Quentin grunted. "Just keep a look out for constables."

The only constables we spotted were watching a small gathering of people protesting about the high prices of basic necessities. A man wearing the robes of the high minister's office stood on a crate and tried to make himself heard. The crowd jeered loudly but they weren't violent.

We found Taaj's shop squeezed between a chandler's and baker's shops. Unlike Tam's stall in Mull, Taaj's larger shop sold more than just spices and herbs. Colorful swathes of silk hung from the rafters like curtains while there were silk hats and bags propped up on the tables. The tang of incense smoke mingled with the spicy and herbal smells in a riot of scents that were quite overwhelming. Kitty sneezed and Quentin's eyes began to water. He offered to wait outside and was soon joined by Erik.

We assumed the man who greeted us from behind the counter must be Taaj or one of his Zemayan relatives. The distinct dark skin was a giveaway, as was the long black hair braided with ribbon. The bells attached to the ribbons tinkled as he looked up at us and smiled.

"Good afternoon," he said with only the faint hint of an accent. "You have traveled far to be here, I see. The ladies are from Glancia?"

"Yes," I said with a smile. "We all are, although not all of us are from there originally."

"It's a long time since I was in your fair land. A very long time." While he wasn't as old as Balthazar, I guessed him to be beyond middle-age going by the fine lines across his forehead and around his lips. "What news do you bring from there?"

"King Leon is dead," Max said bluntly.

Taaj's lips formed an O of surprise. Vance and the others hadn't known about Leon's death, either. It had occurred several weeks ago, and yet the news had not reached Noxford, or at least, not widely. It was a reminder that Freedland was very remote and trade infrequent between the two nations. It was also an indication that perhaps the Freedlandians didn't care what happened in a distant kingdom. Not only were they geographically distant but ideologically as well.

"What do you wish to buy today?" Taaj asked. "Spices? Silk?"

"Information." Dane dropped a pouch of coins on the counter. We had agreed to the sum on the way, although Max and Kitty thought the Zemayan should only be offered payment if he was reluctant to talk. Dane had argued that Taaj had no reason to be reluctant, but it was only polite to offer something in return since we weren't going to buy anything. Max became convinced but Kitty did not. She was overruled.

Taaj eyed the pouch but did not touch it. "I am just a humble spice and silk merchant from Zemaya. What information could I give such well traveled folk as yourselves?"

"We want to ask some questions about magic," Dane said.

Taaj busied himself with the bags of spices, shuffling them and inspecting them as if their contents had been moved. "You think because I am Zemayan that I know about magic?" He shook his head. "Few Zemayans believe, nowadays. Many of the ancient stories about the sorcerer have been lost, while others have been turned into children's tales to frighten them into good behavior. Magic is an ancient, mostly forgotten, belief."

Balthazar rested both hands on the head of his walking stick in front of him. "You haven't forgotten."

Taaj peered at Balthazar through his dark lashes. "You seem certain of yourself."

"Is your name Taaj?"

Taaj nodded.

"Then I am certain."

Taaj stepped back from the counter and regarded Balthazar warily, as if he were the sorcerer. "How so?"

"May I sit? We have traveled a long way to find you. My legs are tired."

Taaj hesitated before rounding the counter carrying a stool. He waited for Balathazar to sit then prompted him to answer. He was almost twitching with the effort of containing his anticipation.

"You went to the prison mine in Gull's Wing," Balthazar said. "You showed an interest in the story of the prisoners' escape and subsequent disappearance."

"They were later caught."

"You asked the tour guide, a former guard, if any of the prisoners had unearthed something in the mine just before their disappearance."

"So?" Taaj asked on a breath.

"So we think you wanted to know if one of the prisoners dug up a gemstone containing the sorcerer's magic."

Taaj returned to the other side of the counter, his steps slow, as if he were delaying his response. When he finally turned to us again, the wariness in his gaze was still there. "I have a minor curiosity about magic, that is all."

Balthazar muttered something under his breath and stamped the end of his walking stick into the floor. It was the most cantankerous display he'd shown in weeks. Despite the length of our journey, and its arduous nature, he had not once complained nor wished it to end. He had not tried to hurry us to

Noxford or to this point. But now that we were so close to answers, yet being denied them, he was letting his frustrations out.

"We need to tell him everything," I said. "Now is not the time to hold anything back."

"Agreed," Dane said. The others nodded too, even Balthazar.

Dane told Taaj all we knew about their memory loss, Leon's admission just before his death, the information we'd received from Lord Barborough, and finally what we'd discovered so far on this journey.

Taaj listened intently without interruption, although he nodded at the mention of Lord Barborough, as if he knew him or knew of him, and he looked surprised when Dane admitted they were most likely the escaped prisoners from Gull's Wing.

After a lengthy silence, Dane added, "We understand if you don't want to tell us anything knowing we are prisoners."

Meg stamped her hands on her hips and glared at Dane. "No, we do not understand. There is some evidence they were imprisoned on wrongful charges. They are good, decent folk, or the three of us would not be here still." She indicated Kitty, me and herself. "We would not care as much as we do about these men if they were terrible people. Now, we have paid you, and we will give you more if you wish it, but we have little more to give. Please, we are begging you, tell us how they can get their memories back."

Taaj blinked in surprise. "But you know how. He has already mentioned it." He nodded at Dane.

As one, we all leaned in a little. "We require the gem and wishes," Theodore said. "Is that correct?"

Taaj nodded. "The guard who killed the king—"

"Brant," I said.

"Brant told you the truth. He has the remaining wishes. He would have gained them when he killed the king."

I looked to Dane but his face remained passive.

Max, however, swore under his breath. "We should have imprisoned him when we had the chance so we know where to find him."

Taaj's eyes widened in alarm.

"Brant is not a nice man," I assured him. "But none of us would have imprisoned him."

Taaj didn't look convinced. "He cannot use the wishes without holding the gem. This you also know."

"We weren't sure," Dane said.

Taaj cleared his throat. "Do you not have the gem? Is that why you didn't ask Brant to wish for your memories to return? Because he couldn't without it?"

"They did have it," Kitty said. "But someone stole it."

Taaj's brows rose up his forehead. "Do you know who?"

Dane shook his head.

"We couldn't trust Brant to wish selflessly," I told Taaj. It was important that he knew he was helping worthy folk, not greedy ones like Brant and Barborough. "That's why Dane didn't tell him where he hid the gem. Brant couldn't be trusted not to use a final wish for his own gain. But as Kitty says, we no longer have the gem anyway. It was stolen. Your information is helpful but useless."

"Is there no other way for them to regain their memories?" Meg asked. "Can they strike a deal with the sorcerer?"

Taaj's bells tinkled as he shook his head. "The sorcerer is not a thing to be bargained with. It is not a human with thoughts and wishes, hopes and dreams, disappointments. Its magic is complex and vast, yet its rules are simple. The finder of the gem receives three wishes. Those wishes cannot be used to create more wishes, they cannot be used to make the wisher immortal, and they cannot be used against the sorcerer. When the three wishes are all used, the gem mysteriously disappears, to be found again by the next fortunate person."

"So we must find Brant for the wishes and the thief for the gem," Meg said, watching Max.

"Do you know who might have it?" Taaj asked.

"No," Dane said. "It's most likely someone back in Glancia who found it and thought it a pretty jewel."

Taaj sighed. "Pity."

"Thank you for your time," Dane said. "We appreciate you not asking for too much in exchange for the information."

Taaj smiled. "My pleasure. It has been an interesting and

enlightening experience meeting you. I have learned more from you than I could ever hope to learn in my lifetime from books. You have confirmed my life's beliefs, and for that, I am truly grateful." He bowed. "I have also learned how magnificent the sorcerer is. To change the geography of an entire continent to fulfill a wish is proof of the sorcerer's power."

We agreed, although no one displayed the same level of enthusiasm and awe as Taaj. It was one thing to simply study magic without being touched by it but quite another to have one's life changed because of it.

"Where are you staying?" Taaj suddenly asked. "I might think of something else that could be useful to your quest."

Dane gave him the name of an inn we'd passed on our walk to Taaj's shop, not the one where we stayed. None of us corrected him.

Outside, no one answered Quentin or Erik's questions. Dane asked them to wait until we were safely back at the inn. We remained alert as we headed there, looking out for constables who might recognize us, as well as Taaj in case he followed us, and Brant.

Now that we knew he wasn't lying about possessing the wishes, we'd be one step closer to success if only we could convince him to join us in searching for the gem. How we'd keep him from using the third wish for his own advantage was a point that required further discussion before he could be reunited with the gem.

Balthazar looked exhausted by the time we reached the inn. He sat heavily on the bed in the room we all crowded into and rubbed his knee. Dane and Max relayed to Quentin and Erik everything Taaj had told us, but I tuned out and joined Balthazar on the bed.

"Are you all right?" I asked.

He gave me a weak smile. "I will be."

"Are you tired? Do you want us to leave you alone to rest?"

"I want you to pass me the map."

I frowned. "Why? We know the way home from here."

"Just pass me the map, Josie." He pointed to the tube made of whale bone on the floor in the corner of the room.

I fetched it and handed it to him. He removed the lid and tipped out the rolled map. Instead of spreading it out on the bed, he set it aside. Then he reached his hand into the tube and pulled out a thin, circular piece of wood and set that aside too. He reached in once more, up to his elbow, and withdrew a small object.

The gaps between his fingers glowed.

I gasped so loudly the others fell silent and turned to me.

Balthazar opened his hand to reveal a gem the color of freshly spilled blood, pulsing and glowing softly as it drew on the magic contained within its victims.

CHAPTER 15

"**Y**ou've had it this entire time?" Quentin cried.

Theodore groaned. "Balthazar, how could you?"

Balthazar dropped the gem back into the map tube and replaced the false bottom to hide it. "It was safer to have everyone believe it was stolen."

"Safer?" Max snarled.

"While Dane was the only one who knew of its hiding place in Mull, his life was in danger. Or, more specifically, the lives of those he cared about." Balthazar didn't look at me, but I felt the weight of his words nevertheless. "Brant, or anyone who wanted the gem, could have threatened to harm someone to force Dane to give it up." He lifted his gaze to Dane. "What would you have done? Let Brant or Deerhorn harm Josie? Or give up the gem?"

Dane's cold glare forced Balthazar to look away.

"This way, no one could be made to give it up because no one knew who possessed it," Balthazar went on. "I don't regret my decision to take it. Anyway, what does it matter who has it or where it has been this entire time? It's useless without the wishes."

"Brant has the wishes," Max snapped. His big chest heaved with his deep breaths, as if he'd just fought a hard battle. "He could have wished for our memories back by now."

"You know why we couldn't trust Brant," Theodore said. "I think Bal did the right thing."

"I agree," Erik said. "This changes nothing. We did not know that Brant had the wishes for certain until today. At least we do not need to return to Mull to find the gem. We have it here. All we need to do is find Brant and tell him to use a wish to return our memories."

Quentin agreed. "Considering Brant followed us from Glancia to Vytill, he shouldn't be too hard to find again. He'll be looking for us."

Max crossed his arms. "You should have told us, Bal."

Balthazar replaced the lid on the tube. "We still have the same problem as before—how do we stop Brant from using the third wish for his own selfish purposes? We cannot afford to have another Leon on our hands."

"So what do you propose we do?" Meg asked.

No one had a suggestion and eventually most gazes fell on Dane. I was painfully aware that he hadn't spoken since Balthazar revealed he had the gem. The firmness of his jaw gave away his thoughts on that, but he did not voice them. Not even when the silence became suffocating.

It was Balthazar who eventually broke it. He'd been the only one who hadn't turned to Dane for a solution. "I wanted to be sure before suggesting this, and now I am. Taaj's information convinced me."

"Convinced you about what?" Quentin asked.

"He confirmed that Brant inherited the wishes by killing Leon. That means Brant's killer will inherit the wishes."

I gasped. "Bal, no."

Kitty covered her mouth and Meg paled. "Dear Hailia," she muttered. "You can't."

"I needed to be sure," Balthazar said again. He had thought this through. Not just since leaving Taaj's shop, but for a long time. Perhaps from even before he stole the gem. Indeed, I suspected this was why he had stolen it in the first place.

Balthazar patted my hand, as if confirming my thoughts. "I needed to be absolutely certain that Brant had the wishes and that his killer will inherit the remaining two. We now know that to be true."

"Who'll do it?" Quentin's question, spoken in a small voice, filled the room as if it were as loud as an explosion.

He was the first to look to Dane. Once again, the others followed suit.

"That's not fair," I snapped. "Dane can't have that on his conscience. None of us can. Nobody should—"

"I'll do it," Balthazar cut in.

"I know you think it's the honorable thing to do, but think about what you're suggesting, Bal. It's murder."

"For the greater good."

"It's still murder!"

Balthazar heaved himself to his feet with effort. "My decision is made. There'll be no more discussion on the matter."

"But—"

"Enough, Josie!"

I pressed my lips together and appealed to Theodore. Theodore cleared his throat and took up the protest.

"She's right," he said. "If you kill Brant, it will weigh on your conscience, Bal. I can't allow that."

"*We* can't allow it," Dane added.

"You don't get a say in what I do," Balthazar said. "That's enough about Brant for now." He indicated the door. "Let's go downstairs. I'm hungry and thirsty."

The others filed out ahead of us, but Balthazar asked Dane and me to remain a moment.

"You're still angry with me," he said to Dane.

Dane grunted. "Am I that easy to read?"

"Your jaw is so hard I could break rocks on it. Go on. Out with it. Berate me for stealing the gem and lying about it so we can go downstairs and enjoy our meal."

Dane crossed his arms and settled his feet apart. He peered down his nose at Balthazar, who looked every bit like a little old man next to him. It was almost laughable to think he planned on killing Brant. The former guard would overpower him in a moment.

"You should have kept me informed," Dane said. "We're on the same side."

"Are we? We don't know a thing about ourselves, let alone each other."

Dane bristled. "I know who I can trust. I thought I could trust you."

"I like to think I can trust you too, but can I? Who are you, Dane?"

Dane shifted his weight. His gaze flicked to me then back again. I opened my mouth to come to his rescue, to tell Balthazar that I trusted Dane completely, when Balthazar spoke first.

"You're half-Glancian, half-Freedlandian. Do you have an allegiance to one nation over the other?"

"Does it matter?" I asked.

Balthazar ignored me. He only had eyes for Dane. "You're educated, good with a sword, knife, on horseback, with your fists. You're charming when you want to be and have a fierce temper when things don't go your way."

Dane's gaze slid to me again. "Have you two been talking?"

"To be all of those things is…intriguing at best, worrying at worst."

"Worrying?" I prompted. "In what way?"

Balthazar sighed and lifted one stooped shoulder. "I'm not entirely sure. There's something about him. Something out of the ordinary. He's too…"

"Perfect?" I asked.

"No," they both said at the same time.

"It's difficult to explain, but I just have a feeling that something's strange about him," Balthazar said. "It might be something good. We cannot be sure until his memory returns or until we find someone who knows him."

Or it might be something bad, he could have said, but did not.

Dane eyed Balthazar closely, and I suspected his temper bubbled away just beneath the surface, ready to boil over. "The warrior priests are all those things too," he pointed out.

"And I don't trust them. Dane, it's not personal. I don't even trust myself at this point. Does that make you feel better?"

"No." Dane strode out of the room, leaving Balthazar and me behind.

Balthazar indicated I should take his elbow and walk with him. "He'll calm down eventually. He might even come to agree with me. It's not personal, Josie," he said again. "You know that."

"Saying that it's not doesn't make it so. It *is* personal, Bal, and you've hurt his feelings. He trusts you. Or he did before you stole the gem from under his nose."

"He shouldn't have trusted me."

"He has known you for months. He has lived and worked with you every day. That's long enough to make the right decision about your character."

"That's where you and I shall have to disagree."

We headed down the steep stairs, going slowly as Balthazar kept one hand on the railing and I held on to his other arm. I could see the others waiting for us through the open door to the dining room. To my surprise, Dane was with them. I thought he'd stormed off in a fit of temper and needed to cool down.

Balthazar must have seen my surprise. "You soften him," he said quietly. "Why do you think I asked you to stay back just now? It wasn't because I wanted your opinion. I already know it. It was to stop him from making me feel like Quentin after a session in the training yard."

Dane suddenly looked up and his gaze connected with mine. There was no anger in his eyes now, no stiffness to his back or jaw, just the forlorn look of a dog that had been kicked by his master.

It took me a moment to realize that Balthazar's words had sunk in, just as they were sinking in for me. Perhaps Balthazar was right and Dane was too good to be true.

Perhaps the sorcerer had conjured him after all, to keep Leon safe.

* * *

THE DINNER CONVERSATION WAS SUBDUED. Aside from one brief decision that had to be made, we avoided all discussion of the gem and Brant. The decision to remain in Noxford a little longer in order to find Brant was made quickly and without debate. We all agreed that finding him was a priority now.

The following morning, while the men wore their hoods and kept their faces obscured, Kitty, Meg and I made sure our blonde hair was visible. Glancian women were a rarity in Freedland, so we hoped word would spread quickly of our presence. If Brant were in Noxford, he would hear and come looking for us.

Hopefully Lord Xavier hadn't come with him. Facing Brant was never an easy task, but facing them both wasn't something I wanted to do, even when surrounded by armed men.

We headed into the market and moved around the town square. We loitered outside the high temple, but with Balthazar's hood flipped up, there was no opportunity for the priests to recognize him. Discovering his reason for coming to Freedland was no longer a priority anyway. Getting back their memories was more important.

The day drew on and still there was no sign of Brant. Our little party grew restless with frustration. All except Dane. He remained alert, his hand resting on his sword hilt, his gaze scanning the shadows growing longer as the day wore on.

"He's not here," Quentin declared as he sat on the edge of the large fountain in the middle of the square.

Balthazar sat beside him with a groan. "I think you're right. He would have come forward by now."

"Unless he's too frightened," Meg said. "He's just one man and he knows we dislike him."

"Should we split up?" Theodore asked Dane.

Dane shook his head. "We need to stay together. Someone's following us."

We all looked around the square. I spotted several men standing alone who could be watching us, but I couldn't be sure and Dane didn't point any out.

"So what do we do?" I asked.

"Wait for them to declare themselves. If it were me, I'd make a move in the dark."

"Do you think it's Brant?" Quentin asked.

Dane merely shrugged.

Max put a hand to his sword hilt and stood beside Dane. "Who else could it be?"

As the sun slipped below the city's buildings, the square emptied and folk moved to the surrounding streets where food sellers plied their trade. Bakers sold pies from shop windows and honeyed nuts could be bought by the handful from hawker's carts. Theodore discovered he adored figs, while I tried as many exotic Freedlandian dishes as I could, as did Meg. Kitty screwed her nose up at everything that looked too different and refused to try a thing.

The city seemed to come alive in the evening. Perhaps the warmer weather made it more conducive to strolling through the streets when compared to Glancia. Cool autumn nights seemed alien here.

"Oh look, fire dancers," Kitty said, nudging Erik with her elbow.

Erik didn't follow the direction of her pointing finger to the group of scantily clad men and women dancing with fire sticks. Like Dane, Max and Quentin, he watched the people around us, alert for anyone following.

As darkness descended, more entertainers emerged to the delight of the growing crowd. It wasn't just fire dancers, but singers and musicians, poets and orators. More than one politician drew an audience of both supporters and detractors. The two sides sometimes jostled one another, or shouted over the top of the orator, but that was as vigorous as it got. Even the large group led by supporters of the current high minister that walked through the streets, shouting their leader's virtues and policies, was met with nothing worse than fist shakes and shouted rebuttals. It made Mull's riots seem barbaric.

"This is truly an amazing country," Meg said as she watched the rally pass us by. "They've come a long way from their revolutionary days."

I stepped back as one of the high minister's supporters suddenly thrust out his hand. But it merely held a leaflet that he shoved at me before passing another to Theodore. "I can't imagine such a peaceful rally happening in Mull," I said. "Or Tilting, for that matter."

"Nor Merrin Fahl," Kitty added. "And the Vytillians consider themselves the most civilized of all the Fist countries."

Meg watched the procession with wonder. "*This* is civilized. Freedland and its people are remarkable."

I looked at Dane to see if he'd taken note of the procession too, but he was intently watching the crowd from beneath his hood.

I knew the moment something was amiss when his eyes flared. He darted forward, pushing me aside as he did so. "Get back," he growled.

As if they'd been commanded, Max, Erik and Quentin fell in alongside Dane and went to draw their weapons, but stopped on Dane's barked order.

"What is it?" Max asked, squinting into the shadows of a recessed doorway. "Did you recognize Brant?"

"Not Brant." Dane ordered Max and Quentin to stay with us then he and Erik dove through the crowd and disappeared from sight.

I stood on my toes to see where they went, only to receive a sharp jab in my ribs. I swung around and gasped. "Lord Barborough!"

"Don't scream," he said. "I have you surrounded."

As if a veil had been lifted from my eyes, I now spotted all his men. There must be almost a dozen of them, all dressed in the clothes of Freedlandians. I'd wager they were Vytill palace guards, come all the way from Merrin to capture us and take us back to King Phillip.

"Unhand her," Max demanded.

Lord Barborough chuckled low in his chest. "I have only one good arm so do not have her in hand."

Quentin jerked his head at me. "Walk away, Josie. He won't hurt you here."

"Won't I? Would you like to try it, Miss Cully?"

I swallowed as the sharp point dug into my flesh.

"Leave us alone," Meg snapped. "We don't have what you want."

Beside her, Kitty had pulled her hood over her head and was

studying the ground at her feet. Lord Barborough made no indication that he recognized her. Hopefully she was safe.

"I am aware that you may have lied to Princess Illiriya," Lord Barborough conceded. "That's why I'm going to take Miss Cully as prisoner. She will only be released when you retrieve the gem and wishes. Whether you currently have them is of no consequence to me. It's *getting* them that counts."

"This is madness," Theodore muttered as he scanned the street.

"Hammer won't rescue you," Lord Barborough told him. "One of my men is leading him on a merry dance through the city. By the time he returns, either you will have given me what I want, or I will have taken Miss Cully prisoner."

"I won't simply go with you," I said.

The point pierced fabric and bit into flesh. I sucked in air through my teeth.

Balthazar stepped towards me. "Let her go. I'll give you the gem."

I glared at him but he ignored me.

Lord Barborough hesitated, perhaps caught off guard by the admission. Then he said, "Where is it?"

"Careful," Theodore hissed. "Don't trust him, Bal. Wait for Dane—"

"We wait for no one!" Lord Barborough's shout was loud in my ear, and I jerked my head away. The guards stepped forward upon seeing some movement.

Quentin went to draw his sword. "No!" I cried. "Don't." I wanted to tell them not to take on Barborough's guards here in the crowded streets where there were too many witnesses. If we could lead them somewhere quiet and overpower them, we would regain the advantage. I could defend myself against Barborough and his knife. With only one good arm, he would be easy to outmaneuver. But it would be a difficult task for Max and Quentin to fight off all the guards. The numbers were not in our favor and I couldn't see Dane and Erik anywhere.

I hoped they were all right.

"Take me to the gem," Lord Barborough said to Balthazar.

"But do not attempt to use your weapons. If I am slain, the men have orders to retrieve the gem and wishes by force."

Balthazar grunted. "You would lay down your life for your king's greed?"

I heard Lord Barborough's wet smile in my ear. "It's highly unlikely I will die here today. If my life is in danger, I'll ram my knife through Miss Cully's gut. Is her life worth more to you than the gem, old man?"

Balthazar turned. "Follow me."

He led the way out of the main street into a nearby narrow one. We followed in a strange kind of procession, with guards behind Quentin and Max, then Lord Barborough and me, followed by Theodore, Kitty and Meg and more Vytill guards. Balthazar's infirmity kept our pace slow.

Slow enough for me to consider ways to extricate myself. I could get away from Lord Barborough, but the guards were the problem. I didn't want to put Quentin and Max's lives in danger. A distraction would help, but it would need to be a large one.

It came in the form of a voice behind me. "Take their weapons."

I turned sharply and would have earned myself another jab in the ribs from Lord Barborough's knife if he hadn't been ripped from my side. Dane pushed a sword into my hand and streamed past me, cloak billowing, while Erik pushed Lord Barborough to the ground. He landed at Theodore's feet.

"Watch him," Erik barked before joining Dane, now engaged in a sword fight with the guards at the front. The bodies of the rear guards littered the empty street behind. Their deaths had been swift, silent.

The battle was quickly over. With our four guards against the remaining five, it was no contest. They gave up when they realized they couldn't win.

Lord Barborough still lay at Theodore's feet, a sword pointed at his throat. Meg stood over him too, arms crossed, while Kitty wisely melted into the shadows. Her caution was unnecessary. Lord Barborough only had eyes for Dane.

"Where did you come from?" he squeaked.

"The roof," Erik said, sheathing his sword and grinning. "We flew down and landed quietly on your men."

"We didn't even see or hear them," Theodore said without looking up from Lord Barborough. "Not until they'd killed all the guards behind us."

Lord Barborough swallowed and glanced around. The street might be quiet but we were still exposed. Anyone could walk by at any moment.

"Put all weapons away," I said. "We don't want to make a scene."

Dane came up alongside me, his sword already sheathed. He pressed a hand to my lower back, as if to ask if I was all right. I gave him a single nod and he lowered his hand again and stepped towards Barborough. He grabbed him by the front of his jerkin and pulled him to his feet.

"Do not move or attempt to harm my friends," he ordered. "Unless you want me to alert the constables that you have a party of armed Vytillian royal guards with you."

Lord Barborough rubbed his throat where the point of the sword had pressed.

By the light of a flickering torch, I could just make out the hard glint in Dane's eye. "It will be my pleasure to see you arrested, not to mention sate my curiosity," he said.

"Curiosity?" Barborough asked with a jut of his chin.

"As to how a republic treats the threat of royalist invasion from Vytill."

"This is no invasion!"

"Good luck trying to convince them."

If Lord Barborough knew the men were escaped criminals from the prison mine, he could call Dane's bluff and tell him to go ahead and report him, knowing full well it would only bring unwanted attention to us too.

"You five, leave," Dane ordered the guards.

All ran off without a second glance at Lord Barborough. He watched them go with a pained look on his face.

"Follow me." Dane led the way through alleys and streets, around bends, and we ended up back in the busy part of the city where the nighttime revels had become louder, the crowd thicker. The bodies of the other guards would soon be found, and we didn't want to be anywhere near them, but we didn't want to take Lord Barborough back to our inn either.

A minstrel rode past on a small horse, playing a flute, a trail of children behind him, laughing and dancing. Dane waited for them to pass by before rounding on Lord Barborough.

"You will leave the city tonight. Do you understand?"

"I can't." Lord Barborough's voice cracked.

Dane drew himself up to his full height, arms crossed over his chest.

"I can't!" Lord Barborough said again. "The king will have me killed if I return without the gem and wishes."

"Then you'd better make Freedland your new home. Just stay away from us."

Dane signaled that we should leave and he turned away. Lord Barborough grabbed his arm, but Dane pushed him off and Lord Barborough fell. Erik and Max hauled the Vytill spy to his feet before anyone noticed. Lord Barborough looked as though he would burst into tears at any moment.

"Freedland is not such a bad place," I told him cheerfully. "I think you'll like it here. Look how happy everyone is."

"Happy?" he blurted out. "They live with high taxes. There is very little money left over for people like me." He indicated his limp arm. "There is no respect for the nobility, only for money. Industry and trade rule here, not breeding or family. If that's what you call happy, then you are not looking deeply enough, Miss Cully. You are only seeing the surface. People like me are miserable. Open your eyes and you'll see the beggars. Please, you must help me. Give me the third wish. That's all I ask. Please, I'm begging you. Let me return home with my dignity. Let me prove to King Phillip that I'm not useless. If I return with nothing, I will be executed." He licked his lips and inched closer to Dane. "Is that what you want on your conscience?"

"You have no bargaining power," Dane said. "Why would we give you the third wish?"

Lord Barborough closed his eyes, his mouth twisted in anguish. I would have felt sorry for him if he hadn't tried to stab me on multiple occasions.

"Let's go," Meg said. "He doesn't deserve our sympathy."

Lord Barborough suddenly straightened. "Will you get a message to the princess for me? She'll protect me from her father. I know she will."

"Doing so will place her in jeopardy," Theodore said. "You would do that to your princess?"

Lord Barborough went to grasp Dane's arm again, but Dane shook him off. "We are not returning via Vytill. We can't deliver your message for you."

He walked off and all followed except Balthazar and me. I stayed because of the strange look on his face.

"Bal?" I prompted as the others stopped up ahead to see why we hadn't followed. "What is it?"

"He can help us find Brant."

At the mention of Brant's name, Lord Barborough's lips parted in a silent gasp.

"Have you seen him recently?" I asked.

Lord Barborough shut his mouth.

Dane approached, his arms crossed, a frown on his face. "You want to tell him?" he asked Balthazar. "Is that wise?"

"If nothing else, it will let him know once and for all that we don't have the wishes."

Lord Barborough's lips curled in a sneer. "If I believe you."

Dane shrugged at Balthazar. "*If* he believes us."

"It's worth a try," I added. "What does everyone else think? Should we tell him what we know?"

All except Theodore agreed. "We shouldn't help him," he said.

"We won't be helping him. He's going to help us by finding Brant and bringing him to us because I suspect he knows where Brant is. Don't you, my lord?"

Lord Barborough's sneer turned to a smug smile.

Dane nodded at Balthazar to go on.

"We went to a Zemayan here in Noxford," Balthazar explained. "It turns out he was quite knowledgeable about magic. More so than you."

Lord Barborough frowned. "There's a Zemayan here? In

Noxford? But they never venture so far from their homeland except to trade. They don't stay."

"This one did. You can question him for yourself, if you like, but you won't learn anything different from what I am about to tell you. He's a spice and silk merchant by the name of Taaj." He leaned both hands on the head of his walking stick. "We asked him questions about the gem and wishes. It would seem that Brant was telling the truth. He must have the wishes."

Lord Barborough rubbed his chin and jaw. "Because he killed Leon?"

Balthazar nodded. "Unused wishes are inherited by the killer."

Lord Barborough's hand stilled. "So if someone kills Brant, they will inherit the wishes?"

Nobody answered him.

"And the gem?" Lord Barborough asked. "That's needed to use the wishes, yes?"

Balthazar nodded. "You had that part right. The problem is, we don't know who has it, and that is a fact."

He was a very good liar. It was how he'd been able to hide the theft from us all this time without any of us suspecting.

Lord Barborough, however, wasn't inclined to believe him and told him so.

Balthazar merely shrugged. "Believe us or not. It doesn't matter. You won't get the gem from us. Your failed attempt this evening proved that. It will take King Phillip's entire army to get us to give in, but it would be for nothing because we don't have it. All we do know for certain is that Brant has the wishes. We must find him then go in search of the gem. Do you understand?"

"Of course I do," snapped Lord Barborough. "You want me to lead you to Brant because you assume I know where he is. Well I don't. He's gone. He left Noxford two days ago after an incident."

"What sort of incident?" Dane asked.

Max and Theodore drew closer to hear, while Quentin and Erik glanced at one another.

Lord Barborough's eyes narrowed. "This news intrigues you?"

"What happened?" Dane snapped.

"He came here looking for all of you. Like me, he assumed you would arrive in Noxford sooner or later. But someone reported him to the authorities after recognizing him. Several constables tried to arrest him in the main square. He barely escaped."

"Arrested on what charge?" Balthazar asked idly.

Lord Barborough's gaze flicked between all the men and his tongue darted out, licking his lower lip. "Ah. So it *is* related to the pasts you've forgotten. You were all there together, weren't you?"

"What are you talking about?" Max growled.

"It's intriguing, isn't it? As much as you try to distance yourselves from him, you are all just like Brant."

"They're nothing like him," I blurted out.

Lord Barborough chuckled. "That's where you're wrong. Brant was arrested for being an escaped prisoner, and they were prisoners with him. Isn't that so? They're criminals too. It seems they've managed to hide their true natures from you. If I were you, Miss Cully, I'd be careful. Especially of this one." He nodded at Dane. "With the moniker Hammer, there's no doubt he went to the prison mine. He's just a thug like Brant."

"You're wrong. They're good men."

He clicked his tongue, over and over. "I wonder what the response will be if I make it known that I have several escaped prisoners here. Will you all be re-arrested?"

"You won't do it," Balthazar said. "Because you believe we have the gem."

"They can arrest the men and leave the women free. One of them will tell me where to find the gem once my men finish *coercing* them."

Dane's fist connected with Lord Barborough's mouth, sending him reeling. "Why not try calling for the constables? Then you'll know for certain what we'll do to the man who is of no use to us."

Lord Barborough spat blood onto the cobbles. "Get away from me."

Balthazar tapped his lordship's leg with his walking stick. "Not yet. Not until you tell us where Brant went."

Lord Barborough dabbed at his cut lip. "I don't know. He wouldn't confide in me, would he? He most likely traveled with Lord Xavier Deerhorn and his retinue. I haven't seen either of them since the trouble. My guess is they went back to Glancia where Lord Xavier is needed by his family. The situation there is becoming precarious, and the Deerhorns have a lot to lose if events don't go the duke of Gladstow's way."

"What are the developments with the Glancian situation?" Balthazar asked. "Is a war between the dukes imminent?"

Lord Barborough's sneer returned. "Very."

"Thanks to your king's interference."

Lord Barborough showed no sign of surprise, nor did he try to persuade Balthazar that King Phillip had nothing to do with the dukes thinking they had more support from the Glancian lords than they did. Both dukes assumed they could win based on the pledges of the noblemen—pledges that had been falsified by the Vytill king.

With the dukes manipulated into starting a war too soon, their unprepared forces would be decimated when pitted against each another, allowing King Phillip to swoop in with fresh troops and take over. As a distant cousin to the last king of Glancia, he would also have a legitimate claim to the throne, although a somewhat tenuous one.

It was a neat move, and one I couldn't see failing. Vytill was too strong and the dukes of Glancia too ignorant of his machinations.

My country was about to be plunged into war.

Meg's fingers found mine and we held on to one another. She had more to lose than me. Her brother and father would be called to fight. Her sister and mother would be vulnerable to the whims of conquering soldiers. I didn't even have a home to lose.

There was only one way out that I could see. Warn the duke of Buxton, the more sensible of Glancia's two dukes. If he could be persuaded of King Phillip's interference, then he might not engage the duke of Gladstow yet. He might search for a political resolution.

But we could not warn him. We were as far from Glancia as we could possibly be. Even if we left tomorrow, it might be too late.

Dane stepped aside, opening the way for Lord Barborough to leave. His lordship dabbed at his lip again and went to walk off, but Dane put out an arm, blocking him.

"You will not come near us again. Next time, I *will* kill you. Is that clear?"

Lord Barborough swallowed. "It seems I won't be returning to my king with the gem or wishes." His gaze wandered to the fire dancers and revelers enjoying the music and food. There was no disgust in his eyes now, nor distress. Merely acceptance. He pushed past Dane.

When he was safely at a distance, he turned around. "Did it ever occur to you that the sorcerer did you all a favor by erasing your memories?" When no one answered, he grunted and trudged off.

His words stayed with me, however, and I knew from the silence of the others that they stayed with them too.

We kept a wary eye on proceedings as we headed back to the inn. As we moved away from the city square, the streets grew quieter and the crowd thinned, but with so few lit torches lining the way, it was impossible to be certain that we weren't followed.

Quentin was quite sure Lord Barborough had given up, however. "He knows the captain is serious about killing him next time."

"Dane," Dane reminded him. "Not captain."

Quentin went on as if he hadn't heard him. "You and Erik dispatched those guards real quick. I didn't hear a thing. I'd wager they didn't, either. They didn't utter a peep. Did you hear them, Josie?"

"I heard nothing," I said. "Dane and Erik were completely silent."

"I didn't get a good look at the bodies. Did you slit their throats, Captain? You told me once that it was the quickest way to kill a man, but you got to make the cut real deep and do it real fast before he can cry out. Is that right, Josie? Is that how to kill someone quickly and silently?"

"I suppose so," I said.

He fell into step beside me. "Can you stop a man from dying

if you get to him fast after his throat is cut? Or is death inevitable?"

"You can't fix a deep cut through the throat."

Kitty made a sound of disgust. "Must we have this discussion now?"

"Would you prefer they have it later?" Meg asked.

"I don't care, just as long as I am not there. It's too macabre for me." She hooked her arm through Erik's.

He kissed her forehead. "You did well, Kitty. You hid your face when Barborough appeared. He did not see you."

She wrinkled her nose. "Horrid man. I hope the only work he finds here is cleaning out cesspits."

"Or scooping up horse dung," Quentin chimed in.

"Or work in a tannery," Meg added.

They laughed.

I took the opportunity of their distraction to fall back and have a quiet word with Dane. "Did you know Lord Barborough was near?"

"I knew someone was there, waiting for an opportunity to make themselves known."

Theodore turned around, having overheard. "Then why did you leave to chase after shadows?"

"My leaving was the only way to draw them out. Erik had to come with me—or Max—or Barborough wouldn't have attacked."

"You left us vulnerable on purpose?" Theodore asked.

"You weren't vulnerable. Barborough wouldn't attempt to kill anyone in full public view. He knew he'd never escape."

By now the others had stopped their discussion and were listening too. Kitty seemed the most horrified by Dane's admission. "You gambled with our lives?"

"A calculated gamble."

Erik patted her hand. "Trust the captain. He would not gamble with Josie's life."

"So I must stay close to Josie or risk my life being gambled away next time?"

"Not at all," Dane said. "I value your company too, just as I value everyone's."

"Oh. You do?" She looked pleased.

"Of course he does," I said on Dane's behalf when he didn't elaborate. "Everyone in this group has a reason for being here. In your case, who else could we tease about her princess ways?"

She tossed her blonde hair over her shoulder. "Duchess, thank you. Princesses are terrible snobs."

* * *

WE DECIDED over dinner to leave Noxford first thing in the morning. With Brant most likely having returned to Glancia, and with the Glancian war looming, we unanimously agreed to cut short our visit. Balthazar's reason for secretly coming to Freedland would have to remain a mystery.

With Max's past already discovered, that left only Dane and Quentin as potential Freedlanders with something to learn about themselves there. Quentin was quite happy to abandon the search for his family and, to my surprise, Dane readily agreed too.

I sought him out later to learn why.

"Come with me for a walk," he said when I accosted him outside his room.

"Is it safe?" I asked.

"Lord Barborough has no more men who'll follow him, and Brant and Deerhorn have left the city. No one will attack us."

Even so, I put my hood up. Dane did too.

We walked in the direction of the river and once we reached the bank, Dane sat on the grass. He patted the patch beside him.

"Should I lay my cloak down for you?" he asked.

"I'm not Kitty," I said, laughing as I sat.

"She would take offense at that these days."

The river was narrow at this point, but quiet. No boats sailed past in the night, and the docks were further north. A water bird flapped its wings as it settled in the reeds to our right, and the symphony of chirping insects surrounded us, but otherwise, the night was calm.

My heart was anything but. Its erratic beat tapped against my ribs as I waited for Dane to tell me why he'd asked me to walk with him. My nerves stretched thin as he lay down on the grass, hands behind his head, and stared up at the stars. It was a long moment before he spoke.

"I like the sky at night," he said simply. "But I never noticed it in Mull."

I glanced up too. "Why not?"

"I was too busy. There was always something to do, somewhere to go, even at night. I never stopped and gazed up." The moon was a mere sliver and did not offer much light in which to see his expression by. His voice, however, was deep, yet soft and filled with awe. "It's amazing, isn't it? There are so many stars. I didn't realize how many until we began this journey and I looked up properly for the first time."

I lay down next to him and studied the sky too, but I was more in awe of Dane than the stars. He never ceased to amaze me. This softness was unexpected after such a day as we'd had.

"I wonder if I ever noticed the night sky before," he said. "Did I take the time to count the stars, see their patterns, or was I too busy?"

"Is this your way of saying you want to stay in Noxford to find out if you're from here?"

"The opposite." He propped himself up on one elbow and turned to face me. "I'm telling you I want to go home. I want to continue to take the time to gaze up at the stars, but not here."

Home. "Do you mean Mull?"

"Yes." It was barely a whisper louder than my own. "I want to go home to Mull and be with the woman I love."

All the breath left my body, leaving me light-headed and a little faint. "Oh," I managed to whisper. "Do you mean me?"

There was enough light to see him inch closer. His face filled my vision and despite the darkness, I could make out the intensity in his eyes, the shine of his wonder. That was for me. All for me.

The kiss shattered me into a thousand pieces. It enveloped me with its heat and pushed out all common sense. There was just Dane and his body pressing against mine, his mouth exploring, tasting, devouring, as if he couldn't get enough of me.

I couldn't get enough of him, of his kiss. I ached for his

mouth to kiss me everywhere, for his exploration to find the secret places of me and make them his own. As his lips moved to my throat, I arched up to meet him and groaned.

The sound startled some sense into me. I pushed him away only to instantly regret the loss of his touch.

"Josie?" The vulnerable hitch in his voice tugged at my heart. I wished I could see his face properly and that he could see mine so he knew how much I wanted him to continue.

But something had to be said before we got to the point where we couldn't stop.

I clasped his face in both hands and caressed his cheeks. "I don't want you doing something you'll regret later, Dane."

The softest sigh escaped his lips. "I could not bring myself to regret this. But if you want to wait, I will do my best to resist you."

I smiled. "Resisting is the last thing I want to do."

I felt his smile in my hands. It was as though I'd captured it, held it. I certainly cherished it.

"I am worried this isn't what you really want right now," I went on. "It wasn't that long ago that you declared you needed to learn more about your past before we could be together. What's changed?"

"Everything. But Brant, mostly."

"That's not a name I expected to hear at a moment like this."

"I can't murder him, Josie. Not even to get my memories back. Nor can I sit by while someone else does it. Even if Balthazar is the one to kill him, Brant's death would be on all our consciences. My memories aren't worth that."

"So…you're giving up?"

He kissed my palm. "You could say that. Ever since realizing that killing Brant is the only way we'll get his wishes, I've been thinking about what my memories mean to me. I've decided they don't mean as much to me as my future with you."

I opened my mouth but only a gasp came out. I could think of nothing to say. Mere words could not do justice to the sacrifice he was making for us to be together. He was giving up his entire past for me. He was drawing a line under it and turning away. He was facing forwards and embracing the future.

A future with me.

"I've been thinking how my life would be without memories," he went on. "In Mull, I was too busy to truly think, but ever since leaving to go on this journey, I've had a lot of time. I've decided that releasing my memories might be the only chance of happiness I'll get."

"I don't understand."

"Barborough might be right. Perhaps the sorcerer did me a good service. Listen," he said when I protested. "I've already learned that I committed a terrible crime and landed in prison, and that I beat a guard with my hammer. I'm willing to concede that something happened to drive me to do those things. But maybe it's for the best that I don't remember them. Maybe it's for the best that those incidents are lost to me. It gives me a chance to be the man I want to be, not the man I once was, formed by a past that may not have been pleasant, to put it lightly."

"Ignorance is bliss?"

"So they say. Look at Theodore, for example. He has no interest in returning to Dreen to learn more about himself, and he seems happy. What he has discovered so far is enough to satisfy his curiosity. And the other servants who remained at the palace could have left to find out more about themselves, but they chose to stay. They chose to remain ignorant of their pasts. Perhaps they're the happiest of all of us."

I could see his point. But Dane wasn't like other people. He had a strong sense of duty and responsibility, for one thing. "What of the people you left behind?" I asked in a small voice. "What if you have a family?"

He stroked the hair at my temple then his thumb caressed my jawline. "They think I'm dead. As far as they know, I was executed along with the other escaped prisoners. It's more than likely they've moved on. If I was married, my widow could have remarried by now. My showing up alive would cause problems."

He did not mention children and nor did I. Some things were too painful to put into words.

Part of me worried that he was not sincere. That he was taking the easier path because he thought it was what he wanted. I doubted he could truly move forward into a future with me, not wholeheartedly and without regret. Not without wondering what, or who, he'd left behind.

But my reservations were soon shredded along with my resolve to keep my distance. I was weak where he was concerned. Especially when he did such wonderful things with his hands and said such beautiful words that scattered my wits and filled my heart.

"I love you, Josie. I want to be with you forever. I don't want to waste my future looking for my past. I have the opportunity to make new memories." He kissed me lightly, tentatively, as if testing my willingness to continue, to accept him and this new philosophy. "I want to make new memories with you."

I pulled his head down and met his mouth with a hungry, passionate kiss. He returned it, sating my hunger with his own voracious appetite. I buried my hands in his hair as he tugged up the hem of my skirts. He caressed my calf, inching higher, higher.

"Josie…" he murmured against my mouth. "I want you."

"Yes," I gasped out.

His hand stroked my thigh, sending waves of desire rippling through me. "May I…?"

"Hmmm," I murmured. "You may."

* * *

WE WALKED hand in hand back to the inn. I was finally able to see his face as we passed a torch lighting a tavern entrance, and what I saw made me smile. He looked happy. I hoped so. I wanted him to be happy more than anything. I wanted what he said to me on the riverbank to be true, that he was ready to leave his past behind and move forward with me.

We would know, in time. For now, the decision had been made and we were heading back to Mull to make a new life together.

He stopped me in the circle of light cast by the torch at the inn's front door and plucked a leaf out of my hair. "Everyone will know what we've been doing if you walk in looking like you've been rolling around on the ground."

I smiled against his mouth. "Let them. I don't care."

He smiled too and kissed me.

With our eyes closed, we didn't see the assailant until too late. Dane's body suddenly jerked and he arched his back, growling in pain. He shoved me away from him then swung around, drawing his sword in the same motion. Blood dampened the clothes at his back.

There was not one assailant but four. All wore hoods, unlike us. We'd not put them back up after leaving the river. Foolish, stupid mistake.

Dane engaged two of the men while the other two lashed out. Dane managed to fend them off, but only just. Each strike sent him backwards. Each blow and kick beat him down. With a deep wound already bleeding profusely, his movements were hindered. He could not fight them all off.

"Max!" I screamed as loud as I could. "Erik!"

Dane was cut and cut again as he weakened and his assailants struck relentlessly. Help would not arrive quickly enough to save him.

I grabbed the torch from the wall bracket and lunged at the man about to swing his blade at Dane's head. My blow wasn't strong enough to render him unconscious. It merely distracted him enough to miss Dane. But the fire set his hood alight.

One of the others also became distracted by my torch. I swung it from the right, and he dodged left, straight into the point of my surgical knife. He hissed in pain then gritted his teeth and came at me. I ducked out of the way and tripped him up with the torch.

He fell face first onto the pavement in front of the door. Erik opened the door and drove his sword through the man's throat, then stepped over him.

Dane grunted as he fended off another blow, but with only two assailants left, he was able to beat them back alone. When they saw Erik and Max emerge from the inn, they abandoned the fight and fled. Quentin came out too, sword raised in one hand and a piece of paper clutched in the other.

Dane fell to his knees, breathing hard. I crouched beside him and checked his face. It sported no injuries, but his clothes were bloodied. He was in pain and the efforts of the fight had taxed his waning strength further.

"We need to get him inside," I ordered. "Quentin, fetch my medical kit, cloths and warm water. Run!"

Max and Erik helped Dane to stand and almost carried him between them up the stairs. The innkeeper watched on with incredulity while his wife told us we'd have to pay for damages.

"Will he be all right?" Theodore asked as we entered the room, voice shrill with panic.

Balthazar rose from the bed where he'd been resting and moved with surprising speed to clear the sheets off. Max and Erik lay Dane face down on the mattress then removed his doublet, jerkin and shirt. The latter gave them trouble.

"Tear it," I said. "I must work fast."

The gash in Dane's lower back was the worst. His other wounds were superficial. The fact that he'd been able to move after the stabbing and fight back was an enormous relief. It meant nothing vital had been severed. I'd once seen a back injury caused by an accident at the docks where a strong man never walked again.

"Is it deep?" Quentin asked. He already had a cloth in hand, soaked in the warm water from the basin held by Meg at his side. Kitty hovered behind, a hand over her mouth. She looked very pale.

"Deep enough," I said, inspecting the wound. It still bled.

Dane grunted then hissed as I pressed down on the wound.

"Sorry," I told him. "The bleeding needs to be stopped." I did not need to tell them what would happen if he lost too much blood.

"Josie?" Quentin held up the bottle of mother's milk and I nodded without hesitation.

He removed the lid and asked Theodore to fetch a spoon from my medical pack.

"No," Dane said when Quentin presented the spoon to him. "Save it for when it's needed."

"Shut up and take it," I barked.

He opened his mouth and dutifully sipped the mother's milk off the spoon. It felt like a small triumph. I waited until his eyelids drooped and I could feel his muscles relax then I pressed harder.

A few moments later, I dared check to see if the bleeding had stopped. We all breathed a sigh of relief to see that it had.

I gently cleaned the wound and inspected it again. The gash was short but not deep enough to cause any permanent damage except for scarring. As long as it was kept clean and bandaged, it would stay free of infection.

If there was one thing I knew how to do well, it was stitch wounds. Usually I stitched women torn during the birthing process, but I'd once had to stitch a cut similar to this on Max's shoulder. It had healed nicely.

"Pass me the needle and thread," I said to Quentin.

He did so then hovered over my shoulder, peering down at Dane's back. "Can I try?"

"Certainly not. You'll have to practice on the carcasses of pigs before you stitch a live human." I pricked Dane's skin with the needle. He was semi-conscious but didn't flinch. He was far too relaxed to feel pain.

Behind me, however, there was a commotion. "Kitty!" Erik cried.

I glanced back to see that Kitty had fainted and he'd caught her. He picked her up and carried her out of the room.

Theodore sat on a chair beside the window. "I need a drink. Do you think they'll deliver strong liquor up here?"

Meg headed for the door. "I'll ask."

"I'll come," Max said, following her out.

I finished stitching the wound then placed a folded bandage over it. Dane had fallen asleep under the influence of the mother's milk so I couldn't bandage him properly. I told Quentin he could help me when Dane awoke.

"I'm going to stay with him tonight," I said.

No one suggested it was a bad idea, or that Quentin could do it.

Balthazar sat on the bed and peered at Dane's peaceful face. "Remarkable stuff. Will he be all right to move in the morning?"

"He has to be," I said. "Whoever tried to kill him knows where to find him. We have to get away from here." How we would do that without being seen was a question no one voiced.

Max returned with Meg, carrying a tray laden with cups. Erik followed behind.

"We checked outside," Max said with a nod at Erik. "They're gone."

"Who were they?" Quentin asked.

"Barborough's men?" Theodore suggested as he accepted a cup from Meg.

"Doubtful," I said. "We killed half of them earlier and the rest scattered."

Balthazar agreed. "He also had no reason to kill Dane. For all he knew, Dane was the only one of us who knows the location of the gem."

I frowned, trying to think of those moments leading up to the attack. I'd been consumed with Dane and his kiss, but not to the point of completely losing my senses. "They made no demands," I said. "They did not ask for anything, did not tell us to leave the city or hand over the gem. They didn't utter a word. So why did they do it? What would killing Dane achieve?"

Meg set the tray down and picked up the remaining cup. "Could it have been Lord Xavier, out for revenge? Were they his men?"

"Or Brant?" Theodore said. "Perhaps he didn't leave Noxford after all."

Balthazar shook his head. "Again, for all they know, killing Dane would mean never finding the gem."

"Constables," Erik bit off. "Someone recognized the captain and told the authorities. They hear there are Glancian women staying at this inn and so come to arrest him."

Someone had certainly discovered Dane was staying here, most likely because as Glancian women, we stood out. I could have kicked myself for not putting my hood up over my head as we returned home tonight. My blonde hair had most certainly acted as a signal to the assailants.

"They wore no uniforms," I muttered into my cup. "Nor did they declare themselves. Constables would ask Dane his name to make sure they had the right person, then tell him what they were arresting him for. Those men came with the intention to kill, not arrest."

The enormity of our problem dampened everyone's spirits further. We had enough enemies on our trail, and now we had one more, except we had no clue as to their identity. Without knowing our enemy, how could we avoid them?

Balthazar scrubbed a hand over his face then indicated the door. "Erik and Max, stand guard tonight. We leave before dawn."

Dane muttered an unintelligible response from the bed. He was fighting the drowsiness, determined to stay awake. Typical.

I sat beside him, determined to admonish him. But I could not. He was alive, thank Hailia. Alive but broken, vulnerable. I stroked his hair back. "You must rest tonight. Tomorrow, we'll move."

"No. No more." He tried to sit up, but I placed a hand firmly on his shoulder.

"Lie still or you'll open the wound. Please, Dane, do as I ask just this once."

He grunted. "Fine, but you have to listen to me. Just as soon as I am able to stand, I'm going to walk out that front door and make myself known. It's the only way."

"It is not!"

"It's madness," Meg said.

Balthazar, Theodore and Quentin agreed. "You will not be offering yourself as bait to the assailants," Balthazar said.

"It'll draw the attackers into the open," Dane said. "If we're ready for them—"

"No!" Theodore pushed to his feet. "I've never thought you a selfish man until now."

"Selfish?" Dane tried to look at him, but I pressed down on his shoulder again.

Theodore moved to where Dane could see him. "Yes, selfish. If you die, you leave a heartbroken woman behind." He flapped a hand at me.

Dane closed his eyes and sighed.

"Not to mention heartbroken friends." Theodore's voice cracked, but he kept his head high, his back straight. "If you try anything foolish, I will personally chain you to the saddle for the entire journey back to Mull. Is that clear?"

"Quite," Dane bit off. Some of the vehemence of his anger was lost considering his vulnerable position on the bed, however.

I gave Theodore a nod. "I couldn't have said it better myself. So it's agreed. We keep to our original plan and return home to Mull and the palace as soon as possible."

Quentin sprang up from where he was sitting on the floor. "The palace! Merdu! I almost forgot." He pulled out the crumpled piece of paper I'd seen him holding earlier from his jerkin pocket. He did his best to flatten out the creases then held it up. A grin split his face from ear to ear. "Recognize her?"

The piece of paper had the word MISSING written across the top then a sketch of a woman's face. She was a little familiar but I couldn't place where I'd seen her before.

Dane tried to rise from the bed and Balthazar drew in a sharp breath. Theodore reached for the paper and stared at it. "It's Tabitha. One of the maids." He thrust the piece of paper in front of Dane's face then Balthazar's. "It's Tabitha!"

Balthazar took the paper and studied it. "It is," he said. "Quentin, where did you find it?"

Quentin was still grinning. He looked thoroughly pleased with himself as he rocked back on his heels. "I was helping the innkeeper move some barrels to his storeroom. It was real musty with lots of old things scattered about. This was wedged between bits of firewood that he said were chopped last winter. He reckons that paper somehow fell off the wall where it was nailed months ago and blew into the storeroom."

"Did he know her?" I asked.

"Not real well. Her kin posted that. They live near Max's gang's lair, across from the inn with the sign of the goose girl."

"We'll visit them tomorrow," Dane said.

"Tomorrow night when we won't be seen," I countered. "And you're not coming."

He grunted which I took as agreement, although I suspected I'd have an argument on my hands later.

Balthazar leaned back against the wall and stretched his legs out on the bed. He rubbed his right knee. "After we've learned Tabitha's story, we'll leave Noxford."

"I think we need to leave this inn tonight," Theodore said. He nodded at Dane. "Those attackers know where he is. It's too dangerous to stay."

"Where will we go?" Meg asked. "Another inn?"

I shook my head. "I have a better idea."

* * *

IT WAS QUITE an operation to move in the middle of the night. Erik and Max scouted the area while Quentin secured a cart for transport. Dane refused to lie down on it, however, until I reminded him he was jeopardizing all our lives by being visible. Only then did he dutifully cover himself with the blanket and hide while the rest of us placed our saddles, bags and other necessities around him. We led the cart and horses past the Goose Girl inn, through the surrounding narrow streets, and knocked on the door where Max's friends lived.

No one answered.

"That's not the sequence," Dane said from where he was now sitting up in the back of the cart. "Drew knocked four times quickly then paused before a final knock."

Max turned back to the door. "Only you would remember that." He knocked as directed and the door opened a crack.

"Max!" The thickset doorman opened the door wider. "What're you doing here?"

"We need somewhere to stay the night," Max said.

The guard gave a shrill whistle to announce our arrival to those inside. As with the last time, he made the men leave their weapons at the entrance.

The smells of cooking bacon greeted us along with the smiling face of Jenny. "Max! Couldn't leave us, eh? Come in, sit down." She slapped the seat of the stool beside her. "Want some bacon?"

Max waved off her offer and did not take the seat. He looked around and cleared his throat. "Is Vance here?"

"Nope. This is our most lucrative time to pick pockets and

purses. Drunkards are heading home and rich folk are visiting their mistresses. No one has their mind on their money."

"Do you know when Vance will be back?" Dane asked.

"He's back now," came a voice from behind us.

Vance entered, followed by Drew and Gillon. They looked surprised to see us, though not unhappy about it. All greeted Max with slaps on the back. Max returned them awkwardly.

Gillon placed a pouch on the table, the contents making a satisfying clink. Drew emptied his pockets of rings, a set of brass knuckles, a knife, and coins.

Jenny picked through the pieces, frowning. "That's it? That ain't enough to feed us, let alone keep us in the lifestyle we've become accustomed."

"The lifestyle *you've* become accustomed to," her brother Gillon teased. "You don't need more clothes, Jen."

She whacked his shoulder with the wooden spoon then returned to the pan over the fireplace and the sizzling rashers of bacon.

"Gillon and Drew will go out again," Vance told her. "Max, do you want to go with them?"

Max pulled a face at the objects on the table. "I'm no thief."

"If you say so. But be warned, you're going to get a shock when you get your memory back."

Drew and Jenny chuckled. Gillon pressed Max's arm. "Ignore them. We're glad to see you. Are you staying?"

"We need a favor," Max said. "We need somewhere to stay tonight and tomorrow night. We'll leave the city the following day, but there's something we need to do first."

Vance collected plates from the shelf and set them around the table. "You want to stay here?"

Jenny picked the pan up and joined us. "All of you?"

"All of us." Max nodded at Dane. "My friend's life is in danger and we need to hide. But we can't leave until we see someone tomorrow night."

"Why's his life in danger?" Drew asked.

"It's, er, complicated."

Drew crossed his arms and studied Dane. "The authorities after you too, eh?"

Dane nodded.

"Well, well. I didn't pick you as the type."

Jenny forked bacon onto the plates then handed one to Erik. She smiled at him. He took the plate and smiled back.

"What do you say, Vance?" she asked. "Do we let them stay?"

Vance hesitated before sitting. "Two nights only. You lead the authorities here, I'll kill you."

Drew slapped Dane on the back, a little above the wound. Dane tensed and released a breath when Drew turned away. He hadn't noticed Dane's reaction, but Vance did.

"You're injured," he said.

Dane sat on a chair beside Vance. "It's just a minor cut."

"Jenny can put something on it. She ain't gentle, but her ointments work."

Jenny stood close to Dane's shoulder as she placed bacon on a plate in front of him. "I can be gentle if I want." She winked at Dane. "Or rough. It depends on what my patient likes."

Gillon rolled his eyes. "Ignore my sister."

"Josie has already taken care of the cut," Dane told Jenny. "But thanks."

"Any time, handsome."

The cottage was larger than I expected. There were enough rooms for us all to sleep in if we shared, so we were able to rest well into the next day. I checked Dane's wound when he awoke and immediately re-bandaged it.

The others had left us alone and we took the opportunity to simply be together.

Later, we joined Max and the others in the kitchen for supper where Max asked rapid questions about his past. They talked into the evening at which time Dane declared we should visit Tabitha's family before it grew too late.

He insisted on coming, and I didn't stop him. We didn't want to overwhelm them so we didn't all go. In the end, we agreed the party should consist of Dane, me, Balthazar, Erik and Quentin. The latter two were to act as our armed guard.

Tabitha's family lived in the rooms behind the butcher's shop. The smell of blood and raw meat hung in the air, even though the stoop was clean and the shutters closed for the night.

Balthazar introduced himself to the man who answered his knock as the master of the palace in Glancia. The gray-haired, robust fellow inspected him from head to toe then glanced past Balthazar's shoulder to me.

"Glancia?" He screwed up his nose. "Why has your king come here?"

"He's not here," Balthazar said gently. "These are my friends, also from the Glancian palace. We've left the king's employment and are visiting Freedland."

"We're closed. Come back tomorrow." He shut the door.

"We know Tabitha," I called out.

The door reopened and I heard footsteps running from somewhere inside the house. "Tabitha?" the butcher muttered. "My girl? You know my girl?"

Balthazar held up the paper with Tabitha's picture on it. "We recognized her from this."

A small woman with pink cheeks and dark hair pulled tightly into a knot on the top of her head joined the man. "Are you saying…" She clutched her throat as tears welled in her eyes. "Is she alive?"

"She is," Balthazar said. "I last saw her some weeks ago, just before leaving to come here. She's alive and well and living at the palace."

"But…why did she not send word? We've been so worried."

"May we come in?" Balthazar asked. "What we have to tell you should not be said out here."

The man opened the door wide and stepped back. Dane, Balthazar and I entered, while Erik and Quentin remained outside, facing the street.

Balthazar re-introduced himself, then Dane and me. Then he told the butcher and his wife that Tabitha was a maid at the palace and once again assured them she was alive and well.

"She didn't contact you because she lost her memory," he said. "She had no idea about her past, only her first name."

The butcher's wife gasped. "My poor baby girl."

"How did she lose her memory?" the butcher asked.

"She doesn't know. She came to us dazed and we employed her at the palace as a maid." Balthazar showed them the poster again. "It's fortunate that we happened to see this. We're heading back to Glancia tomorrow. We can take a letter to her, if you like."

"Yes!" The butcher's wife sprang to her feet and bustled out of the kitchen.

Her husband leaned forward and lowered his voice. "This is not some kind of joke, is it? Because my wife can't cope if this is not real. She's endured so much already."

"We would never joke about something like this," Dane assured him.

The butcher blew out a breath and his eyes welled with tears. "All this time, and we've not heard a thing. And now this… It's a relief, you understand. We didn't know where she'd gone, she just vanished. We assumed the worst."

I glanced at Dane. Tabitha's story was different to Max's. Max's friends had known he'd been arrested and sent to prison, only to later find out he'd supposedly escaped, been recaptured and executed. Tabitha's family had no idea. Like Balthazar, and some of the other servants whose families we'd found in Tilting, she was simply thought of as missing.

"You didn't know her fate?" I asked.

"No," the butcher said. "She just disappeared the same day as her mistress was sentenced to prison."

"Her mistress?"

"Tabitha worked as a maid to the daughter of a wealthy merchant. The young lady got into trouble with the authorities. More than a year ago now, it was. Feels like a lifetime."

"But your daughter wasn't arrested with her?"

The butcher shrugged. "We were never told she was." The anger mixed with the anguish in his voice told of his doubts. "Tabitha's mistress was their prize; Tabitha wasn't important. Maybe they never bothered to record her."

"Which prison was the mistress sent to?" Dane asked.

"A mine outside Gull's Wing. Nasty place. Few survive it." He looked up as his wife returned with paper and ink. "There was an escape but all the inmates were quickly rounded up and executed. We wondered if Tabitha was among them but we never received a word from the authorities."

The butcher's wife set the paper and ink in front of her husband. "Write this down. Dearest Tabby." She dictated a heartfelt letter to her daughter and her husband wrote it in a barely legible scrawl. "Keep that letter safe," the butcher's wife said as she handed it to me, a wobbly smile touching her lips. "Tabby can read a little. Her mistress taught her."

"What was the name of her mistress?" Balthazar asked, his eagerness making his voice tremble.

"Miss Rotherhyde."

"Her first name?"

"Laylana. Laylana Rotherhyde."

CHAPTER 17

"Why was Laylana arrested?" Quentin asked as we headed off through the dark streets. We'd informed him and Erik of all we'd learned from the butcher and his wife as soon as we left. They'd listened intently until we'd finished then peppered us with questions.

"For causing a commotion in a public place," Dane said.

"Commotion?" Erik asked.

"A lot of noise," Balthazar explained. "A fuss."

Quentin scratched his head. "Is that an offense here?"

"It's an offense in Glancia too, if the commotion is severe enough," I said. "Inciting a riot, for example. But it's hardly the sort of offense someone is sent to a prison mine for. It warrants a few weeks in prison at worst, and a local one at that."

"Maybe Gull's Wing is the local prison for Noxford."

It was a sobering thought that any nation could send offenders to a notorious prison for such a minor crime. Perhaps Freedland wasn't as civilized as it seemed on the surface.

"We must tell Laylana's family," Erik said.

Dane clapped him on the shoulder. "We're heading there now."

The butcher told us the Rotherhyde family lived in the third house on the avenue that ran alongside the river. He did not tell us that all the properties along the tree-lined avenue were enormous. Positioned behind a high wall, the Rotherhyde home was accessed through a guarded gatehouse. Torches lit the drive from the gatehouse to a building that I could just make out through the trees. Beyond it would be the river.

The two guards, however, would not let us through. "I have not been instructed to expect you," said one.

"That's because we are not expected," Balthazar said, his voice strained with impatience and exhaustion. "Can you deliver a message to your master?"

"He does not like to be disturbed without good reason."

Balthazar sighed.

Dane stepped forward, flanked by Quentin and Erik. Erik removed his hood to reveal his very distinctive hair and forehead tattoos. The first guard gulped, but stood his ground. The second joined his companion, his hand resting on his sword hilt.

"He'll want to be disturbed for this," Dane said. "We know his daughter, Laylana."

The guards glanced at each another. "Miss Laylana is dead," said one.

"She's alive and we know where she is."

One of the guards nudged the other with his elbow and jerked his head at the main building behind him. The second guard jogged off. I breathed a sigh of relief. At least they were taking us seriously.

The first guard didn't let us out of his sight until the second one returned. "You can go through," he announced. "Leave your weapons here. And him." He nodded at Erik.

Dane ordered both Erik and Quentin to remain behind then left his sword with them. The first guard escorted us to the house where a footman met us in the wood paneled entrance hall. He indicated we should walk ahead into an adjoining room.

Torches flickered in wall sconces but their light didn't chase away the oppressive feeling that settled over me when I entered the sitting room. More paneling and the mounted heads of dead deer decorated the masculine space. The lady sitting on a chair by the fireplace dressed in fine yellow silk, with feathers in her black hair, was the only feminine thing in the room.

To my surprise, she wasn't much older than me. Nor was the

man seated beside her. He had a youthful face, despite his balding head. These could not be Laylana's parents.

The woman suddenly let out a small squeal. "Dane? Dane, is that you?"

I stared at her, stunned, as she charged forward. The man followed in her wake, his eyes wide. Dane stepped back as they crowded close. He'd gone pale.

"Merdu, it *is* you," the man muttered. "Where have you been? Why didn't you tell us you were alive?"

"Has Laylana been with you this entire time?" the woman cried. She picked up a fan from the table and flapped it in front of her face. "Hailia and Merdu, I am shocked. Shocked! But that's nothing to how your mother will receive the news of your survival. Have you seen her?"

"My...mother?" Dane glanced at me. He looked all at sea, a drifting boat in need of an anchor.

I went to him and took his hand.

Both the man and woman noticed. His nostrils flared. "What is the meaning of this? If you are alive, and my sister too, then you are still betrothed."

Dane's hand released mine as if scalded. Suddenly I was the one in need of an anchor. But my anchor had closed his fist and turned even paler. Dane stared at the man, his throat working but no sounds came out.

It was Balthazar who spoke. "Would you care to explain?"

"Dane and Laylana," the man said. "If you spoke the truth to my guard, and my sister is alive, then their betrothal stands. The agreement was struck two years ago and cannot be broken without severe financial consequences. Is that clear?"

This last he said to Dane, but Dane didn't look as though he was listening. He was as white as snow.

"A chair!" I ordered.

The man slid a chair behind Dane just as Dane collapsed into it. He wasn't unconscious, but he wasn't well either.

The woman flapped her fan at Dane's face. "He used to be more robust than this."

"He's injured," Balthazar said. "He recently lost a lot of blood."

"Do you have smelling salts?" I asked the woman.

She retrieved a small bottle from a sewing basket and passed it beneath Dane's nose. He blinked and rubbed his forehead.

"Do you need to lie down?" I asked.

"I'm fine." His gaze held mine. "You?"

My heart felt like it had a deep hole in it, my thoughts were scrambled, and I'd never wanted to cry as much as I did at that moment. But I smiled and nodded. I wasn't sure if I did it for his sake or mine. The reaction was mechanical.

Dane looked to the man. "I've lost my memory. Laylana has too. Tell me who I am. Tell me everything."

"Lost your memory?" The woman laughed nervously, but it quickly faded upon Dane's glare. "How peculiar."

Balthazar sat without being invited. "Let me explain. They both showed up at the Glancian king's palace without any knowledge of their pasts. All they knew were their names. I employed them. Dane worked as a guard, and Laylana worked in the kitchen garden."

The woman snorted softly, only to try to cover it up with a cough. "Laylana a gardener? That is quite amusing."

The man lifted a finger and she fell silent. "My name is Ewen Rotherhyde, and this is my wife, Eeliss. Laylana is my sister. You must understand, this has come as quite a shock. We thought Laylana dead."

"No doubt you have questions," Balthazar said.

"I do. Firstly, if you have no memory, how did you know to come here?"

Balthazar told them about the poster with Tabitha's picture on it and how that led us to their house.

Laylana's brother drew in a deep breath and let it out slowly. "This is overwhelming. I can barely comprehend it."

Balthazar studied Dane, who in turn studied the Rotherhydes. "It's not just overwhelming for you. Dane has just learned that he not only has a mother but is betrothed to a woman he has had little do with over the past few months."

He did not mention that Laylana's memory kept erasing itself every few days. The insecurity frightened her. Early on, some thought her mad. She'd even tried to escape the palace, then locked herself away in her room. Without daylight and exercise, her health suffered, and I'd ordered her to get outside. That's when she'd started working in the garden and writing notes to herself, so that when she did awaken without her memory again, she was not completely in the dark. One of the footmen had sketched the faces of people she could trust. She'd added notes to those pages to help her quickly adjust to her strange existence. She and the footman had become quite close. While Laylana and Dane had always been friendly towards one another, there'd never been any attraction that I could tell.

Yet he was betrothed to her. He could not marry me. Not until he'd spoken to her and explained the situation. I knew Dane well enough to know that he would want to do the honorable thing and break it off with her gently before making any promises to me.

I glanced at him and felt ill. What if he was too honorable and wanted to go through with the marriage? He was a rescuer by nature, and Laylana needed rescuing more than anyone.

"We know Laylana was arrested and sent to the prison mine outside Gull's Wing," Balthazar was saying. "We also know you were told she escaped, along with the other prisoners, but the escape failed and they were all executed for murdering the guards. But we think Tabitha and Laylana did manage to escape and traveled to Glancia. Dane too."

"I must have been with them in the prison mine," Dane said. "Do you know why I was arrested, Mr. Rotherhyde?"

"Call me Ewen, and my wife Eeliss. Anything more formal sounds strange coming from you." He laughed as if he'd told a joke.

His wife did not. "I think we should take him to his mother immediately. We can explain on the way." She looked to her husband and he nodded.

The footman was summoned and arrangements made for a carriage to be brought around. "We can only fit four," Ewen said, eyeing me. "Perhaps the girl should go home, Dane. This doesn't concern her."

"Her name is Josie, and it concerns her very much. I have another two friends at the front gate. We'll need to collect them."

Ewen asked the footman to prepare two carriages. We followed Ewen to the front door where a maid placed a fur stole around Eeliss's shoulders and handed her a pair of white gloves.

Ewen took the opportunity to study Dane. "You've changed. Palace life has hardened you." He slapped Dane on the shoulder, rather awkwardly. "You look stronger."

"That was probably prison life," Dane said. "You haven't told me why I was arrested."

Ewen dismissed the maid and waited for the footman to leave through the front door to greet the carriages. "I'll tell you in a moment."

The carriages arrived and Balthazar agreed to ride in the second carriage so that I could sit with Dane and the Rother-hydes in the first. Ewen informed the drivers to make sure they weren't followed then joined us in the cabin.

As soon as the door closed, Dane again asked why he was jailed. "And why didn't you want your servants to overhear?"

I didn't like Ewen's smile. It was smug, as if he were pleased to have knowledge of Dane that Dane didn't have himself. His wife's smile matched her husband's. She looked as though she couldn't wait to see Dane's reaction.

Dane sat gingerly on the seat beside me, his lower back not quite touching the leather fabric. I wasn't worried about him fainting again, however. His color had returned and his gaze was sharp as it drilled into Ewen.

Ewen cleared his throat and stretched his neck out of his lace collar. "My sister was very loyal to you. That was her greatest fault."

Beside him, Eeliss rolled her eyes. "She had others."

"It got her arrested," Ewen went on. "She tried to break you out of the prison cell after your arrest. She hired folk from the slum to cause a scene outside the prison, and a small group of mercenaries to take advantage of the ensuing chaos to break into the prison and set you free. Her plan failed and she was arrested too, her trial quickly arranged, and the real reason for her arrest suppressed."

Dane closed his eyes and tipped his head back. "She was arrested because she was trying to free me."

"I see it bothers you."

"Of course it does," Eeliss said. "Dane was always a decent man. He never shirked his responsibilities, never blamed others for his mistakes. His mother brought him up well."

At the mention of his mother, Dane reopened his eyes.

"You owe Laylana," Ewen said darkly. "The predicament she's in now is your fault."

"Do *not* lay that at his feet," I snapped. "She had a choice."

Ewen's lips flattened. "I did not ask for your opinion."

"I believe I am free to give it anyway. Isn't that what your revolution was all about? Giving a voice to the people?"

Eeliss put a hand on her husband's thigh. In warning? To calm him down? It wasn't needed. He chuckled to himself, as if I'd told a joke.

"Why did the authorities want to keep the reason for Laylana's arrest a secret?" Dane asked Ewen.

"If it became known that she was trying to free a prisoner, the public would wonder why a Rotherhyde would risk her life for a nobody."

"Because she loved him," I said simply.

"Don't be ridiculous," Eeliss scoffed.

"I don't understand," Dane said. "Why did it matter if the public knew she was helping a nobody like me?"

Ewen smiled that smug smile again. "They would be curious as to her reasons. Curiosity leads to suspicion, and they would dig and dig until they unearthed the truth. That's what the authorities were afraid of. So everything was hushed up and rushed through. You were both sentenced before we knew she'd even been arrested too."

Dane tilted his head to the side. "What truth?"

Eeliss placed a hand on her husband's thigh again. "We should let his mother tell him."

Ewen gave no indication he'd heard her. He stroked his chin and regarded Dane. "You really have no idea, do you?"

"About what?" Dane's patience was stretching thin, and I'd wager he was still in considerable pain from the cut in his back. The carriage ride had not been a smooth one. His temper would be bubbling to the surface.

"Think about it. Why would a man such as myself betroth my only sister to a nobody?"

"A man such as yourself?" Dane echoed. "Who are you?"

Eeliss laughed until her husband hissed at her to be quiet.

"I'm Ewen Rotherhyde. My family is the richest in Freedland."

"Congratulations."

Ewen's jaw hardened at the note of sarcasm in Dane's voice. "My family are merchants, and I am the head of the family company. Our ships travel to Zemaya and everywhere in between, trading goods. My father also started his own bank, and I have extended our banking interests. I even loan money to the government."

"Is this important?"

"I ask you again. Why would I allow my sister to be betrothed to a nobody?"

Dane shifted in the seat, but I wasn't sure if it was because he was physically uncomfortable or what he was about to say bothered him. "The same reason people usually marry."

Eeliss snorted again. "He means love, Husband. The commodity that only the poor can afford."

"Am I not poor?" Dane asked. "Am I from a wealthy family too?"

"Oh, you are quite poor," Ewen said with delight. "Your father is dead and your mother relies on handouts from those who call themselves friends." His supercilious tone grated on my nerves.

"So why am I worthy of marrying your sister?" Dane asked.

"Because you have something more important than wealth. You have pedigree."

Dane leaned forward ever so slightly. "Who are my relatives? Wealthy folk who cut me off? A minister?"

"Royalty."

Dane went very still. I gasped.

Opposite us, both Rotherhydes smiled those smug smiles as they watched Dane, seeming to delight in his shock and confusion.

When Dane asked no more questions, I took over. "I thought

the Freedland royal family all died in the revolution. Is Dane a distant relative of the last king? Was he so distant that the authorities never bothered to track him down?" The revolution had occurred forty years ago. It would have been Dane's parents who'd somehow escaped General Nox's troops. Dane was certainly no more than thirty.

"You are right in that he is a relative of the last king of Freedland, or of Averlea, as it was known then," Ewen said, watching Dane closely. "But he is not the king's distant cousin or nephew. He is the king's own grandson."

Dane's hand curled into a fist on his thigh. He made no other movement. Not even his chest rose and fell with his breathing.

Eeliss tapped Dane's knee with her gloved finger. "Did you hear my husband?" She spoke loudly, as if Dane were deaf. "You are the direct descendant of King Diamedes. You are the heir. The *only* heir. When the royalist supporters learn of your survival, they'll waste no time in carrying out the plans they were forced to abandon upon your arrest last year. You'll be sitting on the throne in no time. As king," she added, when he didn't respond.

Ewen turned to me. His lips thinned as his smile spread. "And *my sister* will be your queen."

althazar, Erik and Quentin knew something was amiss the moment they alighted from their carriage in front of a cottage at the edge of the city. Dane's pale face was clearly visible by the light of the carriage lanterns.

"Is he going to faint?" Quentin asked me. "Because I don't think I can catch him alone."

"He has learned something about himself," I said quietly. "Something you will never believe."

Dane flipped up his hood and advised me to the do the same.

"Very wise," Ewen said. "If someone who knows your true identity sees that you're alive, your life will be in danger."

"Someone already knows," Dane said as he glanced around. "I was attacked yesterday."

"Merdu! We must get inside." Ewen banged loudly on the door.

Quentin nudged me. "What does he mean by the captain's true identity?"

"Apparently Dane is the heir to the Freedlandian throne," I said.

"Averlea," Eeliss corrected me with a sniff.

Balthazar, Quentin and Erik stared at me. "You joke," Erik said.

I shook my head. "He's the direct descendant of King Diamedes, the last king."

"The tyrant?" Quentin asked.

"Hush," Ewen snapped. "Don't call him that. Not in this house. She'll throw you out. She might throw all of us out."

It just dawned on me who we were about to meet. This woman wasn't just Dane's mother. She was the daughter of the last king of Averlea. She was a princess. I wished Kitty were here. She'd know how to talk to a princess.

I suddenly felt lost again. Give me a wound to stitch any day over meeting princesses.

I glanced at Dane to find him watching me from beneath lowered lids.

"Josie," he began, his voice full of ache. His hand found mine and his thumb caressed my knuckles before he released me.

I wanted to reach for him, but the door opened to reveal a woman. At first I thought her too young to be Dane's mother. But as she stepped closer upon seeing him, I noticed the small lines around her eyes and lips, the strands of gray in her dark hair.

She emitted a small squeal before throwing her arms around him. He rocked back with the force of the embrace, his arms at his sides. Slowly, he raised them and embraced her too.

"We must get him inside, Yelena," Ewen said, making a shooing motion. "He has been recognized. There has already been an attack."

"Attack!" Yelena took Dane's hand and pulled him into the cottage. "Why were you not more careful?"

"He has lost his memory," Ewen said. "He has no idea who he is."

I hung back as Ewen and Eeliss followed Dane and Yelena. Erik, Quentin and Balthazar remained on the porch too. Like me, they must feel uncomfortable intruding on an intimate moment between mother and son.

Our hesitation cost us. The door was slammed in our faces.

"They do not have manners," Erik said, turning his back on the door and crossing his arms.

"I don't understand," Quentin said with a pout in his voice.

"What don't you understand?" Balthazar asked.

"Should we call him highness now?"

The door reopened to reveal Dane. "Come in."

"I'm not sure we should," I said.

"You should."

I glanced at Balthazar and he nodded, but it was Dane taking my hand and drawing me in that got my feet moving.

"Quentin and I will keep watch," Erik told him.

Dane gave a nod of thanks.

"But I want to go inside too," Quentin whined as Dane closed the door.

Going by the glares I received from Ewen and Eeliss, there had been a brief debate over whether I should be allowed inside. Dane had won.

The cottage was small but neat. It reminded me of my own house back in Mull with a modest entrance hall, a parlor to the right, a kitchen ahead, and staircase leading upstairs. Yelena stood in the parlor, gazing at Dane.

"Come, my son," she said, her hand outstretched. "We have much to discuss."

A low fire made the cottage feel warm, welcoming. It was a comfortable and clean space, although there were not enough chairs for all of us. A woman wearing an apron rushed in behind us, only to stop and stare at Dane.

"Merdu and Hailia!" she cried, tears blooming in her eyes. "You're alive!" She clasped his hand and bobbed a curtsy at the same time. "Welcome home, sir."

Dane nodded his thanks and waited for an introduction.

"Martha, fetch refreshments," Yelena said. "And cake. We have much to celebrate tonight." She beamed and took Dane's hands in her own. "My dearest boy is home. My son, my only hope, has come back to us alive. Everything will be well again."

The maid hesitated. "There is not enough for everyone, madam. Sorry, madam."

Yelena's rapid blinking was the only sign this news bothered her. "The Rotherhydes will not be staying."

"But we must!" Eeliss cried.

"I wish to be alone with my son."

Eeliss's gaze slid to me. "Then Dane's friends will leave too."

"No," Dane said. "They stay with me."

Yelena's only reaction was a slight stiffening of her jaw. She did not look at me. It was as if I wasn't even there. Understandably, her entire focus was on Dane.

"The betrothal will go ahead," Ewen told Yelena. "Laylana is also alive. She has been living with him."

Yelena drew in a deep breath. "That is good news. I am very happy to hear it. Of course the betrothal will go ahead."

"We need to talk," Dane said. "Things have changed. My memory loss—"

"Nothing has changed," Ewen said with triumph. "You heard her. The betrothal will stand."

"Don't interrupt my son," Yelena snapped.

"We require an assurance from Dane."

"*I* have given you an assurance. Is my word not good enough for you now, Ewen?"

Ewen hesitated then gave a small bow.

His wife curtseyed. "Thank you, madam. We are so very happy to see you reunited with your son and to hear that my dearest sister-in-law is alive and well too."

"Yes," Yelena said with a tilt of her chin. "It's wonderful news and should be spread. Ewen, make it known to our friends that Dane has returned."

"Any instructions?"

"Not yet. I need time." She looked to Dane and gave him a small smile. "New plans must be formed."

Ewen and Eeliss left, both casting me one more glare before exiting.

"They have been insufferable this last year," Yelena said after they'd gone. "But that will change now that you're back." She touched Dane's cheek. "Everything will be well again."

"We need to talk," Dane said. "About my memory loss."

Martha entered with a tray carrying cake and four cups. "I wasn't sure how many to bring in here, madam."

Yelena indicated we should all sit. "I suspect these are my son's friends, not his servants. Serve the cake, Martha, then please leave us."

Martha did as ordered then bobbed another curtsy. She didn't leave immediately, however, but smiled at Dane. "I will serve your favorite breakfast in the morning. Fried eggs and cheese between two slices of bread."

Dane thanked her, but I hardly heard him. He seemed to have forgotten, but I had not. He'd made himself fried eggs with cheese between bread at my house once. The eggs and cheese had been an odd combination and I'd wondered at the time if it was something he'd eaten in the past. Now here was the proof, as well as the woman who made it for him.

Martha left and Dane turned to his mother. She had the same strong cheekbones as Dane, the same olive skin, and the set of their brow was identical. His eyes were blue, however, while hers looked black in the candlelight. She was beautiful with an elegance and imperiousness that reminded me of Kitty.

She smiled gently at Dane and I expected her to put down her cup and embrace him again. But she remained in her seat, her back straight, her hair perfectly arranged, like the princess I knew her to be.

Former princess. Her father the king had been deposed, her family murdered, and the man who'd ordered their executions took charge of the new order. She must have been young when it happened, a mere child. I couldn't begin to imagine how it must have affected her.

"I have longed for this day," she said with conviction. "I never believed that you'd died. It didn't feel as though you had. Not in here." She tapped her chest. "A mother knows these things."

Dane set down the cup on the table beside him. "There is a lot I need to tell you before you tell me more about myself."

"Of course. I will listen without interruption. But first, will you introduce your friends?"

Dane apologized. "This is Balthazar, master of the palace in Glancia."

Yelena's brows arched. "I've heard about the palace. Is it as beautiful as they say?"

"It's a glittering jewel," Balthazar said.

"Outside are Erik and Quentin, both guards from the palace. Another guard is also traveling with us, along with the former king's personal valet, and two women from the village. And this is Josie Cully from Mull in Glancia. She's the village midwife, daughter of the former doctor, and someone very important to me."

"So I've noticed," Yelena said. "Welcome to our home, both of you. Miss Cully, I suppose I have you to thank for taking care of my son after his memory loss?"

"He's more than capable of taking care of himself," I said.

She looked pleased. "I'm glad all his training paid off."

"Training?" Dane prompted.

"You have been taught all the arts required of someone in your position. Sword fighting, fist fighting, horse riding, leadership, diplomacy, dancing, as well as an education in economics, mathematics, geography, history…" She laughed softly. "Forgive me. Sometimes I get carried away when discussing my favorite topic. Of course, you must have known you had a better upbringing than the average man."

Dane shook his head. "Let me explain what I *do* know of myself. But first, I must ask you to try to believe me."

"Why would I not believe you?"

"What I have to say is incredible."

He started with the day his memories began and told her how events unfolded from there. She listened as he described how all palace servants awoke in exactly the same predicament on the same day, including Laylana. He mentioned the sorcerer, magic, and Leon's dying confession. She didn't interrupt as he explained his reasons for coming to Freedland, knowing he and many of the other servants were from this place. He told her what we'd learned from Sander at the prison and finished with the events that led us to the Rotherhydes. He didn't mention that Brant had inherited the unused wishes and that we had the gem in our possession, nor did he tell her Laylana's memory continued to fail regularly.

She didn't say anything for a long time. So long, that Dane leaned forward.

"Yelena? Are you all right?"

She nodded weakly. "Please call me Mother."

"Mother," he repeated somewhat dully. "Say something."

"You are right in that it is incredible. But I believe you. It makes sense of everything. I never thought you had died trying to escape. But if you had survived, it meant there must be a very good reason for you to disappear and not make contact. While I didn't *think* it was your choice to maintain silence, sometimes I had doubts." She shrugged one shoulder, the movement languidly elegant.

"How long was I in the prison for?"

"Six or seven months before the supposed escape."

We'd heard as much from Sander, yet it still shocked me to hear how long Dane had been there. It must have felt like a lifetime.

"So if the escape was the sorcerer's doing, the high minister lied about your executions." She huffed out a humorless laugh. "He lied to ensure we would give up all hope and not go looking for you."

"Or to avoid panic among the people," Balthazar said. "It would have been frightening for the public to know a thousand dangerous prisoners were in their midst."

"They should not have lied to us," Yelena said.

"No, of course not. If you'd known about his disappearance, you would have searched for him."

"We would never have given up. We would have searched the length and breadth of the Fist and beyond."

"We?" Dane asked.

"Our friends. Royalists who wish to see you back on the throne."

He sat back heavily, hissing in pain from the cut.

Yelena set down her cup and rose. "You're wounded. From the attack?"

"It's all right," he told her.

She signaled for him to stand. "It should be cleaned and dressed."

"Josie took care of it."

"Until you have a wife, you're my responsibility." She sat again. "Martha is very good at treating injuries."

"Josie is a doctor."

"Doctor's daughter, I believe you mean." She smiled at me.

"I'm glad he was in capable hands in his absence. I thank you for all that you've done."

I felt as though I ought to curtsy and leave the room.

"Speaking of wives," Dane said. "About the betrothal to Laylana."

"Oh, that. You don't have to worry. It's a mere formality."

"You don't wish me to marry her?"

"Of course I do. A promise is a promise, and I owe the Rotherhydes much. They have funded our cause for years and have promised to continue once you retake the throne. What I meant was, you can continue to have a liaison with Josie after your marriage. It's quite common—"

"No." Dane put up both hands. "Enough." He squeezed the bridge of his nose. "You must understand that everything has changed. I am not the same man now."

"Of course you are. You simply don't remember a time before the Glancian palace. Son," she said in earnest, "I know this feels sudden for you, and overwhelming. We don't need to move quickly. You can have time to resettle, to learn about yourself again. Laylana will have to travel from Glancia, for one thing. How long is the journey?"

Dane expelled a breath. "Laylana won't want to marry me, and I don't want to marry her. But that's not all. You've told me I am the heir to Freedland, that I'm descended from royalty, but...I am just the captain of the palace guards. I know nothing about being a king."

"I will guide you. As will Ewen and our other friends."

Dane grunted. "I've only just met him, but I can assure you, I wouldn't take the advice of a self-centered man like Ewen Rotherhyde."

Yelena wrapped her hands around her cup. "Ewen has been very good to us. We owe him."

Dane closed his eyes and blew out a deep breath. When he reopened them, the old Dane had returned. He was once again the commanding captain of the guards that I knew so well. "On top of all that, I don't want to plunge this country into another bloody civil war."

Yelena's nostrils flared. The moments slipped by in heavy

silence as she glared at her son. "There will be some bloodshed, certainly," she finally conceded. "But we have support from several important families, wealthy families, who are fed up with the high taxes and other restrictions on trade. They have promised us money to hire mercenaries. We have the numbers—"

Dane shot to his feet. "I want no part of your second revolution. Josie, Bal, we're leaving."

Yelena stood too and drew herself up to her full height. While she was tall for a Freedlander, she barely reached the middle of his chest. "Please don't go yet. You're right. I'm rushing you. You're not ready for this. Please, sit down and finish your tea. Tomorrow, we will discuss everything further after you've rested in your old room."

Dane shook his head. "I won't feel differently tomorrow."

"Perhaps not, but you will feel differently once your memory returns. Don't make hasty decisions in the meantime."

"I don't know when that will be, or if it will happen at all."

"You must not make decisions based on what you only remember today. You might regret it."

"She's right," Balthazar said.

Dane looked surprised that Bal agreed with Yelena. He turned to me and swallowed. My heart melted at the sadness I saw in him. He wanted to find his family so badly. He had wanted to learn about himself, and had thought the worst thing that could be learned was his reason for being jailed.

Yet this news shook him to the core. If he'd been all at sea before, he was now drowning.

I took his hand, offering myself as his lifeline if he needed it. His fingers closed around mine tightly.

"Yelena's right," I said gently. "You owe it to yourself to re-learn everything you have forgotten. Only then should you make your decision." I didn't tell him what that decision should be, nor would I ever tell him what I thought he should do. It must be his decision alone. But he must be fully informed to make it. "Hear what she has to say." I turned to his mother. "Don't tell him about your plans for a second revolution. Tell him about himself, about his life. Let him get to know you again. Am I right in thinking you are the only family member he has?"

Yelena's gaze lifted from our linked hands to meet mine. It was impossible to tell if she was grateful I'd encouraged him to stay or if she resented the value Dane put on my opinion. She sported the same unreadable expression as her son when he was trying to keep his temper in check.

Dane leaned down and lightly kissed my cheek. "I'm sorry I dragged you into this," he whispered. "I wish we'd never left Mull."

"I'm not sorry," I whispered back. "It's going to be all right."

He settled in the chair again and faced his mother. "My apologies if this is painful for you, but I want to start at the beginning. How did you escape from General Nox's army? I'd heard the entire royal family of Freedland—"

"Averlea," she corrected him.

"I thought they all died."

"Executed, like animals." She spat out the words as if they were bitter poison. "My parents and two brothers were beheaded in front of that traitor's supporters."

"Nox?"

She lifted her chin. "They told me he did not even stay to watch. Coward."

"And you?" Dane asked. "How did you escape?"

"The master of Merdu's Guards helped me, with a little assistance from my maid."

"The master of the warrior priests from Tilting?" Dane looked to Balthazar.

Balthazar stared at Yelena, but she didn't notice his interest, or mine and Dane's. Her gaze had become distant as she picked up her story.

"He didn't think I should share the fate of my parents and brothers, and I wasn't as heavily guarded as them. The benefits of being a mere girl," she sneered. "The master smuggled me out of the castle before the executions took place. He took me out of the city to a noble family who supported my father. I hid on their estate during the following months. They were tumultuous times. Nox claimed I'd been executed behind closed doors in deference to my age and gender because he didn't want royal supporters thinking I'd survived. It was the first lie of many under his regime. They are still lying about executions." She lifted a hand in Dane's direction.

"The noble family raised you in secret?" Dane asked.

"Only for a brief time. They endured much in the months after the revolution. They were stripped of their title and estate and forced to live alongside villagers who'd once worked for them. I did too. It was degrading." Another sneer twisted her lips. "But word of my survival secretly spread, and other royalist supporters came in search of me. Some had not fared as badly, and I was moved between families to keep me out of Nox's clutches. The years passed. I grew up but my true identity remained hidden. I pretended to be a governess working for the former noble families who'd managed to flourish through careful diplomacy and wise decisions."

"The Rotherhydes were one such family?"

She nodded. "Ewen's father was my greatest ally. He kept my secret and hid me in plain sight while increasing his own wealth under the new regime."

"The Rotherhydes had been nobles?" Balthazar asked.

"Mere barons."

"The new regime has been kind to them," Dane said. "Ewen claims they're the wealthiest family in Freedland."

Her lips pinched. "His father took advantage of a bad situation, and Ewen is continuing to seek out opportunities to further his family's business interests. They should be congratulated for beating the ministers at their own game."

It seemed to me that the Rotherhydes were better off now than they had been under King Diamedes. They'd taken advantage of the bad situation, as Yelena put it, but they were also taking advantage of her desire to return the royal family to the throne by betrothing Laylana to the heir. With his sister as queen, Ewen could expect more favors to fall into his lap.

I looked to Dane, but his eyes were hooded as he watched his mother.

"Whatever you think of the Rotherhydes, you must be agreeable to them," Yelena told him. "Laylana is a good match for you.

She'll make an excellent queen. She's courageous, charming and good natured. She might not be a great beauty, but beauty is not as important as bearing and nobility. She adored you, of course. It's not surprising that she tried to help you escape after your arrest. Unfortunately she wasn't quite clever enough to orchestrate it. If only she'd confided in me..." She closed her eyes and released a deep breath that seemed to release much of the tension from her shoulders with it. Dane's arrest and imprisonment must have been nightmarish for her.

Dane scrubbed a hand over his mouth, as if stopping himself from blurting out something he would regret. He'd promised not to make any decisions about his future yet, but it was costing him not to tell his mother yet again that he wouldn't marry Laylana.

Balthazar rested both hands on his walking stick as he leaned forward. "The authorities didn't trouble you in all the years since the revolution? After all, some of them knew you escaped."

"I changed my name and remained low. Dane was birthed in secret. No one knew our true identities except for a few trusted supporters."

"Did Dane grow up knowing he was the heir?"

"Of course."

"Why was he arrested? It can't have been to get him out of the way if they didn't know who he was. Did he commit a crime?"

Yelena turned away from him to look at Dane. She was answering these questions for his sake, not for Balthazar, and she wanted us all to know it. "They were false charges of assault."

"False?"

"The authorities discovered who you were somehow and sent someone to assassinate you. You fought back and were arrested."

"But how did they learn his identity?" Balthazar asked. "Could he have let it slip himself?"

"No! He would never do something so foolish."

"Out of arrogance, perhaps?"

Yelena's nostrils flared. "How dare you call my son arrogant to his face?"

"You forget that I know him quite well too. Perhaps not as

well as you, but enough to know that he can be arrogant and imperious at times. Perhaps that arrogance got the better of him in a tavern one night and he boasted—"

"My son is not stupid. He wouldn't let something as important as that slip, no matter how drunk he got."

I refrained from asking her how often he got drunk. It didn't sound like Dane, and I was curious, but now was not the time.

"Then how did the authorities come to discover his identity?" Balthazar pressed.

"And how do they know he's back in Noxford now?" I asked.

Yelena squeezed the bridge of her nose, just as Dane had done moments before. "I don't know, although I have my suspicions. Just before your arrest, you had a visitor, Dane. I was out, and when I returned, the visitor had gone. You'd sent him away with instructions to hold his tongue. Either he didn't or someone got to him and made him reveal your whereabouts."

"The visitor knew who Dane was?" Balthazar asked.

Yelena nodded.

"How?"

"Who was he and what did he want?" Dane's question came over the top of Balthazar's. Both sat forward, as did I. I could guess who the visitor might be, but I needed confirmation. I held my breath.

"He was an old priest," Yelena said.

I kept my gaze focused on her and did not look at Balthazar. Nor did Dane.

"He was a priest in the order of Merdu's Guards, so he told you," Yelena said to Dane. "He brought with him a document from his order's library. He'd stumbled across it one day and thought it...interesting. He came here to have it verified."

Dane sucked air between his teeth and finally looked to Balthazar.

Balthazar's knuckles were white around the head of his walking stick. "The document was an account written by the master of Merdu's Guards who saved you from General Nox, yes?"

"Yes," Yelena said, unsurprised that he'd reached that conclusion. "The account of my escape had been written down so that the truth would be recorded if something ever happened to the master. His successor should have read it and known that a member of the Averlea royal family lived."

"But the successor never read it," Balthazar said. "The warrior priests were ashamed of their failure in the revolution. They'd fought on your father's side, and lost. They're a proud order, and failure doesn't sit well with them. They did their best to try to forget about their involvement, and that meant burying all accounts of the war. Over time, no one remembered that you'd been saved."

With every sentence, Yelena's eyes had widened a little more. By the end of his account, she was staring at Balthazar as if she'd only just noticed him.

"*You*," she growled. "*You* were the priest who visited Dane that day."

"I suspect so."

She launched out of the chair and flew at him. "You dog!" Her hand slapped his cheek and her other hand descended, but Dane grabbed her by the wrist and pulled her away.

He forced her back into the chair. "Calm yourself."

She looked like a wild animal with her ragged breathing and bared teeth. The princess had vanished beneath the first sign of real, raw emotion. It was then that I realized she hadn't even cried yet.

"This is your fault," she snarled at Balthazar. "If it hadn't been for you, my son would never have been arrested. He would never have been taken from me."

"You don't know that," Dane said.

"It's too much of a coincidence for it not to be the case. You were arrested the day after the priest's visit."

"You said yourself that it may not have been deliberate, that someone could have got to him and made him reveal what he knew."

"He should have kept his mouth shut."

"But why would someone make him reveal anything?" I asked. "They would have to have an inkling that he knew something worth telling."

She did not have an answer for that. I wasn't even sure she'd heard me. She was still glaring daggers at Balthazar.

I crouched before him and checked his cheek. It was red but seemed fine, and he smiled to reassure me. As I rose, I caught a glimpse of movement by the door. Martha stood there, hidden from Yelena but not the rest of us. Tears dampened her cheeks and she pressed her apron to her mouth in an attempt to silence her cry. Her longing gaze followed Dane as he sat again.

"Balthazar must have wanted to speak to you that day," Dane said to Yelena. "He wanted confirmation of the master's account of your escape."

She shook her head. "It wasn't just an account of my escape that he'd found. There was an addendum added by the master. He was still alive when you were born, so I wrote to him and asked him to record your birth. I sent him the certificate of your birth and told him he could find us in this very house. He died soon after that, I believe."

"And your letters and the account were as good as lost."

"I didn't know that. I didn't know my situation was forgotten by the world outside Averlea."

"Do you know what Dane and I discussed that day?" Balthazar asked.

Her jaw hardened and she looked away. For a moment, I thought she wouldn't answer him, but eventually she gave in. "Nothing that Dane didn't already know. You asked if the document spoke the truth, and Dane confirmed it. He told me you were shocked and worried about what it would mean for Averlea."

"Did you think I wasn't in favor of him returning to the throne?" Balthazar asked. "Is that why you assume I betrayed him to the authorities afterwards?"

"Dane wasn't sure of your political alliances. He said you were thoughtful, as if trying to determine what it all meant for Averlea, and for the Fist Peninsula in general."

"But you think I informed the authorities of his existence anyway, whether intentionally or otherwise."

Yelena raised her chin.

Balthazar lowered his head.

Dane rested his elbows on his knees and clasped his hands. "I know you, Bal, and you're not a cruel man. If your coming here led to my arrest, it wasn't your intention. Don't blame yourself."

The gaze Balthazar lifted to Dane's was a haunted one. "What if I thought getting rid of you was for the greater good of Freedland?"

Yelena scoffed. "For the greater good? I've heard that excuse time and again. The revolution cost countless lives. Hundreds of soldiers died, on both sides—perhaps thousands. It upset the natural order and uprooted the lives of dozens of families whose only crime was to support my father. How is any of that good?"

"Your father was cruel to the people." Balthazar's accusation cut through the air like a knife and ended Yelena's lecture. It was like him to say exactly what he thought, but now was not the time.

"Bal," I hissed.

Yelena shot to her feet, and Dane rose too, ready to stop her if she tried to strike Balthazar again. "You believe what you've read in history books written by the victors, by Nox's people," she spat. "I won't listen to such lies in my house."

"Sit down," Dane said.

She pointed at the door where Martha stood, the apron stuffed into her mouth, wide-eyed shock on her face. "Get out of my house, old man! Go!"

"Enough!" Dane snapped.

Yelena blinked long and hard at him. "Pardon?"

"I said that's enough. Balthazar is my friend. Whatever happened in the past is forgotten."

"Not by me."

"He went to prison too. Does that not speak of his innocence? Does that not say something about what the authorities—"

"I won't have a stranger disparage my father's name in my house."

Dane's jaw hardened. He did not like to be interrupted. "You have to understand that everything is different now. I am different."

"You are *not* different. You are still my son. You are still the heir."

Dane tapped his chest. "*I* am different."

She crossed her arms and regarded him down her nose. "Yes. I see that. You would never have said a word against me before."

"I have not said a word against you now."

"You are disagreeing with me."

I wrapped my fingers around Dane's hand before he said something he later regretted. He let out a breath and released his anger with it.

Yelena's hard gaze took in our linked hands. She suddenly turned her back to us.

Balthazar pushed himself to his feet. "I'll join Quentin and Erik outside. We'll make our own way back to Vance's place. It's late and we're all tired. Yelena, I apologize for any discomfort I've caused. Sometimes I forget that I should keep my opinions to myself."

She gave no indication that she'd heard him.

"We'll follow later," Dane said to Balthazar. "I want to learn more tonight. I still know nothing about my father. Josie, will you stay?"

I hugged his arm. "Of course." I was as curious as he was about his father. The man who could match Yelena must have been interesting indeed.

A shout from outside startled me. It sounded like Quentin's voice.

There was a thump against the door and more shouts, followed by the clang of metal against metal.

Dane rushed towards the door but it opened before he reached it, crashing back against the wall. Quentin landed on his back on the entrance hall floor.

Martha screamed.

"Run, Dane!" Yelena cried. "The back way!"

But her shout was lost amid the clash of metal and Erik's cry of pain. Then he too fell through the doorway, knocking over Quentin as he tried to rise. Armed men wearing constable uniforms barreled in after Erik. One pressed his sword point to the Marginer's throat while another disarmed Quentin and pulled him to his feet.

Dane, sword drawn, engaged the constable standing over

Erik. Erik kicked the constable while he was distracted and jumped to his feet. Dane dispatched the constable amid more screaming from Martha and shouting from Yelena.

Balthazar pointed his walking stick at a door that must be the rear exit, but it too opened, and armed men streamed through. I counted almost a dozen, and they were not constables. They wore soldiers' uniforms.

Merdu and Hailia, save us.

But the god and goddess weren't listening. The soldiers came up behind Dane, Erik and Quentin, just as more constables entered through the front door. Dane managed to parry a strike, but for every blade he deflected, another four came at him.

Erik was equally inundated and Quentin was once again on the floor, doing his best to fend off two men larger than himself.

We could not escape. Not even if we all took up arms and Max was here to help. I counted fifteen soldiers and constables at least.

Martha went to her mistress, but Yelena didn't seem to notice her. "What is the charge against him?" When no one answered her, Yelena shouted, "What is the charge?"

Dane parried another strike and shoved a soldier into one of the constables, giving himself some space. But instead of continuing the fight, he put up his hands.

"I surrender!" He dropped the sword. "Leave my friends and family alone. It's me you want."

"No," Yelena whimpered. "No, no, no. Not again."

I clung to Balthazar, my heart pounding and my head screaming at me to do something to help Dane. But nothing could be done. Erik and Quentin both lay on the floor, bleeding but alive. The soldiers and constables did not continue the fight.

They looked to the sergeant, the last man to file into the cottage. No, not a sergeant. He wore all black with gold braiding at the shoulder of his doublet, similar to Dane's captain's uniform.

He regarded the scene and us with cool indifference.

"Captain?" asked the soldier with his blade pointed at Dane's throat. "What do you want me to do?"

Merdu, he was asking whether he should kill him right here!

"No!" I cried. "Please, don't. He's done nothing. You don't understand, he can't remember—"

"That is murder," Yelena spat at the captain. "If you murder an innocent man then you have to murder all of us witnesses too. She is a Glancian noblewoman and the old man a priest from Merdu's Guards. Do you want the warrior priests and the entire Glancian nation to know you murder innocents?"

The captain showed a flicker of uncertainty as his gaze raked over her. I wondered if he'd been told who she was.

"Let them go," Dane said. "They're not important. My name is Dane. It's me you want."

The captain sheathed his sword. "Dane March, you are under arrest for leaving the place of your incarceration before your sentence is complete and for the murder of the guards at Gull's Wing prison."

"But he has no memory of those events," I pleaded. "You cannot arrest a man for a crime he isn't even aware he committed."

"Josie," Dane said with gentle firmness. "Look at me."

I did, and my heart cracked in my chest. He was so tall surrounded by Freedlandians, so sure and confident. But I knew it was all for my benefit. I knew inside he must know his fate was precarious. I tried to be brave for him too, but I suspected I failed miserably.

"I'll see you soon," he said, attempting to smile.

He was led away between two soldiers. He didn't struggle or look back.

"No!" Yelena screamed. "I can't lose him again!" She charged towards them but was forced back by the constables.

"Captain," Balthazar said as the captain went to leave too. "What happens now?"

"He will be tried in court and if found guilty, sentenced to hang." He followed his men and Dane out into the night.

Martha sobbed and collapsed onto a chair.

Yelena let out a scream that sliced through my already frayed nerves. I went to comfort her, expecting her to collapse too, but she shook me off. She paced the room, her hands balled into fists at her sides, her breathing labored.

"Josie," Quentin said from where he was bending over Erik. "He's injured."

"It is nothing," Erik said as I rushed to him. His side was damp with blood.

I tore his clothing to see the cut better. It bled profusely. "Yelena, I need cloths and clean water. Quentin, we need to get him back to Vance's. This needs stitching and my medical pack is there."

"I'll find a cart." Quentin ran off.

I pressed on Erik's wound in an attempt to stem the blood.

He squeezed his eyes shut and breathed heavily.

"Yelena," Balthazar snapped. "Josie asked for cloth and water."

I turned to see Yelena still pacing, muttering to herself. She hadn't heard him.

Martha rose from the chair. "I'll fetch what you need. I've cleaned Dane's scrapes many times, although never sword cuts."

She bustled out, and I turned back to Erik. He was pale and getting paler. My hands were covered in his blood, and it was still oozing from the wound. The cloths and the water would not be necessary if I couldn't stop the bleeding.

"I can speak to Ewen and the others, mobilize the mercenaries," Yelena said as she continued to pace. "We'll storm the jailhouse. We will *not* give up."

Balthazar and I glanced at one another. He looked grave, his face haggard, his back crooked as he leaned heavily on his walking stick.

"Sit, Bal," I ordered. "I can't have two unconscious men on my hands."

He sat and swallowed heavily as he watched Yelena. She kept pacing but at least she'd stopped muttering. Her eyes had hardened again and she once more looked to be in charge of her own mind. It was a relief. I was afraid Dane's arrest had sent her mad.

Just as it might send me mad if I did not have Erik to worry about. Yet as I knelt beside him, my hands covered in his blood, my mind cleared. I knew precisely what I had to do to free Dane and keep Erik alive.

Martha returned carrying a basin and cloths. She knelt beside me, just as Yelena passed her. She stepped over Erik's feet and opened the front door.

"Madam?" Martha asked. "Where are you going?"

"To rescue my son." Yelena disappeared into the darkness outside.

Martha whimpered then swiped at her tears with the back of her hand. "I should go after her and make sure she doesn't harm herself."

"She'll be all right," I said. "She has something to do to keep her mind occupied."

"And Dane?" Martha started to cry. "Will he be all right? My mistress can't get him out of this, for all her talk. Her supporters are not ready."

"He'll be fine. I know a way to set him free."

"How?"

I looked to Balthazar but he gave no indication that he followed my thoughts. I didn't care if he agreed with me or not. My mind was made up.

"Magic," I said. "I'll use magic."

Now Available:
THE RETURN OF ABSENT SOULS
The 6th and final After The Rift novel

A MESSAGE FROM THE AUTHOR

I hope you enjoyed reading THE PRISON OF BURIED HOPES as much as I enjoyed writing it. As an independent author, getting the word out about my book is vital to its success, so if you liked this book please consider telling your friends and writing a review at the store where you purchased it. If you would like to be contacted when I release a new book, subscribe to my newsletter at http://cjarcher.com/contact-cj/newsletter/. You will only be contacted when I have a new book out.

SERIES WITH 2 OR MORE BOOKS

After The Rift

Glass and Steele

The Ministry of Curiosities Series

The Emily Chambers Spirit Medium Trilogy

The 1st Freak House Trilogy

The 2nd Freak House Trilogy

The 3rd Freak House Trilogy

The Assassins Guild Series

Lord Hawkesbury's Players Series

Witch Born

SINGLE TITLES NOT IN A SERIES

Courting His Countess

Surrender

Redemption

The Mercenary's Price

ABOUT THE AUTHOR

C.J. Archer has loved history and books for as long as she can remember and feels fortunate that she found a way to combine the two. She spent her early childhood in the dramatic beauty of outback Queensland, Australia, but now lives in suburban Melbourne with her husband, two children and a mischievous black & white cat named Coco.

Subscribe to C.J.'s newsletter through her website to be notified when she releases a new book, as well as get access to exclusive content and subscriber-only giveaways. Her website also contains up to date details on all her books: http:// cjarcher.com She loves to hear from readers. You can contact her through email cj@cjarcher.com or follow her on social media to get the latest updates on her books:

facebook.com/CJArcherAuthorPage

twitter.com/cj_archer

instagram.com/authorcjarcher

pinterest.com/cjarcher

bookbub.com/authors/c-j-archer